PRAISE

"Paul Jessup is the ghostpoet of weird, writing words of unease that rattle like bones and whisper in dark corners."
—Lavie Tidhar, author of *The Circumference of the World*

"I am not sure *Daughter of the Wormwood Star* is actually a novel—to read it is to enter a sustained and fevered dream that is not spun out of plot and characters, but instead of madness, bliss, and passion. No, this beautiful book is too weird and magical to be a novel: this book is a spell. Read it and be ensorcelled!"
   —Wendy N. Wagner, author of *Girl in the Creek* and *The Deer Kings*

"[Paul Jessup] uses language to great effect to heighten the more surreal aspects of his world."
   —Eric Lahti, author of *Better Than Dead*

"Jessup's prose sometimes recalls Harlan Ellison at his most extrav- agant, invoking a lurid, elastic environment steeped in ritual yet with delirious magic as well as weird science."
—*Kirkus Reviews* for *The Silence That Binds*

Cancer Eats the Heart

Paul Jessup

Underland Press

This book is published by Underland Press, which is part of Firebird Creative, LLC (Clackamas, OR).

The emptiness is where the real fear lies . . .

Edited by Darin Bradley
Book Design and Layout by Firebird Creative

This Underland Press trade edition has an ISBN of 978-1-63023-131-6.

Underland Press
www.underlandpress.com

Cancer Eats the Heart

For my Mom & Dad

who always supported my writing, even from a young age

thank you

PROLOGUE: 1986

HIS parents had no faces, only sharp blobs torn in the places where their eyes and mouth should be. Toby Miles had no clue they'd died three nights before, suicide. They couldn't take the pain of watching him slowly die from retinoblastoma. His mom blamed herself, for taking so long to get it checked out, and by then it was too late. It had spread to both of his eyes, crawled across his face, and nestled inside of his cheeks and his nose. Each day the doctors changed how long he had to live, and each day it grew shorter and shorter and shorter. Time was running out.

Even though he was blind, he kept seeing his parents, day in, day out. Right there, talking to him and walking about. They moved backwards, as if they were stuck behind an unseen mirror. And when they spoke, their words were harsh whispers.

His favorite nurse, Joanne, said that couldn't be true. And even after she explained to him what happened (in the most gentlest way possible), they still showed up and hung around in the shadows. Dimmer and dimmer the world grew, while they shone brighter and brighter. What they said to him didn't make sense. To watch out for the one who walks behind the Doors of Night. To resist his promises, and go gentle into the fire beyond life. Death, after all, his mother said, was not the end. They were proof of that.

He wanted to ask her what happened to their faces, and he wanted to know why they were naked in his hospital room. But he worried that it would somehow break the spell, and they would be gone from him if he asked too many questions. And he didn't want to be alone in that dark once more. The dark was a lonely place, and he was a lonely boy who needed company. The nurses weren't always around, and when they were they were so sad, it left him feeling way worse than he had before.

After all, he knew that he was the reason why they were sad. He was the reason why his parents had been sad, too, but they weren't sad anymore. Maybe that was a good thing when it came to death, your sadness gets left behind. It was a thing of the physical world, and had no place outside of the body, and its messy chemical constructions. Anger would be gone, too, he assumed. And even though the rest of the world was sad at his condition, he was angry.

So much had been stolen from him, and it wasn't fair nor right, nor good. Why did everyone else get to grow up, grow old, go to college, get a job, get a life and family of their own? All of that gone, taken from him by the great thief known as cancer. He raged in that darkness of his vision, fumed and hollered and shouted. Eventually, those emotional outbursts frightened away the ghosts of his parents. He threw things at the nurses and cursed, and even they came less and less each day. They did what they could and what they felt like they had to do, but they'd also stopped just dropping by to say hello and see how he was doing.

He didn't blame them, of course. One day, he was so sick of needles, he slapped the shadow of the nurse who had come to put an IV in his arm. She fell crumpled to the floor, sobbing. Others came and escorted her out, and then a doctor came by, yelled at him, and jabbed him several times with a needle. The doctor kept saying that Toby's veins were no good. They kept collapsing, and he kept fishing, and they wouldn't bleed at all. Eventually, after nearly ten tries, with Toby dizzy from all the pain, the doctor found a good vein in his thumb, and hooked the IV port up to that.

He wondered later if the doctor had done this on purpose, after what he did to the nurse. He knew he should feel bad about all of this. But, no. Instead his anger welled up even greater, a slow burning light inside of his body. He saw it when he looked down, a little candle spark of fire, right where his heart should be, sputtering in the dark. It was the only thing he saw for days, his vision drifting further and further away, until all was lit by the lamp of his hate.

That hateful lantern of a heart is a beacon in the night for all the wrong kinds of creatures. Creatures that exist on the skin of our world, pressing up against the thin membrane, and looking for the wounded that would let them in, and give them flesh to wear. It came to him on a rotten Saturday, when his medications made him vomitsick with that underskin ant feeling. Woozy, dizzy fury fluttered about in Toby's heart, the lamp of hate the brightest it had ever been.

At first he thought it was a hallucination. Doctors said that might happen, after all. It'd been forever since he'd seen the ghostly blobs of his parents, and he wondered now if they'd ever been real at all. Was it dream, a lingering thing, something that would always haunt him? So when the bones made of light first appeared he shut his eyes to try and force it away into the darkness.

But even with eyes closed the skeleton stuck around. It stood in the center of his room, not moving, not speaking a single word. He opened his eyes again, and the rotted lumpy shadows of the world returned, with the bones still there. It looked like the after image of the sun at first, like when he was younger and snuck a peak at the eclipse, and saw yellow blotches for days. They made curious shapes back then, sometimes a skull or bones. Almost exactly like this entity here.

His dad had said that it was just a random series of splotches and nothing more than that. "Come on, champ. It's like looking at a quilt or a rock and seeing faces that aren't there. Doesn't mean nothing more than nothing."

That thought made him miss his dad so much. The heartlight fluttered again, bright and then brighter still, now tinged with a deadly combination of sorrow and hate. The skeleton nodded at him, and spoke. The splotches moved like a jaw on a real skull. "Hello there."

Its voice all smoke and lightning.

"Hi? Are you really here?"

"Yes and no, but I would like to be really *really* here. And to do so, I need you to lend me a hand. I had a body here for awhile, a little girl no older than yourself. But I got kicked out of her something fierce, because she didn't have the right kind of heart. But you've got the right kind of heart, Toby. I know that, I can see that. You've got the kind of heart that could keep me going forever."

Toby wasn't sure what to make of all this. The meds left his brain in a constant fog, and right now he was trying everything in his power not to throw up. He hated throwing up, and that seemed to be a common occurrence these days. Way more than he liked, that was for certain. And yet, even under all that, this whole conversation felt *off*. It was like the day his mom said they were going home to take a shower, and they would be back in the next few hours. That was the night they died. That whole night felt off, too, just like tonight.

"No, thank you," he said, and he meant it.

"You haven't even heard my proposal yet, so how can you be so certain? This is a gift I'm giving you, in exchange for your help and services. I want to do miracles in this world, Toby. But I cannot."

"Why."

"Because I need flesh and bones to do that. I was wondering, could I have yours? You probably won't need them for much longer anyway."

No no no no no. This was wrong.

"So if I'm not long for this world, what's in it for me?"

Everything ached and his vision danced. He wanted this vision to leave him now, so he could get some rest and feel slightly better.

"Eternity is in it for you. You let me inside, and I can keep your body going for a long, long, time. Might even stick around after this world is gone and done for, and the whole universe is a cold dead emptiness, you would be the only thing left alive. No more pain, no more sorrow, nothing of that sort. Now, I can't heal all of you, that's only a gift I can give to others, and only after I have your bones and body under my will. But I can make the pain drain away, and I can make it so death has stopped and will never claim you. What do you say?"

"Will I still be blind?"

"In a way, yes, we'll still be blind."

"And I won't die? Will that mean the cancer will keep growing, and I'll be in here, trapped in a living corpse? Unable to pass onto the next life?"

"Oh my, how horrible that would be. Of course not, Toby, my dear, of course not. When I come in, I can freeze it in place with a single word. It's not as good as my other gifts, but as far as things go, it's a much better deal than what you have now. Wouldn't you say?"

He wanted to be left alone, and told the creature as much.

"I'm sorry, Toby, I can't do that. I'll be here, waiting patiently for your answer."

"All right, then. Tell me your name. You do that much, and I will give you an answer."

The creature whispered something horrible sounding. It was mostly a word, constructed out of strange syllables that would be impossible to create in a human mouth. The tongue went into all the wrong places, and Toby wondered if a bird would be better suited to say that name. The sounds of it made him shiver all over, and his blood felt colder than usual. He couldn't help it, he couldn't hold on anymore, he leaned over onto the edge of his bed and vomited into a lone bucket, one that had been placed there for that very reason.

"I . . . I'm sorry . . ."

His mouth tasted bright and pink and he hated it.

"Don't be, my child. Don't be."

"I can't say that name . . . how about I call you Mister Bright-bones?"

The skeleton smiled.

"That is a perfect name. I couldn't have chosen a better one myself."

And then he held out his bony paw of light, and Toby leaned over and grabbed it and said, "Okay, yes. You can use my body. Just promise me I'll still be in there, and I'll still be able to experience life as much as I can."

"I promise. Everything I do, you will do, too. And everything I taste, you will taste, and you will understand. You will be able to see as I see, not with the limitations of the physical world and your damaged eyes, but instead with the ethereal shadows of the world that hums behind sight."

And then a whisper, filled with dark secret knowledge. "Everything in this world is a shadow. All they see is shadow. I will show you the sun, and you will be astonished at how beautiful it all can be when we pull back the skin of this world and reveal the bone and sinew that's underneath."

And Toby did understand. He'd seen his own muscles and bones before his eyes completely went. He'd peeked during operations, and watched what should never be watched with childlike glances. The secrets we hold inside of us, the wonders of the world beneath the flesh. But he had seen it, and he was in awe of the beauty he saw.

Everything was a top, spinning, as Mister Brightbones walked into him. The two skeletons merging. And Toby slid away from the waking self, and only stayed a whisper, hovering around the edges of his thoughts. Watching, but not touching. Not doing. Yet, still alive.

Even now, decades later, long past his expiration date, still alive.

1

BETWEEN the knotted trunks of the trees a shadow danced in the fog. At first Nix thought it was another scarecrow, moving in the wind. She'd come back for a walk on her property to see if she could figure out who planted them there in the first place. Creepy things, with ragged old clothes, scattered along the various paths. The first one freaked her out something fierce, and she was about to call the cops and have them come and take a look at them when she saw that shadow.

It was something human shaped, a little shorter than her, twirling about and flailing in a wild, almost erratic manner. It reminded her of when her own arms would spasm during a multiple sclerosis relapse, the way they would involuntarily jerk about, like she was punching the air.

Just the thought of it made her reach over and grab her left shoulder and give it a small squeeze. It was always the left side, wasn't it? Like her sickness played favorites, of all things. It was understandable, she always liked her left side as well.

The fog drifted and the dim clouds moved a bit to reveal a teenage girl of about sixteen, give or take a few years. A purple wig perched delicately on top of her bald head, and as she danced it would slip aside and reveal shaved skin and esoteric tattoos. Her body was gaunt, her clothes so big they bloomed around her. Her eyes sparked with embers and fire, and seemed to call the lightning in the sky towards her. She was a roman candle of a girl, burning brightly in the evening light.

Nix shifted her weight a bit and accidentally stepped on a dry twig. The sound was a gunshot in the air, the crows scattering from branches above. The girl turned around and looked directly at Nix and grinned. Her clothes were filthy, mottled, and ripped. Her skin had patches of mud and dirt caked across it, and Nix wondered if she'd taken a shower recently. Dead leaves clung to her hair and arms.

And it dawned on Nix, then, that this girl was homeless. A mothering sensation welled up inside, and she wanted to run over, give her a hug, wash her up, take care of her and feed her. This feeling was very odd and alien, and unlike any other emotion she'd felt in the past. Like it came from outside of her body, sinking tentacles of oxytocin under her skin.

"Hello," the girl cried out and smiled, waving. "Howdy, howdy, hello! Pleased to meet you, new best friend."

Nix couldn't help but smile back. "Why, hello right back. Are those your scarecrows?"

"Yes, yes indeedy, that's my ring of protection."

"What are they protecting you from?"

The girl frowned for a moment, and looked to the sky like she was thinking really hard on this, and that it was the most important question in the universe. "It's not just protecting me, you know. It's protecting you as well. "

"Fair enough. Can you tell me from what, though?"

The branches around them rustled in a feverish sound, as a few cracked and tumbled about with the force of the storm. It was a right chill air, what everyone around Dark Rivers called the Witch Wind. The teenage runaway wrung her shirt in her hands, and looked nervously toward the ground. "Mister Brightbones."

The name sounded weird in her head, and Nix didn't like it. The girl was in trouble, and even if the scarecrows were part of some delusion, she had a feeling that Mister Brightbones was a very real danger. Probably someone that abused her, and was probably the reason she'd run away from home in the first place. She had so many questions . . .

Nix tried to stand on her left leg, as the arch of her foot screamed in pain. The muscle felt like it was being stretched close to tearing, so she took her weight off of it and sighed. Stupid multiple sclerosis, always acting up at the worst possible time. "I would say let's go back to my place and get you something to eat, but I can't walk right now, and I don't think you're any shape to help me out. No offense, but it looks like you can barely hold up your own clothes, let alone a grown-ass woman like myself."

"Will you be okay?"

Nix leaned against the tree and looked up at the sky. It would rain any moment now—you could taste it in the air like pennies. "Yeah," she said, "I just need to rest for a hot second, and then hopefully I'll be all right. While we wait, why don't you tell me all about this Mister Brightbones?"

"Okay."

And then the girl sat down right next to Nix, and leaned her head against a large knotted burl of the tree. "I'm Daphne Valentine, by the by."

Nix laughed. Daphne had always been her favorite Scooby Doo character. "My name is Phoenix, but all my friends call me Nix."

"Phoenix?"

"Yeah, my full name is Phoenix Fox. I think my parents expected me to be a super hero."

"And you're not?"

"Naw. It's hard to be a super hero when you've got all this going on." And she motioned at her body with her cane. "Having a chronic illness is less like a super power and more like a super bummer." Yeah, it was a bad joke. She had a tendency to make them when nervous.

Daphne frowned and crossed her arms across her chest. "Oh, okay . . . I guess. Well, my parents didn't expect me to be a super-hero, but they did expect me to be dead by now. I'm sick, you know, like you but different. I've got my . . . cure? Well, I guess you could call it that, but it's not what you're thinking. Mister Brightbones, he was the one who give it to me, and it worked like gangbusters. It was a miracle, and I was so relieved and filled with joy. Until he had me pay the price. It was . . . it was . . . awful. You don't have any idea what he had me do, and I wanted to do it at first, he has that kind of power over you, and you get drunk with it, you know? Like your body is filled with lightning. But after a while, it got to be too much. The things he asked me to do grew worse and worse, and I just couldn't live with myself anymore, after all I'd done, and the price he had me pay for a little miracle cure. I had to get out, I ran and kept on running, and I never looked back, even though I know he's out there looking for me. He doesn't like it when his children leave him. That's what he called us, even the adults, even a woman in her fifties . . . he called us his children."

There was a pause for a brief second or two, as the crows returned to the trees above.

"I owe him everything, for this little miracle cure, but I also fear him, and fear what he needs from me, what he wants me to do when he finds me again . . ."

Daphne closed her eyes, like she was fighting back tears, and Nix knew that kind of emotional pain, and respected the silence. Sometimes you needed the quiet, she understood that. And she understood the pain of searching for a drug that works to heal you at all costs, and that need to do even the most horrible things to get better. Infusions that made her blood burn like ice and shiver all over crying out in pain, pills and needles and electric shocks testing out her nerves and making her bones jump beneath her skin.

After all, if Mister Brightbones had approached her and offered her a cure for multiple sclerosis? Well, then, she would take that little miracle without hesitation. And if the cost was too much and she had to stop? That would be like the world ending.

"You know," Nix said, carefully breaching that silence as best as she could. "You don't have to continue on with the story if you don't want to, I get it."

And Daphne opened her eyes, a deep green with a gold ring around her iris. "Thank you," she whispered. "He's coming for me, you know? And he always finds me. It's why I have to be prepared, and why I set up my sentinels. After all, this storm is his storm," and she pointed at the crows in the trees, "And those crows are his crows."

And at that moment the sky opened up, drenching them both completely.

2

THE walk back to Nix's house wasn't easy going. She kept slipping in the mud, and the rain drenched them both completely—their clothes hung damp and heavy on her limbs. She should've listened to the weather forecast before going out earlier, but it was just near the end of August, and most of the bad rains didn't usually come until at least October. Though, she guessed she should've known something was up, after all the temperature dropped drastically in the morning, and the fog was a good sign that rain was going to come back soon. At the time she thought nothing of it, and just loved the atmosphere of the woods.

On their way back she'd made up her mind, that Daphne was going to stay here with her for as long as it takes to keep her safe. She had no idea who this Mister Brightbones was, but that child was terrified and lost and all alone in the world. Her heart roared like a mother bear at the thought of it, her instincts to protect and save this poor wounded cub overpowering.

She'd never had kids of her own. Multiple sclerosis complicated things, and left her filled with guilt at even the thought of it. It felt dangerous and irresponsible. and it's why she'd left so many relationships, once they got serious enough that they thought of starting a family. It was an irrational fear, that was certain, and yet there it was, clinging to her.

Maybe she should've adopted. Or maybe she should've just had a child with her last husband, like they'd discussed over and over again. *After all, they say your MS goes into remission while you're pregnant. And if it gets to be too bad, I can always take over and do double duty for the poor tyke.*

But she couldn't let him do that, could she? No, no. And so she ended it like she always did, and then went into a full blown relapse from the stress and depression. That last one was a doozy, and for about a month after she had to go about in a wheelchair, and even hired a live-in nurse for a while until she got better, and her MS went back into remission.

Best not to think about that anymore, what's done is done. And now she had Daphne here, fully grown and needing her help. She could be a mother to her, and protect her in a way that made her heart sing. It was something she needed, even though she told herself over and over again through the years that she really couldn't do it after all. Funny how that was. One person made the impossible possible . . .

There was a moment during the walk when the mothering feeling felt foreign and strange, like alien chemicals poured into her brain and manipulating her? Her stomach turned, as she bent over and dry heaved for a second, her cane holding her balance so she wouldn't fall over. The feeling didn't last too long, and the world righted itself again, her thoughts grew pleasantly furry, and she leaned back into that mothering instinct. Of course this was a natural feeling, of course. This girl needed help, and she was going to help her.

Their clothes were in the wash right now, and Daphne had borrowed some of her pj's and a nice cotton robe. The outfit was comically too large on her, with her sleeves dangling down past her knees, hiding her bony thin exterior. When they'd first gotten back Nix insisted that Daphne eat something, anything. The girl kept protesting, saying she wasn't hungry yet, and that food would just make her sick. Nix still shoved a sandwich and an apple at her, and that was that. She didn't sit there and make sure that she ate it, even though she probably should have.

She had better things to do.

Like getting that guest room set up for her new guest. She told Daphne to stay there, watch some TV, or go online if she wanted. She gave the kid the WiFi password, and pointed her toward the laptop perched flat on the coffee table. Daphne saluted her, laughed and turned on the TV, the blue light shouting shadows across the darkness. She flipped through the different streaming channels, smiling and kicking her feet in that enormous, ratty robe, as Nix walked back, wandering the labyrinthine halls of the old farmhouse.

It wasn't going to be easy to fix up this room, was it? Her aunt had died there a few years back. That's how she got this place, inherited it a little afterwards and didn't have the heart to clean the room up or change the sheets. Everything was still in the exact same condition, with the pictures on the bedside table covered in a thick pile of dust. The first thing she did was shoo her cats from the bed, moving them reluctantly from the blanket and scattering them onto the floor, their nails clacking on the rough wood.

One cat was named Doctor Death, since he had velvet black fur with a white skull design over his kitty face. His sister was called Sherlock, and had skyblue fur, and a tail always poised in the shape of a question mark. The two looked at her for a brief moment, cleaned a paw or a tail, and then shuffled off into the darkness beyond the door.

After the cats moved on, Nix lifted up the blankets and sheets and gave them a good shake. Dust flew all over the place, and she had to open a window and let the cool air in. This place always felt so dusty, even when she was a kid and she stopped by to visit every summer. The corners clung with cobwebs, with dead spiders and the remains of their prey strewn throughout like pebbles. This would take forever, but she had to do it.

And then she turned over the bed, and sat down in shock. That was not what she was expecting, not at all. There was a stain in the shape of her aunt's corpse stretched out like a ghost under the sheets. No, no, no. How could that still be there?

She stared at it for a moment more, touched it briefly with the palm of her hand and then stepped back, as if it had shocked her. Brown, deep and rooted into the mattress, shaped just like her shadow. Everyone always said she looked exactly like her Aunt Doreen, right down to the color of her hair and the shape of her body. Would she be able to fit into that shadow? Like a key in a keyhole?

Oh no. That thought brought back the memory of the day after they took the body away, and her nephew climbed up into the bed, and asked if he could sleep in a bed like this, too, someday? And she remembered her sister, Sammy, choking back a sob and saying, "Maybe, someday." Trying hard not to worry the poor boy. And yet,

Nix could tell that she was wrecked at the thought of her son lying in that same bed, leaving that same stain behind, and dying of mysterious causes during a bad dream.

Her aunt had also been childless, alone, and somehow the strongest woman she knew. At one point she'd even asked Nix to come and stay with her and care for the plum trees out back. Looking back she really wished she'd taken her up on that offer, but alas, Nix was too young and stupid to imagine living out here in the middle of nowhere. She complained about the town being too far away, that she would never be able to see her friends, and that she would miss all the after school activities like dances and all that other *stuff*. How stupid it all seemed now in retrospect.

She should've done it. Maybe everything would've turned out differently? Maybe her aunt would be alive now, the two of them living here, taking care of Daphne. Hiding her from Mister Brightbones, whoever that was.

She'd had a bad dream that night aunt died. Oh god, why was she thinking about this now? She hadn't thought about it in so long, not even the day of the funeral. That stain, that, that must have brought it back to her. The house in the dream was not this house, but some strange place she'd never been to before in real life, but always visited in dreams. It was a house that was made of night and shadows, a large attic always filled with the buzzing of flies. The walls had the scratch of mice echoing in them, and she knew whenever she had a dream like that it meant something important.

Her dream aunt walked and led her through the hallways and corridors, talking as she moved along. It was odd how she remembered this so clearly, the way her aunt's face looked like wood and bone and windows, like she was made up of the same architecture as the dream house.

"You're like me dear," she said, "You've got a place inside of you connected to everything. It's solid, see, feel that." And she knocked on the floorboards, and the skeleton of the house muttered and creaked. "Dream houses don't do that. Look, I've pissed off the wrong kinds of shades and they're coming for me tonight, probably a little after this dream is done and over with. No, no, don't give me that sad look child, this life has been good to me, understand? I did shit that you wouldn't even believe, shit that Oliver Haddo himself was too scared to even ponder. Trust me, once this corpse kicks off and the body's rotting in the ground, I'll still stick around. I got that kind of ghost you know, the kind that even death won't pick up and take home."

And Aunt Doreen laughed, and crushed a fly in her fingertips. It all came back so strongly to Nix now, like she'd never even forgotten a single moment of it.

"Look, something's going to be coming for you soon enough. I can't see it quite clearly, the oracles can be shit like that, more interested in riddles and taunts and less interested in the specifics of things. But I see it, right? A blur of the future, all blind and clouded with lightning. It will start with vampires, and end with a great emptiness. The emptiness is where the real fear lies, my wonderful Nixy niece."

And then her aunt leaned in close, pulled Nix's face right up to hers, so that their lips were barely touching. It was so vivid now in her mind's eye, more vivid than any dream or memory she'd ever had before. Was it because she'd touched the stain?

"I can only hope that the blood you drink will make you powerful enough to destroy it. There is a fire inside us, the both of us, one that can keep us burning past the mortal coil that claims all those other losers out there. We got to use that fire, and hope it's enough to burn the void with light."

And then the bedroom door swung open and startled Nix out of her memory. Daphne stood there, arms akimbo and a crazy grin on her face. She had a bit of red smeared near her lips, and it looked like ocher lipstick. "Wowee, boy! I'm feeling a lot better, thanks for the food!"

Nix nodded, and yes, Daphne did look better, she really did. Some of her had fleshed out more, and looked a little less like a bony wraith. Her cheeks were chubby and flushed, no longer pale and hollowed out like a skull. Her eyes brighter, and she noticed little bits of stubble around the edges of the wig. That's odd, she could've sworn that wasn't there before.

"Oh, no problem at all. If you want more, feel free to help yourself."

Daphne grimaced and then ran over and hugged Nix tightly, and said, "Oh, you don't look so good! Are you all right? If you need me to go, I can go . . ."

And the smell was overpowering, an earthy, sickly sweet scent that subsumed her senses completely. Like rotting fruit, buried under rain soaked dirt and covered in month-old meat. Nix tried not to gag, and gently moved out of the hug and sighed. "No, no, I swear, it's fine. This room just has a lot of . . ."

"Ghosts?"

And Nix laughed. "Yes, that's it exactly, it has a lot of ghosts." She was more shook up than she'd originally realized. It had been a while since she'd been here, thought about her aunt Doreen, or even that dream. And yet, the wound was still fresh in her heart, and hadn't scarred over or healed in all that time. She wasn't sure what to make about that. The pain was bright, yes, but . . .

She liked having that connection to her aunt. As if they were still tethered together somehow, and Doreen's ghost would walk out of the stain in the bed and say hello. She really hoped she would dream of her tonight, that would be nice, to see her again. Even if it was only a figment of her sleeping mind.

"I have an idea," Daphne smiled, her lips still closed and hiding her teeth. "We should so camp out in the living room, make a tent and everything. Doesn't that sound like fun? And we can leave this bedroom for another day."

Nix leaned back against the wall and looked at the pictures of her aunt dotted across the room. She'd been the one to find Aunt Doreen dead on the bed, rigor mortis just starting to set in. She'd driven all the way out here that day on a hunch after that dream, and saw her and there was no mistaking it. It wasn't like she was sleeping at all, her eyes were lifeless and tinted gray, her body completely motion-less. Not even the echo of breath, the stillness and silence haunting, like she was made of papier-mâché.

"All right, yeah. We can do that."

Daphne ran over to hug her, and Nix turned her head and put her hands up. "Wait, wait, wait. When was the last time you took a shower?"

Daphne hemmed and hawed, twisting the bathrobe in her hands like a puzzle box. "Been a long while, I guess. Why? Do I smell?"

Nix snorted and said, "Yeah, you could say that. Why don't you get yourself cleaned up, and I'll get blankets and sheets all ready to make our fort."

"Dealio, my deario."

And then Daphne turned around and ran off to search for the bathroom. The scent left with her, and for a brief moment Nix wondered if she'd noticed that smell earlier or not. Maybe not? She couldn't remember. Maybe she just didn't realize it, or maybe the rain had washed the scent away and it was just now noticeable after they'd dried off for a bit?

Maybe. Just maybe. Oh well, best not to dwell on that now. She got up, put the sheet and blanket back on the bed to cover up the old stain. She would put them in the washing machine later, but for now she wanted that shadow out of sight and out of mind. She had enough things to worry about. There was a teenage girl to care for, and the thought made her smile. Maybe she could be a mother after all, and her MS wouldn't be a problem.

Besides, it wasn't like Daphne was an infant and needed constant care. That always scared her the most, especially since she was prone to dropping stuff without even realizing. It was the damnedest thing, she would be holding a bowl, and walking into the kitchen, and then it would tumble right out of her hands. It wasn't slippery, it wasn't like she let it go . . .

It just was there one moment, and then shattered on the floor the next. Her neuro said it was probably due to weakness in her muscles, something that was slowly getting worse and worse through the years. She definitely couldn't hold or cradle an infant like that, it was far too dangerous.

But a teenager? Well, that was a different story. Teenagers were made of stronger stuff, and were used to getting broken.

3

NIX quickly dug through the linen closet, and brought out every single hand-me-down quilt, bedsheet, and pillow her aunt had left her. They smelled of old cloth, a sweet mildew smell, that brought back memories of spending the nights with her as a child growing up. Right before bed they played a game called Grab the Ghost, where she chased aunt Doreen through the halls of the house, a pale sheet twisted about her body like a funeral shroud, as banshee howls escaped her pursed lips. Such a happy memory.

The sound of running water filled the house, as steam rolled out from underneath the bathroom door. Nix thought of twisting herself in a sheet once again and running through the halls for old time's sake, but quickly changed her mind. It would be too easy for her to lose her footing, for the sheets to trip her and then she would be on the ground again and in pain. There'd been too many falls through the years, and it made her sore at the prospect of even a slight tumble, and it made her miss her aunt even more so than ever before.

Hah. No. Wait, this was a silly thought. A creepy thought. But, well . . .

Maybe she should go back to the guest room, lay down on that stain herself, and see if Aunt Doreen would come and visit her? Yeah, no, no, no. That's not a good idea. She shook the thought from her head, sauntered into the living room, and tried to ease her mind away from all these thoughts of death that hung around in the guise of pale ghosts and old dreams.

Best way to do that was to go online and be stupid.

She sat squat down on top of the pile of pillows, and pulled the laptop over and opened it up. It was still toasty warm against her lap, and after a few moments of waiting, the screen lit up, and revealed an incognito window Daphne had left open from earlier. She knew she shouldn't look, she should just close it right away and check her email, or do anything else, like browse YouTube for dumb cat videos. And yet . . . she was curious. After all, this was a stranger in her house, no? She should look, just in case it was anything too disturbing.

The web page was done up in a language she didn't understand. At first glance it looked like it might be in Hungarian or Russian, but that wasn't quite right. She copied and pasted some of the text and put it into google, hoping it would help her out somehow. Maybe give a bunch of results in the same language, as well as website URLs that could help her pinpoint the country of origin? It took google awhile to trawl through the records, far longer than usual. She had never experienced it going on for that long . . .

And just when she was about to close the tab and open up Reddit, it stopped and showed a small handful of pages in English. Pages about different customs involving wraiths, phantoms, and vampires in folklore. What a strange thing to come up, and from such a strange page. She closed out of google, went back to the other page, and tried to see if she could figure out what it was about just by looking at any images plastered across the website.

It was hard to make them out. They were blurry, yellowed, torn and taped back together, scanned in on an old low DPI scanner from probably the early 2000s. Pixels were sheared and smeared, and at points you could see the dots blown up out of proportion. She squinted, pinched and zoomed in to get a better look. Faces, rows of faces, howling and screaming, or maybe laughing. And someone sitting in a chair in the center of the group, levitating. A pair of crutches laid on the hardwood floor beneath him like a cross. She shivered, briefly, and realized that there was a body curled up next to the crutches, blood pooling around a gashed neck. Was that also blood smeared across the faces in the crowd? No, of course not. That might just be the scanner, and the low resolution causing grainy distortion in the images.

She looked at another picture, and another, and another. Skulls glowed in the shadows like faint lanterns. A tall thin man in a glass coffin with his eyes closed, while two figures in gray placed a black shroud over the body. More bodies on the floor, more blood. What was going on here, why was all this happening . . .

One image was just a row of skeletons, their bones rearranged into strange formations. Triangles of femurs and ribs, skulls placed in the center and cracked with a hammer. Large stones placed in their skeletal mouths. Another image had several bodies lying in a large field, and on closer inspection (pinch and zoom, pinch and zoom) she saw they were burnt black and ashen. On one you could still see the fire roaring up toward the unforgiving sun, and in the background someone danced with a skull pressed close to their chest. Was this evidence of spontaneous combustion? Oh, if only she could read the accompanying text.

And then the bathroom door slowly creaked open down the hall, and startled her so badly she almost jumped in the air and threw the laptop across the room. If only she could ask Daphne questions . . . like what language was that, did she speak it? And did that page have anything to do with Mister Brightbones? But, no. She couldn't ask that, not without betraying the trust of someone who had recently escaped horrific abuse. Probably the same kind of abuse she saw in those distorted, old pictures from the late '90s or early 2000s.

She gently shut the laptop, placed it back on the desk, her heart thundering rapid in her chest, and then sat back down on the floor, and looked up at the ceiling. Tiny plastic stars glowed green in strange constellations. Her aunt had placed them up there when Nix was only eight years old and still obsessed with outer space. She'd climbed up on her rickety old ladder, and waited for Nix to point out a spot for each new star. "This will be our Sistine Chapel," Aunt Doreen told her. "And God will be so damned jealous of how beautiful our night sky is compared to his, he'll come down here and take notes."

There was a soft padding sound as Sherlock ran into the living room, followed by Daphne wrapped up in a clean robe, still drying her face and hair with a ratted blue towel. "Wow, we got a lot of great stuff in here! I bet we could make a regular castle from all the blankets and pillows."

Nix nodded, the images of the burning bodies still tugging strongly on her mind. She reached out for Sherlock, and petted the blue cat without thinking, as a soft purr rippled across her palms in soothing waves. "I wonder where your brother is," she asked the cat, "It's not like him to wander around this house by himself."

Sherlock purred some more in response, and leaned into her palm, greedily seeking attention.

"Oh, I think I saw that other cat earlier, when I was eating. Skull design on his fur, right?"

"Yeah, that's Doctor Death. Or, Doctor Dee, as I sometimes like to call him. Why? Where'd he go?"

"Dunno, he seemed like he was spooked about something, though I'm not quite sure what it was. Like, I saw this shadow moving on a window pane, and he just freaked out and took off running."

"Oh. And Sherlock stayed behind?"

Daphne shrugged. "Guess so. I dunno."

"That's so odd. Usually they run around in pairs, the perfect brother and sister, fighting over food and snuggling up with each other when they're napping."

A cold sensation spilled through Nix's stomach, chilling her. The images she'd seen on the webpage flickered in her head like grim movies, as her hand trembled while she petted Sherlock some more. Was that tremor multiple sclerosis, or something else? She felt the shiver running over her arms and her legs, like how the body shakes when freezing cold or in the throes of a fever. What had she invited into her house?

She gulped, looked up and caught Daphne's gaze, and almost barked out a laugh. Her eyes, green with that gold ring around the irises, that tight-lipped firecracker smile, dimples, and the lopsided wig, all of it . . .

What an absurd thing to feel threatened by, even if only for a little bit.

That creepy website must've really gotten into her head, yes, and Doctor Death was probably out back hunting mice in the barn again. Whenever he disappeared for a day or two, that's usually where she found him, surrounded by half-eaten mice corpses, their heads scattered about. Sometimes she would catch him playing with the mice skulls, batting them about and nipping at their heads. That must be it—she was being so silly.

"You okay?"

"Sorry, I was a bit spooked for a moment there," and then she realized she had to confess. "Look, I went to go and check my email, and I saw that website you had up, and it had me really freaked out. Those images, that text . . . what were they, and why were you looking at them?"

Daphne glanced at the ground, chewed on her lip for a brief moment with her eyes closed. Sherlock's purrs disrupted the silence as Nix rubbed her ears, and wished Daphne would say something, anything.

"I'm sorry you had to see that," she said finally, her voice a rough whisper. "But it's none of your damned business, okay?"

And then she lifted up her head and opened her eyes. The gaze caught Nix unawares, and reached into her chest, and wrapped around her heart, and squeezed, briefly. Breathless, heart thunder, the tremors in her muscles quieted down to a mere whisper. In her head she saw only Daphne's eyes, and felt all worry leave her body. What was she thinking about, again? She felt like it was important or dangerous, and yet now her mind was completely blank. She tried to focus on it, to drink in those images again that disturbed her. Something was there, a warning, and if Daphne did not want her to think about it, well, then . . . maybe . . .

And then the thought was gone again, replaced by Daphne's eyes. The gold of the irises spun in spirals, and Nix realized that Daphne had opened her mouth, teeth so sharp, like a cannibal's grin. She leaned in, no longer petting the cat, baring her neck to Daphne without even thinking about why she would want to do that. It felt like the most natural thing in the world, didn't it? Like her whole life had led her to this moment, when she could give herself over to Daphne, completely and wholly. Please drink me, she thought, just open me up and drink me . . .

She'd never wanted oblivion so badly before, and she realized she desired the long untroubled rest of the dead. That was it, she realized, life was so tiring, what with multiple sclerosis, and her bills, and her loneliness, death would be this release from all of it. And it would be such a treat if Daphne would be the one who gave it to her.

"No," Daphne said, her voice all wine and opium-coated, "Sleep, sleep, and dream deep. There will be none of that tonight."

And yes, Nix wanted to sleep more than anything else. Maybe that would be just as restful as death? Yes, that made sense. A long good sleep, like dying a tiny bit and putting your whole life on pause. That would do for now. After all, she was so sad all the time, and it was hard to be sad in dreams.

"Shouldn't we make up the fort first? So we have someplace to crash."

"You've had a rough day."

"Yes, I did. My multiple sclerosis was being so stupid."

"Of course it was! And you deserve a nice little rest, all right? So crawl into your room and get some sleep, and I'll stay out here and hold down this awesome blanket fort. That will keep both of us out of trouble, so you can get a good night's rest."

"Okay. That sounds nice."

And then a rubber band thought snapped in her mind, alerting her to a brief danger once again. She wasn't safe, a darkness slid around her new friend like a living shadow. It hovered just on the edges of her vision, but she couldn't catch it, could not bring it close and intimate to see what it meant. She felt Sherlock purr beneath her fingertips and said, "Something . . . something's wrong. I think Sherlock here should come with me and sleep in my room."

Daphne seemed a bit hurt, but nodded and said, "Oh yeah, sure thing, you take her with you and keep each other company for the night."

"And maybe Doctor Death will come and keep me company, too."

A sharp pain at that thought, something she was trying to avoid thinking about again. Daphne's eyes pulled at her, moved through her heart and squeezed again, briefly. She crawled over, gave Nix a kiss on her cheek. A gentle thing, the red ochre across her lips staining Nix's face with a smear in the shape of her mouth. "Be safe, be careful," and then she leaned in, whispered in her ear, "Mom."

"Mom?" Nix gasped. And in that moment never realized how badly she'd wanted to hear that word, and how much it scared her at the same time. "Mom."

"I hope that's okay?"

"Yeah, I think so. Mom."

"Good, that makes me feel so glad. My own mom, my real mom, she's . . . she's gone now. And for a while I had a foster mom, I guess you could call her that, Mama June? But. Well, she's not the good sort of mom. Unlike you, you are the good sort of mom, aren't you?"

"I am. I am the best kind of mom."

After all, you could just ask her kitties. Sherlock and Doctor Death were always excited to see her, purring and wrestling about for her attention. Daphne might just be like that, and that would be perfectly okay by her. And then, she thought about Doctor Death in the barn, playing with mouse skulls, surrounded by corpses. She thought of the time he had a crow in his mouth, and dragged it bloody across the dirt. Maybe Daphne was like that, too. A predator that plays with her food.

"Was Mama June related to Mister Brightbones?"

"Yes and no, but I don't really want to answer questions about that. That was my past, okay? And thinking about it's like opening up an old wound and poking at it. If I do it too much, it'll infect me, and neither of us want that, do we?"

And Nix nodded. Of course, that makes sense. All families have secrets. She guessed this new family would be just the same in that respect, and that was perfectly a-okay in her book. "I guess I should go to sleep now, huh. I am feeling really tired."

"Oh wait," and Daphne leaned over the couch, and reached around in the satchel she'd brought with her to the house. "I need you to wear this." She pulled out a necklace of bones, and they clanked like wind chimes as she placed them around Nix's neck.

"What is this? It smells kind of funky."

"It's a dreamcatcher, I made it myself," and then she lifted another one from the neckline of her own shirt, "See, mom? I'm wearing one, too."

Nix tucked hers back into her shirt, so it rested cold and sharp against her chest. "It doesn't look like any dreamcatcher I've ever seen. What's it made of?"

"Mouse bones and owl bones and some sticks from a yew tree. I charred them each a bit, you have to do that, you know, or the magic's inert and they won't really work."

"The magic's inert? What are you talking about?"

The fog in her head swished about and cleared up for a bright second. Her heart raced, and the danger of the situation reared its ugly misshapen head once again. She thought of running, or maybe tricking Daphne outside and locking the doors and windows. She hadn't been in control of her thoughts, and she didn't like that at all.

And the word mom . . . it felt manipulative, and . . .

The eyes met hers once more, and the lazy fog rolled back in and blanketed her thoughts. Later, she would think maybe this was multiple sclerosis acting up. It might be—she's had brain fog from it in the past? And yet, she knew that wasn't it. Deep in her bones. This was something else, something terrifying.

She just had no idea how bad it was going to get.

"Maybe I was wrong in calling them dreamcatchers, they don't really catch dreams. They're a bit more like . . . oh huh. I dunno how to say it? Dreamcatcher just feels right, but it's not quite there yet, oh damn. Let me figure this out. It's a bit more like a protective amulet. It keeps the lost boys and their pets from getting in your head while you're asleep."

These words made no sense, and yet made perfect sense at exactly the same time. It was a paradox of thinking, one that her mind was primed to accept as just perfectly fine and normal. "Is this connected to your scarecrows outside? Your, what did you call them again? Your sentinels?"

"Yes. But I shouldn't tell you more than that."

"Why?"

Daphne leaned in, kissed Nix directly on the lips and said, "Good night, Mom."

And that was it, she fell deep into the darkness beyond dream.

4

THE dreamcatcher did not work. The minute she laid down on the rickety bed and crawled into sleep, she saw something strange and flickering on the edge of her dreaming mind. She followed it, moved through empty passages, broken doorways, followed a cat through the passage of shadows, until she came to a familiar grave-yard. She'd dreamt of this place long ago, the night she'd fallen from the top bunk on their bunk beds and cut her ear in half on the edge of a dresser. She still had the scar from when they'd sewn her ear back on, without any anesthetic, as her dad held her down kicking and screaming and they applied needle to severed skin. This dream place was not a good dream place. It was all connected and wrapped up into that one night . . .

Maybe it was an ill omen? She wasn't sure.

And the dream sharpened. Vine-choked mausoleums stood guard along the pathway, their edifices coated with Medusa faces etched in stone. Primitive, fang lipped, wide eyes, like the old Gorgon coins of ancient Greece. It was neither day nor night here, but some hazy in-between time, the light a bruised twilight dawn.

And there, as if he was waiting for her all this time, was a boy on a gravestone, sitting in the center of a large spotlight. The twilight oozed inky black outside of the amber light, focusing all attention on his beautiful, feminine features. Long gold curls, lips chapped and cracked, as a blindfold stretched across his high cheekbones, with two silver buttons right over where the eyes should be. A loose gray hospital gown draped over his body and fluttered in an unseen wind, as he grasped an old IV, still connected to a port on the back of his hand.

Fog rolled through the tombstones, a living thing.

"I can't see you . . . step closer."

He whispered these words, his voice dead leaves under foot and stone scraping against stone.

"Who are you?"

She did not walk closer.

He leapt off the tombstone. She thought maybe he was about nine or ten years old? He had to be twelve, at the latest, she was sure of that. And somehow, maybe this was dream logic, but his movements unsettled her. Like a spider, dipping his head down into a webby cocooned corpse and drinking deep.

"Oh, child," and he grinned all teeth. "You know who I am. I'm certain your little guest told you all about me. In fact, that's partly why I'm here . . . I can't see you right now, either of you, and I need you to do me a little favor."

Hard to think, to see, to feel in this dream. She couldn't control it, it felt unconnected to her thoughts, to her body. She was in his domain. "No."

"Well, my, my, my. That was very rude of you. You haven't even heard my proposal."

The spotlight followed him as he floated up to her, the fog carrying his body, as he lifted right up to her face, and placed his hand on her cheek. His fingernails were so long, far longer than she'd ever seen on a living body. She had seen nails like that on a corpse once, but that was a long time ago, when she'd worked in a medical school. "What proposal."

She knew she didn't want to betray Daphne. There was a connection there, a silver thread between them. When the girl called her mom, it felt so right, like she'd been waiting her whole life for that moment. Destined to be a mother to an orphan . . .

"When I came to Daphne she was dying of cancer. Did she tell you that?"

And Nix couldn't remember exactly what Daphne said, only that she was sick. "I, I think so. She told me you helped her . . ."

He tapped her cheek gently, and Nix felt it. A real touch, real skin on skin, the bones beneath his fingers pressed against the bones beneath her flesh. Was this really a dream? Or was this something else?

"I *cured* her. I can cure you, too, you know. Would be the easiest thing in the world."

"I . . . I . . ."

This couldn't be real. This had to be her mind playing off of what Daphne had said earlier. How could this be Mister Brightbones? He was a child! And how could he cure her? There was no cure for multiple sclerosis. And yet, she felt something break inside of her. Like a glacier cracking in the summer heat, slowly opening up to the waters outside. He couldn't do that . . . he was lying . . .

"I don't lie, my child. The truth means the world to me, it is all and everything. Do you understand? You need to trust me, and understand when I say this. I can *cure* you and it would be so simple."

"Then do it."

"Aha, but I *need* to find you first," and the word *need* rolled around in his throat. "I have no idea how she's doing it, but that girl child, Daphne, she made it so I can't see you. Destroy these *things* that blind me, and I will come to you, and give you my greatest gift."

The dream swam and blurred, as someone shook her violently in the waking world, a ship on the seas of blankets and pillows.

"What's in it for you?"

A pause as the world shook some more. Someone was trying to shove her out of this dream, but she clung on, fingers against the frames of sleep, holding tight. She had to hear this, had to know what she would be giving up in order for her to be cured of her MS. One thing she learned throughout the years was that all medication came with a price, and very rarely was it only financial.

"Everything."

And then she let go, the dream sliding away in cloud of wings, revealing Daphne's face where a moon would be, hysterical and screaming. Her face streaked with tears, as she shouted over and over again, still shaking Nix's body. "Don't go, don't listen to him, you stay here, Mom, you stay with me, you're mine, I will keep you safe, Mom, stay with me, stay with me."

The blurry aftersleep world sharpened into focus, now headache bright with temples throbbing to the rhythm of her blood. This always seemed to happen when her sleep was disrupted mid-dream, as if being pulled into this reality tore something in her mind, giving her a minor migraine. She grabbed Daphne's hands with her own, stopping the queasy motion. "No, please," she said, and tried her damnedest not to vomit from the combination of pain and motion sickness. Everything spun briefly, and then righted itself as she laid down and covered her head with the blankets.

Her mouth had a crusty afterparty taste to it. Was this a hangover? She hadn't had anything to drink in years, and yet that was exactly what this felt like, a hangover. Even the small table lamps rung out with pain, as the images on that webpage flickered in her mind, briefly, running around the headache, and she felt like vomiting again.

Yes, this was most definitely a hangover.

"I'm sorry," Nix said, "I just don't feel so hot right now."

She thought back to yesterday, in the evening when Daphne convinced her to go to sleep, and it seemed like some kind of rotten fugue state. Had she been drugged? All that warm fuzzy feeling had since left her, and that need to please Daphne and call her daughter was gone as well. She pulled back the blanket, and looked at that pale stranger in her house, leaning across her bed, and realized she had no idea who this girl was at all. She'd taken her in out of need to care for another soul, yes. But then . . . what had happened? Something had gotten into her mind, dulled her senses, made her feel drunk and suggestible. And it was not something she imagined, no. It was visceral and real, and the way she felt this morning was certain proof of that.

"You dreamt of him, I can tell," Daphne said.

Nix decided to take a lesson from Perseus in the battle with his own Gorgon, and turned and looked at the window instead. She saw Daphne's reflection there, but didn't feel that fuzzy draining feeling from looking at her eyes. Good. She could stay in control of her body now. That was important, she needed her thoughts to be her own.

"You don't have to say it," Daphne said, "I can tell. You did dream of him. Whatever he told you, it was a lie, you understand? His promises are wrong, broken things."

"He cured you, didn't he?"

And Daphne shook her head in disbelief. Her reflection opened her mouth wide, revealing those cannibal teeth, and a terrifying sensation washed over Nix as she remembered . . . remembered . . . wanting to give herself over to Daphne, and let her drink her up with those beautiful teeth, those beautiful lips.

"No, he didn't cure me, not exactly. If I don't feed every other day, my cancer comes back and I step closer and closer to the grave."

"Feed?"

"Yes, yes, yes. On blood. Please don't hate me, Mom, but I have to do it, or else I'll die. Human blood, animal blood, all of it. I don't want you to have the same fate I have, it's horrible. The price is too steep."

Nix wanted to turn away, to not look at her reflection any more. Maybe Perseus was wrong, maybe that Gorgon could still turn you to stone, even with a reflection. But she wouldn't turn around, could not look her in the face. Pile of salt, hypnotized, subservient to Daphne the vampire once again. No, no, she had to have her own thoughts. She looked at the ground instead.

"Death is what feeds this cure that Mister Brightbones gave me. Though I like to call it a curse more than a cure, I don't revel in death like the others did. They had me, they had me . . ."

"What?"

"I drank up my own mom, right there in the hospital when Mister Brightbones came for me. It was the first and last step, after that this thing inside of me, this cure, this curse, this . . . whatever the hell it is! It came to life. It fed me and changed me, and I could tell that not only was my cancer gone, but my hair was growing back, my ulcers and sores were healing, I could walk so easily again, no longer tired whenever I moved even the slightest finger. But the hunger grows, it wants more death, to feed until the light goes out and gets sucked inside of me. That's the unspoken promise of what he does."

Just turn away, Nix, just turn away from the reflection, turn away and walk outside. Don't look back, drive into town, get on a plane and leave this whole mess behind.

But . . . could she get around Daphne?

"It is like a ghost, or a demon, or I don't know what. It speaks to me at night, I can hear it whispering in my blood after I feed, the voice like a burning fire all crackles and light. When I dream, I dream the ghostly dreams . . . I haven't had my own dream in decades."

"Decades?"

Damn it, she turned and looked at Daphne, her heart loud, hungry, a drum in her ears. So far, she felt like herself, still connected to her own body and thoughts. Maybe she could fight it, stay herself long enough to get out of here.

"How old are you?"

"About a year or two younger than you," and then Daphne leaned back and smiled at the ceiling. She kicked her legs out, and laid back with her head leaning off the bed. "Funny, isn't it? It was decades ago he changed me. And here I am, still in this tiny body. It makes it hard to get by, no one takes me seriously at all. Just a teenage runaway, with the soul of a middle-aged woman, and a thick blood lust that can't be quenched."

Nix chewed on her fingernail, looking at Daphne's legs as she kicked them in the air. She's that old? "When were you supposed to die?"

"Several lifetimes ago."

Well, now. The gift of Mister Brightbones didn't seem so bad, did it? Killing animals, that was nothing, she'd had hamburgers for dinner the other night and felt not a lick of guilt about it. Sure, the idea of feeding on death itself seemed kind of creepy, but how was that any worse than pumping her body full of chemicals? Right now she had an infusion every few months that made her freezing cold, nauseated, and so immunocompromised that even the sniffles turned into a full-blown sinus infection or pneumonia. She felt it in her veins, too, like music, and it messed with her dreams . . .

And even after going through all of that, her relapses still happened, just a little less frequent than they used to be. Not to mention the steroid infusions she had to get every time a relapse came back! That medication was something else. It wracked her body and mind, and when it drained from her system she could barely move out of bed for the rest of the month. It felt like getting hit by a truck.

"You're able to live off of animals . . . right? So maybe . . . maybe it's not too bad."

"Cats, squirrels, dogs . . . but it's not quite enough. Their deaths are not the same as our deaths, and this thing inside of me wants *human* death. This is just pushing back the inevitable . . . eventually I'll have to feed on a human or my cancer will come back and take me this time. I don't know if I could do that again . . ."

"Oh."

And yet, Nix couldn't shake the thought of it. A cure.

"You don't want this. You don't want Mister Brightbones to come here, no. You can't even come close to understanding what this means, what you will have to do, who he is . . ."

"He seemed so harmless in my dream . . . was he like that in real life, I wonder? Like a little boy with curly blond hair . . ."

And then Daphne shot up, put both of her hands on Nix's face, and forced her to look directly in her eyes. Golden, dancing, iris, blue, green, flecks of brown sparkling, and then a warm feeling spilling throughout her entire body. Everything turned numb and distant, her thoughts slowly fading into the shadows again, and she tried to grab a hold of it, to grasp onto the frame of her thoughts like she'd held onto the frames of her dream . . .

But it was no use.

"Mom, listen to me."

"I'm listening."

Her own voice sounded strange to her ears, like someone else was talking through her mouth. Some distant, brain-dead thing.

"You don't want this cure."

"I don't."

"You don't want to bring Mister Brightbones here."

"I don't."

"Good. Now, come on, we're going to go outside, and you're going to help me make sure my scarecrows are still up and keeping those nasty crows away from spying on us. Come on, Mom! Grab your cane, let's go already."

And then she watched her own body move without thinking, following exactly what Daphne told her to do. This was perfectly fine, wasn't it? Everything was okay now. Nothing was wrong, it was just what she'd always meant to do. Pick up her cane, walk out with her daughter, and make sure the world was all right and good once again. She smiled and said, "I'm glad we're a family."

5

THE next month or so blurred around her in waves, deep under and drowning in the numb moments. She barely clung onto the memories of her actions, and each night she dreamt only of empty static. Each day was the same, she walked around the perimeters of her farm, cleaned up any animal corpses that Daphne had emptied of blood, and then checked on the scarecrows. If they'd moved at all, she'd reposition them in just the right way, to make her daughter Daphne happy. She did not want to upset the poor little girl, she'd been through enough, hadn't she? And this life here, this was the good life. A life they both deserved, after so many hardships.

She would then go into town for a while, mostly to have someone to talk to. Since Daphne slept most of the days away she'd gotten lonely during the daylight hours, and needed some company, any company at all. She would walk the two miles down to Main Street, her hip hurting a bit from the walk, but she was careful not to fall or trip. There, she would hit the bakery and talk with Anna and see what she'd been up to during the week, and hopefully score a free muffin or two to take back with her. Daphne could not each such things, so they were all for her. What wonderful treats!

They'd gone to school together, her and Anna. And for a little while, when they were drunk and careless teenagers she'd made out with Anna's brother. Something Anna still teased her about to this day, even though her brother had been dead for a few years now. An overdose, which wasn't too uncommon in a small northern town such as Dark Rivers. She still stung at the thought of Anna finding him that rough winter morning, knocking on his shack, using her key when he wouldn't come to the door. That was the year of Nix's very first multiple sclerosis attack, too. Don't you dare tell her those things weren't connected, Nix knew better.

Still, even with all that between them, it gave her something to look forward to, coming into town most days and talking with Anna. Even though at the time her mind was thick and muddy, she still tried to carry on conversations, and Anna would remark about it, and ask her if everything was all right? Was her MS acting up, was that it? Was she on some new medication maybe? And what was all this gossip about a teenage girl come to live with her . . .

And each time Nix brushed it off and said yes, it was her multiple sclerosis, of course it was, what else could it be? She didn't like lying to Anna, no, but she couldn't explain it away herself, either. For the most part she felt happy and content, even though something felt wrong underneath it all. Like a rotten buzzing baritone that you could barely hear under the sweet music, souring it just slightly.

And Anna nodded each time, and gave her the muffins and a weak smile, and then said maybe she should stop by in the afternoon sometime, once the bakery had closed for the day. She could bring Hank and their kids, wouldn't that be nice? And Nix of course said, yes, that would be really nice, they really should do it. But whenever Anna called or texted to try and set something up, Nix's head would be all abuzz again and clouded, and she just ignored it until the next day. And Anna, that sweet friend that she was, wouldn't even bring it up or question what had happened.

After hitting the bakery she would drop by the grocery store and pick up some food for the day, and maybe a little more for the rest of the week if she had the money. Most of the cashiers were too young for her to recognize, and quite a few of them had been replaced ages ago by self check out aisles. She avoided self-checkout, of course— she needed the communication. Even if it was with some little pimply boy that would stare at her like she was from outer space and not from around here. It was okay if they didn't talk back, sometimes it was just nice speaking and being heard and that was that.

She didn't really talk much with Daphne, it was more like Daphne talked toward her, told her things, her words crawled under skin and wrapped around her bones. She tried to shake this away, but that felt wrong, so she just listened and that was all okay. Everything was all okay. It was all perfect, wasn't it? So perfect and wonderful and great.

Afterward, she would hit the bookstore that used be an old movie rental place, back in the dark ages when people still rented DVDs and VHS tapes. The store was owned by one Danny Forrest. He'd inherited it when his parents died not too long ago. They'd passed from that awful car accident (bad snowy roads, one of those rough blizzard winters where they had to call in the national guard to help clear it out and save those trapped in their homes without food or heat). Back then it was still a rental place, and just barely on its last legs. When Danny came in, he turned it around, right quick, and made it into a semi-profitable bookstore. That was in the early 2000s, and he'd been in his mid-twenties at the time. He was only two years younger than Nix and Anna, but they'd never seen him at school. He was one of the few home-schooled Jehovah's Witnesses that congregated on the edges of the town.

Using their money and his wits, it became a destination for readers and writers alike. It was called *Something Old*, a joke because they sold books in the digital age, and did not have a website, nor did they put any of their books on eBay or Amazon. If you wanted that rare signed copy of Anaïs Nin's *House of Incest*, you had to come here and get it. Keeping with the theme was the lack of any WiFi or internet, and a $150 charge if he saw you using your phone at any point. The music was a ten-record turntable, with selections from his personal vinyl jazz collection that he'd hunted down and squirreled away through the years.

When she walked in every day, the little bell tinkled overhead, and the smell of coffee and old books hung heavy in the air. This was her favorite place in the entire world, and she didn't hesitate to tell him that. This was once an apartment building, with the first floor acting as the business area for the rental place. After Danny was done with renovations, he'd turned it into three stories of shelves and tables and chairs. Each floor relegated to different time periods of books, and as she moved between the floors she felt like she moved through time itself. She hadn't moved between floors in the last few years, though. Stairs where her sworn enemy now. The worst part was how random it all was, she would be walking fine down the stairs, and then fall without any reason at all. The first few times were so painful, she just decided never to risk it again and kept away.

Because of that, if she needed a book on another floor, Danny would run up and search for it himself. He didn't keep track of stock on the computer like a smart business owner. He just let the books stack up in a chaotic mess, and searching things out became a certain sense of joy and discovery. She envied him that ability, to hop between floors with ease, and rustle through all of those books like a literary archaeologist.

He always gave her a free cup of coffee, and she would browse around for a bit, take a book down and read for the rest of the day, while she waited for whatever treasure he could bring her way. Several other people congregated on the first floor as well, each one lost in the pages of their texts, barely noticing anyone else around them. It was not a lonely act. Even without speaking they were connected in that moment, and it felt wonderful.

Sometimes someone would buy something and leave, other times an older gentleman she didn't recognize would stomp in, his beard a frazzled gray mess, a knotted old walking stick clenched in his hands. He would take off his pointed leather hat, as if it were still impolite to enter a building while wearing your cap, and place it in his coat. As it got further and further into September, his coat became heavier, and his beard tangled up in the sunset tones of dead leaves.

Danny called him Old Wick, which seemed like a very weird name, indeed. Even weirder still was the fact that Nix had never met this man before September. Where'd he come from? People didn't pop up into a place like Dark Rivers without her noticing. After all, she'd lived in this town pretty much her whole life, as did most of the residents who clung around here. Escaping was hard. Sure most of them would go away to college for a bit, and maybe they would have a job or two in a big city . . .

But then always, always, they ended up back here, back home. Whether they liked it or not. Danny would jokingly call this place the Bermuda Triangle, or the Ninth Circle of Hell, because people kept on coming back, even when they knew better. It seemed to be a curse, and the minute someone got away, death would happen. Death that would bring them back, and then they were stuck, unable to leave ever again.

Not that Nix minded it much. Sure, in her early restless years she wanted to get out of here so bad and see the world. They all did, there was something in the blood of teenagers and young adults that made them want to explore everything. A burning, restless feeling that eventually slid out with the hours of old age. It did not die, as so much melt away. A calm peace remained after, and an appreciation for the dense forests, the charming people you've known your whole life, and the way the birds perched along the edges of the window and sang in the odd hours of morning. A town like this was alive in a way that was different than a larger city, in a way that most people did not understand. There was root and magic here, it dug into you, singing to you. Powerful, drunk stuff.

She never told anyone this, not even Daphne, nor Anna, nor even her parents, no. Not even to her sister Sammy. Although, maybe once she'd mentioned to Aunt Doreen in a dream? But that didn't count, after all, that was only a dream. Anyway, she honestly believed that her multiple sclerosis would be far worse if she'd ever actually left Dark Rivers and went somewhere else. Once cut off from the magic here, she knew it would deteriorate quicker than quick. After all, she'd known a lot of other sufferers around her age and younger that were in wheelchairs already, or could barely talk, or had gone completely blind. One, a poor girl of eighteen, had fallen into a month-long coma during her third relapse. These things terrified her, that one day she could wake up blind, or not wake up at all, all because she had multiple sclerosis.

Anyway, she'd spent her whole life here, her family as well, and they'd never seen Old Wick before this month. One time she'd asked Danny about him, and Danny just shrugged and said "All I know is that he lives on the hill by the lake," and that was it. She couldn't get anything else out of him, no matter how hard she tried, how far she pushed, he seemed to be lost and confused whenever she brought it up. Much like how she'd felt during these blurry days, when Daphne had a hold on her. Maybe somehow that was connected. But she wasn't sure how, not just yet.

6

WERE Old Wick and Mister Brightbones the same person? No, of course not. How silly of her to even think that. After all, he did not resemble the Mister Brightbones she'd seen in her dream. Though, that was a dream, wasn't it? Why would she assume he looked the same in dream as he did in real life? He could be one in the same still, couldn't he? Dreams were deceiving, after all. That was why they were dreams.

Was that why Old Wick showed up in Dark Rivers around the same time as Daphne? Because he was really Mister Brightbones, sniffing her out?

And yet . . .

No, Old Wick walked around in daylight, and Mister Brightbones was the same thing as Daphne, wasn't he? He was the one who cured Daphne, made her into a vampire. Of course he wouldn't be able to walk in the raw sun! Daphne could only go out on overcast days, and even then it drained most of her energy, and she had to go to sleep yet again. When it was a sunny day, even the slightest touch of sun on skin set her limbs ablaze.

Yes, that settled it. Old Wick was not Mister Brightbones.

But that left the question . . .

Who was he, then?

7

NIX kept asking Daphne to turn her into a vampire, too. She wanted it more than anything else, to be able to walk without a cane and dance again. To see perfectly with both of her eyes, and not be blind in one and color blind in the other. To no longer drop random things, to run again . . . run again! Oh she wanted to run and to bike and get a good night's sleep, and no longer worry about not being able to urinate, or having to urinate too much, or having an accident like before when she couldn't hold her shit in while on a long walk.

Daphne said no each time. "I'm not the one who does it," she said, "Only Mister Brightbones can do it. I don't even think he's a vampire, I think he's something else. That thing you saw in your dream? That's what he looks like even now, but when you see him . . ."

"Yes?"

"You'll understand what I mean. He's not clear, you know? He gets all . . . fuzzy and indistinct. You ever look at a cloud and think you see a unicorn or a dragon, even though you know it's just a cloud?"

"Yeah."

"It's kind of like that, but you're seeing a human boy, and you know he's something else, something far more horrible than that. True me, you don't want to meet him. You don't."

And she thought of asking Daphne if somehow Mister Brightbones could come here, and then decided against it. Whenever she even broached the topic of her life before today, she would wince and clam up and not speak for a day or two. Those days she felt the weirdest, as if not hearing Daphne's voice deadened her on the inside, her mind crawling with rough depressive thoughts about Daphne, and if she would ever love her again. And then the next day, after the conversation left the air, Daphne would be all smiles and happy, and everything would be right with the world once again.

Even though, on some underwater level she knew that it was not right after all. That the world may never be right again, not with Daphne here, and not with Mister Brightbones out there, looking for her. And most definitely not with Old Wick, whoever he was, and whatever it was he wanted with the small town of Dark Rivers.

8

IMAGINE her surprise, then, when an old Crown Vic pulled up beside her during her daily walk into town. It was obviously an old cop car, the doors painted black and the logo long since scraped away. It slowed down, she was just near the edge of town, on the train tracks near main street. Leaves rustled under her shoes, and the wind sounded alive as it moved through the trees. Normally, at any other point in her life, she might've felt terrified at this occurrence. She would run and keep on running, or even just walk proudly by, not looking at the fogged-up window slowly pulling down to reveal the rough Santa Claus grin of Old Wick. His face a pile of beard and wrinkles, his eyes sparkling a mischievous blue, all silvery and placid lake still.

But she was not feeling normal right now, so she did not run, she wasn't terrified. Her mind held silent and serene and not ready to panic. After all, Daphne had numbed her to almost all things, and kept her docile in her thoughts and in her heart. She felt a tug of fear, but it felt so far away and distant, as if it were happening to someone else. She wanted to feel that thought, and for a moment tried to chase it, to maybe reclaim herself through her old fears and anxieties . . .

But she was disrupted when Old Wick coughed and said, "You look a bit lost, ma'am. I'd seen you before, up at the coffee place? I always figured you for a local, so I'm not sure why you have that look on your face."

Another shadow of an emotion, just out of reach. Embarrassment? But it was too far away to experience it completely. Instead she tried to smile, but even that was damn near impossible. It was as if her cheek muscles were on the other side of the world. Maybe this was multiple sclerosis affecting her, and not Daphne? She wasn't sure which thought was more comforting, and which more terrifying.

"What look on my face?"

"Oh, oh, I'm sorry, I meant no offense at all, my dove. I just meant I was worried about you, that's all. Are you lost?"

And then she thought about it, and realized, she was kind of lost, wasn't she? But not in the way he thought, it wasn't a physical kind of confusion, where she did not know where she was or where she was going. No, it was more a mental sort, where her mind and her body became a labyrinth to herself, and moving about in the once-familiar place had become confusing and meandering. She tried to remember her dream house at times, and found that it was mostly gone now, with entire floors missing. Had Daphne done this to her?

"I, I guess maybe I am. But not in the world . . ."

"In yourself, I know, I can see it in your eyes. Look, I can probably help you. Do you want my help?"

"I don't know."

And she really did not. She tried to figure out how she felt, if she wanted to do one thing or the other, but really all she wanted was to help Daphne. She wanted to go back and watch the coffin in the basement, and make sure she slept all right. Or maybe even guard the outside, and make sure no crows came to spy on them during the day. When was the last time she had a thought to herself? Even in the bookstore, or the grocery store, when she was talking with her friends, and walking alone, Daphne always seemed to be there, hiding in the corner of her mind, just waiting to make herself known once again.

"All right, let's try a different tactic, then, lost girl. Do you want to come over to my place for some tea? It's all organic, I gather it myself in my garden. Some of the best tea you'll ever taste, I promise you that!"

And for a moment then, the mist slid aside. She saw herself reflected in his eyes. Haggard, alone, somehow lost within herself, and felt a tinge of fright at what she'd become. How did this happen to her? Did the mist of Daphne age her so much? And in his eyes she saw herself change, just a little, just a tiny bit. She saw her old self, the self that was wracked by multiple sclerosis, yes, but also full of her own agency. She wanted to be that person again.

"I guess that's okay."

And even though some distant part of her tried to warn her, and sent her images of missing women she'd seen online, found dismembered or choked to death, it was as if her thoughts were screamed across a long, vast, hallway . . . she walked over to the passenger side, and got into the banged-up car. It sputtered and coughed exhaust, and Old Wick smiled at her and said, "Wait until you see my house. It's had a lot of names, you know, some stretching back a long while indeed."

"Oh?" And still, she felt perfectly okay making small talk right now. How odd. She actually saw herself, watched herself talking like everything was perfectly fine and nothing strange was going on at all. Of course she got into cars with strange Santa Claus-looking old men and went to their houses. Maybe . . .

Maybe she could at least find out why he was in Dark Rivers before he killed her? That thought seemed so absurd, it made her laugh a little.

"Yes, it was once called Haddo House, named after an old magus who used to live there, Oliver Haddo. You ever hear of him?"

"No?"

More images flashed in her mind, this time of *Black Dahlia*, and the grim images of satanic panic from her childhood, and then the Manson murders she found online. Part of her mind tingled at this moment, as if her fear was getting to her, finally.

"He was a contemporary of Aleister Crowley, Yeats, and all those other Golden Dawn era occultists. Not quite as popular mind you, but still a bigger name in the occult circles."

One more warning in her mind. One more. She remembered how her great-grandma on her mom's side disappeared in Cleveland in the 1940s, right around when the Torso Killer was out doing his thing. She was never found again, and no one knows what happened to her. They never found her grave, and none of the bodies were identified as hers. She should . . . get out . . . so that . . . doesn't happen . . . to her . . .

"So it's an old house?"

"Oh, my dove, you have no idea. Come, let's go and take a look, and I'll give you the grand tour. I think it might wake you up some, so you're not quite as lost. That sound good?"

She almost said no, almost. But that numb curse placed on her thoughts was too strong, and Daphne had done too good a job of making her a docile servant. The last of the murderous images dashed out of her head, and she was a doll again, a doll in human skin.

"Okay, I guess it sounds good. And then I'll no longer be lost?"

"I hope so," he said, "But one can never be certain on these things. I'm going to try my best, but the rest is up to you, my dove. You're going to have to meet me halfway."

And then he put the car into gear, and turned around, and drove back the way he'd come. She saw the hill on the edge of town, with that one old house sticking out of the pine trees. It was a late nineteenth-century, neo-Gothic kind of building, with strange arches and Addams Family flourishes. She'd seen that house all of her life, and she'd always wondered who would live there. Some people said it was haunted, and one friend of hers in high school claimed a coven of hippie witches had lived there and practiced weird cannibal rituals lost in time. No one really believed that stuff, but they told it all the same.

She'd never met anyone that had lived there before now. In a way she was oddly excited, and needed to know if those rumors were true.

"The Cannibal House."

"Yes, I've heard it called that. I told you it had a lot names through the years. Want to hear a few more? Let's see here, we got the Hollow House, and Hallow House, that was all a play on Haddo House after he died. You know how he died, right?"

"No?"

"He died by his own hand . . . not just a normal suicide, mind you. He'd found out had cancer in '68, the kind that was like a long slow death, and he decided he was going to do something about it. This was a ritualistic human sacrifice, you understand? One last occult ritual to end all other occult rituals."

That part screaming *get out* was louder now, and yet still far away. She tried to shake the cobwebs from her thoughts, so she could listen to the warnings and maybe wake her body to screaming. This felt like a dream now, like one of those bad dreams where you can't control your body and it moves on its own.

"Do you know what he was doing, what that spell was? Do you have any idea?"

She shook her head, and it felt like moving through water.

"No, I guess not," he sighed, "It's a bit of a grim story, that's for sure. Oh, here we are."

And then he pulled into the dirt road climbing up that hill, the pine trees speeding around them in a whirlwind of dust, the Cannibal House perched above, a vulture built from wood and masonry.

9

THE house disoriented her, in a way that was subtle and hard to distinguish from multiple sclerosis at first. Compound that with the woozy fuzzy feeling Daphne had drilled into her head, and it took a bit before she realized that the walls were slightly off kilter, and the doors a little too small for their frames. The ceiling slanted about at seemingly impossible angles, and the floor rose slightly when it reached the walls. The whole effect was dizzying, and she had to sit down on one of the chairs in the innermost parlor.

She noticed, too, that the wallpaper was a deep burgundy color, and was one of those old patterned wallpapers that became more complex the more you looked at it. The patterns were the same color as the wallpaper itself, just slightly fainter, so that at first you thought you were hallucinating different pictures, or maybe if you could focus just right, then they would disappear. It didn't help much that she had problem seeing red in her left eye, that multiple sclerosis had damaged the ocular nerves so badly that it was blurry and lacked saturation. It made this weird effect even more pronounced, and it distracted her, she kept trying to focus, closing one eye, then the other, to see if she could bring these images into clarity.

Old Wick coughed to get her attention. "What do you take in your tea? Sugar? Milk?"

Oh, that's right. She came here for tea, not freaky wallpaper.

"Just plain, thank you."

For a brief second she felt her mind clear, as if the wallpaper had teased consciousness back into her thoughts. She saw what looked like a pattern of women crawling up the walls, their faces obscured by their long hair, chains dragging behind them. She jumped back, a bit startled, as the fog settled back into her thoughts again.

"What's up with that pattern?"

"Do you like it, my dove? One of the reasons I brought you here was to see that, it has an odd effect on most people, I find it almost meditative. Oliver Haddo himself had it designed, and then placed on this very wall, before he brought all those young women here near the end of his days."

Old Wick walked over to a tea cart that had been left out, and plugged the electric kettle into the wall. "You know how hard it is to find one of these around here? Bunch of barbarians living in the States, I swear. I had to scour the internet and finally imported a kettle from Canada, of all places."

"What women?"

"Hmmm?"

"You just said a bunch of young women came here during the end of his days. What young women?"

Her heart beat a steady rhythm in her chest, like a low slow battle drum. She had a feeling if it weren't for Daphne's influence on her, it would be going rattle fast. Another faraway down-the-hall part of her was screaming to get out, that she shouldn't be here. But it was all static and broken down, and barely even reached her thoughts. Maybe if she stared at the wallpaper some more? No, no. She did not want to do that. That wasn't helping her in the right way, and she felt she would be trading in one enchantment for another.

"You didn't hear the story about the cannibals? I thought you knew all about this, since you called this place the Cannibal House."

"I didn't know it was real. I thought it was gossip, just a rumor."

"Well, it wasn't. I told you Oliver Haddo killed himself, yes? As a sacrifice?"

"Yes, I think so."

"Well, then. He'd been planning that for awhile, ever since he'd gotten his prognosis and a date for his own death. Could you imagine what that would be like? To know practically the exact hour and date you were to die? Awful. Anyway, back in the '60s and '70s, a lot of young hippies sought out old occult figures like Haddo. They were looking for something, a key to break reality, to transcend it all in an era of bliss and magick. You look throughout that decade, and you see it all over the place. You have Manson, of course, but you also have Anton LaVey, Father Yod and the source family, the Ant Hill Gang, and so many more. Oliver Haddo was no different."

"And they were the cannibals?"

"In a way, yes. When they showed up he knew exactly what he wanted to do. He had to become a god, and decided to choose Bacchus, and found a bunch of old texts explaining rituals of ecstasy and destruction, and under his guide, those poor women became maenads. They held long orgiastic festivals of wine and LSD, they would buy bulls from the local farms and rip them apart and devour them limb from limb. At times they would disembowel crows with their bare hands and read the entrails to see the future."

Everything felt underwater and distant. She tried looking at the ceiling, at the walls to regain her own thoughts, her own mind. Daphne's voice spun about in her head, her eyes diamonds, telling her to come back home already, to protect the sleeping Daphne. She'd told her about vampire hunters, and how they weren't the usual sort you read about in horror novels. They weren't on a holy crusade, no. They were thieves, collecting bones they cut out of living vampires, to power dark unseen spells. They would trap their vampiric prey with a horrible glare, hold them down, their faces blank except for one large mouth that took up almost the entire head, smiling. According to Daphne they were in the shape of people, but were not people. Nix wasn't sure if she believed her about all this stuff when she first told her, it seemed so absurd and horrific.

Then again, she'd watched Daphne drink the blood of a wild raccoon until it died, twitching in her arms, her eyes lighting up like thunder clouds filled with lightning. As her skin plumped up and her face glowed a little, no longer looking sick or cancerous. She felt like this was connected to that somehow, but she had no clue how or why. The house. Haddo. Old Wick. The vampires. The vampire hunters. How did they all mesh together?

No clue. She was still confused and foggy headed from Daphne, from the house, from her chronic illness. Still, she pressed on.

"How do you know all of this?"

"I'll give you a tour later, you might be lucky enough to see it yourself."

"Wait . . . what?"

He walked over and knocked on the wall. The house murmured and seemed to shift for a moment, and then moaned a little like an achy old woman. "This house is not what it appears to be. It feeds on horrific things, records them on its bones and plays them back when it wants to relive its greatest hits. It's not just alive, you know. it's also endlessly hungry, and has gotten quite adept at luring and feeding on misery and suffering."

"I think . . ." Daphne pulled on her mind, and she couldn't resist it any longer, "I think perhaps I should go?"

"Oh? You do seem a bit less out of it right now, so I guess I can take you back home if you want. I really did want to show you around, I think you might even recognize some of these rooms and corridors. I have a feeling you've seen them in your dreams."

Her dreams, was this the house she'd dreamt of all those years? The one where Auntie Doreen walked with her through the maze-like hallways and warned her about all this horrible stuff going on? She wanted to see it, she needed to see it . . . maybe she would dream of the house and Aunt Doreen again if she walked through the halls and saw it in person.

And yet the call of Daphne to go back home was even stronger.

"Here, just try some of the tea first, and I'll finish my story."

He poured the boiling mixture into a small, smoky gray teacup. One for her, one for him, and then dipped in an old Victorian-style tea ball. It was metallic, and connected to a chain, the looseleaf tea floating around inside of it.

"Okay."

"So, where was I? Oh yes, so he trained them in the old bacchanal rites, and then led them through several days of ritualistic orgies and manic ecstasy, building up into a crescendo on the final night. *His* final night on this planet earth. He donned a bull mask, and rose up in front of them, and in their frenzy they ate him alive with their bare hands. He hoped that in doing so he would become Bacchus . . . but instead he fed his misery into the house, the pain into this house, nourishing it with his sorrow. Then the women turned on each other and did the same thing. It was really awful. To be fair, I hope you actually don't see any of this, out of all the ghosts that repeat themselves in this house, this one is by far the worst of them all. Only a twelve-year-old girl survived. I found her in the newspaper, an old article, she was discovered walking through town, covered in blood, unable to speak."

Her stomach filled with ice and lurched about, as the world grew smaller and smaller around her. The dizziness of the house didn't help this at all, and she was lightheaded again. Which could've been from MS, or it could've been from her medications, or it could've been from the house itself, or yet again from Daphne. It was impossible for her to tell, and it made her hate her MS even more than ever before, for muddying up this reality.

"Who was she?"

"I don't know, to be honest, I really don't know. This was around '68 or so, and the newspaper didn't list her name, on account of her being a minor and all that. but it's odd, you know."

"What's odd?"

"You look just like her. You're older, you know, but you both have the same face. Curious." He shook his head, as if clearing away stray thoughts. "But of course, you're too young to be her."

He looked down in his lap for a moment, and then dunked the tea ball in and out a few times, and then set it on the small end table beside him. "Tea should be done steeping now, you'll probably want to drink it soon. It tastes kind of bitter and nasty if it gets too cold."

She nodded and followed suit, and then said, "After this, can I go home?"

He grinned and then sipped his tea with his pinkie out. He didn't slurp or anything, but instead silently enjoyed it, and then set it back down on the saucer once again. "Of course. Let me tell you another story . . ."

And this time she audibly groaned. This wasn't a conversation, this was a monologue, and it seemed like he was telling these stories to keep her here longer than she wanted to stay. And she needed to get back, needed to return to her daughter and keep her safe. Even if she didn't actually believe in vampire hunters in the first place, especially not ones that were that cruel.

"It will be a short one, I promise, and then you can go back home."

"Okay."

"And before I start, I have a present for you. Promise me you'll take these home with you and place them by your bed? They might help with that lost feeling you have swimming around inside."

He reached into his pocket and found what looked like two little wax men. Their faces were blank except for a thumbprint for a mouth, and each of them had a tiny black ribbon pinned to their waxy chest. They smelled like burnt candles, their wicks blown out long ago.

She took them and held onto them as she drank some more of her tea. It tasted funny, like a forest fire. "What are these?"

"Just superstitious nonsense, that's all, Like that dreamcatcher you wear around your throat."

She touched it, and realized that the bones were hidden under her shirt. How did he know what this was? She muttered a thank you and placed the waxy figures in her satchel.

"Now, let me ask you a question: have you ever owned a pet mouse?"

She remembered back when she was a kid, Aunt Doreen had given her a pet mouse that only lived a few years. His death had been a horrible thing, and she didn't like being reminded of it.

"Ah, yes, you have. Good! Now, I had a mouse when I was a kid, too, a little white mouse I won at a fair. How perfect for a little boy! We were the best of friends, for an entire year it was pure happiness. And then, I caught this wild mouse in the woods, and I thought, how great! They're going to be good friends. I knew you couldn't just throw two mice in together, so I put a cardboard divider between them, and slowly introduced them to each other over many weeks. After about a month I thought it would be good to remove the divider."

He sighed with his whole body.

"I didn't even get a chance to exhale, that wild mouse tore the other one apart before my very eyes. It was awful, I've never seen anything like it before in my life. Not until I saw that ghostly display here, showing the last days of the bacchanalia. It haunts me to this day, the one mouse screamed so much as it died, it . . . I still have nightmares."

Nix realized she didn't want her tea anymore, so she set it aside on the end table next to her. "I'm sorry . . ."

"You brought a wild animal into your own house, too? Didn't you? A feral mouse in the shape of a teenage runaway."

She turned and looked away.

"I really think you should take me home now."

10

WHEN she came back, she went to her room on the first floor, and placed the weird little figures on one of her dressers, near her bed. They felt odd, like they didn't belong anywhere. Not just in her room, anywhere at all. They did not fit into this existence, and she tried to puzzle out why that was the case. These sorts of things never creeped her out before. She'd had tons of little straw and wax dolls, worry dolls, China dolls, puppets, and her mom had even had a ventriloquist's dummy perched on the couch when she was a kid, growing up. If none of those things made her feel so wrong, icky, or creeped out . . .

Then why did these?

She decided it was best not to think about it, and instead to go about her day, finishing up her chores, and then get a good night's sleep. Sadly, it would be a long while before that happened again. Every night after tonight she would wake to the sound of scratching in her room, and at first she thought it was a mouse in the walls? But the sound wasn't coming from the walls at all, no. It came from the dolls, over on her dresser. She wondered if they'd moved, or if it was only a trick of the light.

And in those late-night hours, she wished she'd gone downtown like she originally planned each day. She missed seeing her friends and hanging out at Something Old. Maybe she should drive into town tomorrow instead of walking. Yes, it was a bit tricky, what with her eyesight and all of that. But . . .

She didn't want to get stopped by Old Wick again, and be driven someplace else. Her mind was too weak right now, her willpower melted down to a candle stump, all from Daphne's influence. She knew she would just go with him again, and again, and again, and maybe end up dead or part of a cannibal feast, and some part of her mind screamed in the numb dark corridors of her thoughts.

Would she even be able to go to Something Old without him being there? Trying to talk to her, to maybe get her to go back to his place once again? She didn't doubt it. But at least Danny would be there, and he would be able to help out, maybe snap her out of this zombie state.

If only.

11

THERE were moments in that numb month when she had whip crack clarity, and saw her situation real and true. It shook her, when she realized she'd become thrall to a vampire that had probably murdered and drank both of her cats. Poor Sherlock, poor Doctor Death. It was all her fault, wasn't it? And when she remembered the times she offered herself up to Daphne in bright revelation, neck bare and blood pumping, as Daphne refused to drink, to drink deep and devour her . . .

She locked herself in her room, arms shaking, whole body a tremor of nervous terror. She piled up everything in front of her door—chairs, bookcase, and a dresser she had to push with her back, all grunting and weak-muscled. Panic thoughts, ways to escape ran around in her mind. Would she get to her car in time? Did it have enough gas to go and keep on going? Would her MS behave itself long enough to keep her peripheral vision in check, so she wouldn't get into an accident during her escape?

Running away on foot was an impossible proposition. She would clutter, fall, trip, and slide, and Daphne would be on her quick and nimble. Her eyes would focus on Nix's features, and Nix would try to look away, but it wouldn't take much . . . even the slightest glimpse, and she would be back in thrall again. So instead she would barricade herself away in these moments, and try desperately to think of a way out of all this.

And each time she turned to Mister Brightbones. Someone who could cure her. Someone who would give her the same powers as Daphne, yes. And then she would no longer be in thrall to that strange homeless girl. Could she do it, actually become a vampire? Yes. But it wouldn't be so horrible, would it? To be cured, to be free . . .

She never realized until she met Daphne that she would do anything in order to be normal again. She'd gotten so used to her disabilities, they barely even registered. And then, here, all of a sudden, the promise of healing, of normalcy . . .

Eventually, the clarity faded away, somehow, and the fog came back even without Daphne staring into her eyes . . . maybe she'd drunk enough of her that it clung to her blood, and waited silently to be activated yet again. No matter the reason, she would zombie over to the pile of refuse in front of the door and pull it away. She would then open that same door to reveal Daphne smiling each and every time, her body blocking the doorway.

"You can't get past me yet, Mom," she would say, "Not until you give me a kiss!"

And Nix swam over to her, and planted one right on her cheek. Everything had a warm glow with a sour tint to it, and at moments she felt suffocated by love and tenderness, and the scent of rot that clung to everything now that Daphne had moved in.

Once she was lucky enough to have that clarity in the middle of the night, waking up all alone to the sounds of scratching yet again, that dream of black static humming in her thoughts. Daphne did this to me, she thought in that bright and clear night.

She knew she could summon help in her dream, that she had done it countless times in the past. But who? She took off that dreamcatcher from around her neck, and threw it across the floor. It clattered, skittered, and stopped against the wall. At first she wanted to dream of her aunt. If anyone could come here and help her, surely it would be Aunt Doreen?

And yet, right before that last moment of slumber, when she slid under to the garden of dreaming, she had a different thought. A dangerous thought, yes, but one that was always at the forefront of her mind. She wanted to see Mister Brightbones instead. She wanted to be cured. Aunt Doreen could wait for another day. She smiled, it would all be better now, wouldn't it? She ignored the sense of apprehension as she walked through a vast, darkening hallway of a dream, vague gray curtains like molted flesh fluttering in tatters on either side of her. Shadows of tall, twisted statues grinned at her from behind the cracked glass of old windows.

This wasn't the graveyard from before, and this wasn't the dream house of the dead. This was someplace else, someplace other. This had to be Mister Brightbones's home turf—there was no other explanation for it. She'd never visited anywhere like this before, not in dreams, nor in real life. It had an alien sense of uncanny about it, and the unease rested like a splinter in her eye, a visceral physical feeling, even here, in this dream. The walls whispered through open wounds, and she wanted to turn back, to run away. This was a bad idea. Why did she do this? Why not just walk away and leave Daphne behind?

Eventually, she came to a vast indoor garden. The ceiling domed overhead, and more twisted, deformed statuary prowled through this dreaming landscape. Vines clung from everything, and bore diseased fruit, and corpse-scented flowers. In the center of it all sat that boy, Mister Brightbones, reading what looked like a very long scroll, half unfurled in his hands.

She cleared her throat, hoping he would look up and recognize her. He did not.

"Yes?"

"I need your help."

"That is painfully obvious. The question is, so what? I cannot do anything to help you if I can't see you. I have sent my crows, and even they are blind to your location."

"That's the thing, Daphne put up scarecrows . . ."

"Aha, oh, she's a clever child, far more cleverer than we suspected. Good, it will be good to bring her back into the fold. Why don't you just destroy them? I know you've got your difficulties, but I assume you can still start a fire, or even knock them over with a big enough stick."

She twisted her shirt, wringing it between her hands.

"I would, but she's enthralled me."

"That makes sense, your dreams have been a black static to me, a closed doorway without keyhole to enter. How did you get here tonight, then?"

"I woke up around midnight with a clear head, and I tossed off the dreamcatcher and thought of you before I went back to sleep."

"She gave you an owlbone charm as well? Clever girl, she's thought of everything. Well, then, well, then. If I came to you, would you accept me, drink of me, and be healed?"

She nodded and said yes without even a second of hesitation.

"Good, good, good. I knew you were reasonable and smart, you have that way around you. Hold out your hand, palm up."

She walked over to Mister Brightbones, who then set down the scroll and turned to look up at her. "Are you ready? This will probably hurt."

"Is this your gift?"

"No, this is *a gift*, but it is not *that gift*. That is not a thing for dreaming." He tsk'd a few times. "That one requires meat and sinew, blood and bone, burnt offerings. Things that cannot be done here, in this liminal place, but instead in the physical world, with all its trappings and rules that bind it together."

"Oh, okay." And she tried so hard not to let her disappointment show through. "What is this, then?"

"A trick to keep Daphne out of your head. Are you ready?"

Nix nodded, and kept her dream hand steady, palm facing up all vulnerable and ready for pain. Mister Brightbones pulled a key out from under his tongue. It was old and iron and rusted, and had large teeth without too many gaps along the edges. He then spit on it, red, bloody spit, and it burst into flames in his fingertips. "One, two, three."

And then he placed the key in the palm of her hand, and forced it shut into a fist. He held her hand closed with his tiny, boyish, fingers gripping tightly, so impossibly tight that she could barely move. At first she thought it was just a little hot, this wasn't so bad after all. And then, yes, the fire spread, that lighting burn against the palm, the heat pushing against bone itself, the metal melting and fusing with her skin. She had never felt so much pain before in her life, and it was physical and real, and not just a thing in a dream. She held onto the pain, held onto her thoughts, she was going to pass out, it was too bright, too much, and she bit on her cheek, to try and ground herself in this reality, one pain replacing the other.

"Hold onto it," he said, "Just a little longer, you're doing so well."

She smelled burning flesh and wanted to vomit.

"There, there, you can open your fist now."

And she did, and he pulled the key back. It took a few tries, it really had melded with her own skin, and she saw it stringy and stuck, as he yanked and it tore. Small bits of blood pooled on her palm, and she saw a ragged burn shaped exactly like that key. It still stung, yet the pain was smaller, and smaller, a distant throbbing ache compared to the burning metal of before.

"It feels real."

"It is real. Tomorrow, when you need to have your thoughts to yourself, dig your thumb into the burn. This will sever the hold Daphne has on you, if only for a bit while the pain rings out in your mind."

"Is the pain . . . necessary?"

"Yes. No good magic exists without pain, for that is the price we pay for our little *tricks*. Remember, when you have your own thoughts and well-being, you need to go and destroy those scarecrows, so I can come and find you. Understood?"

"And you'll cure me?"

He leaned over, placed his hands on either side of her face. "Yes."

And then she woke to the bared knuckles of sunlight, and that frothy hangover feeling in her body again. Daphne hadn't come in yet, had she? She waited for a moment and listened quietly to the breathing of the house. No noises, no movement, she looked around the room and saw nothing was disturbed. That meant Daphne was probably elsewhere, already asleep in the basement once again, far away from the bright sunlight. Nix walked over and grabbed the dreamcatcher and slid it back over her head before she started work for the day.

Already, she felt Daphne's thoughts weakly spinning around in her mind, vague impressions of the various chores she'd wanted Nix to do during the daylight hours. Clean up a few dead cats she'd drank dry, perhaps bury or burn them. After that, check on the sentinels, and then watch over her sleeping body for a while, to make sure it was protected. The commands gave her that restless numb feeling again, and for a moment, she rose her thumb, placed it over the burn on her hand. It smelled ripe, of freshly melted skin and hot iron, and kept it there, not pressing down just yet.

The wound was real. This was all really happening.

She pressed down, and the pain swept the icky cobwebbed feeling from her mind. For the first time in forever she felt no compulsion, no overwhelming need to do exactly as Daphne had wanted her to do. The thought of feeding her sickened her now, and no longer held the same allure it once had. She was in complete control of her thoughts, and it terrified and exhilarated her at the same time.

12

NIX stood in front of the scarecrows, motionless with her thumb in the palm of her hand. It came and went in waves, Daphne's thoughts drowning out her own thoughts, pulling them under, into the deep sea of her mind. Each time, she pushed her thumb against the burned key, and each time the pain sharpened everything, and she was herself again. As the day wore on, hour to hour, she felt the influence of Daphne leaving her blood, leaving her mind, slowly turning to a dim echo in the distance.

It was about three in the afternoon now, the sun bright in the sky and casting long tree shadows across the forest floor. She'd come here five times already, and stood here in this exact same spot, motionless and staring at them, watching their tattered rags tumble about. She neither fixed them nor tore them down, not yet. She wanted to, she felt the urge to do either, or both at the same time. On one hand, freedom, on another hand . . . betrayal.

Yes, Daphne had enthralled her and controlled her thoughts, and yes she did horrible things, and kept her own gift of a cure out of reach . . .

But Nix couldn't help it. She cared for that damned urchin, no matter what she had done. Doing this last act, it would bring Mister Brightbones here, and he had done something horrible to Daphne, or made her do something horrible, and for the longest time Nix assumed it was abuse . . .

But what if it wasn't? She wouldn't talk about her time with him, would never explain why she left, why she was on the run. Only that he wanted her to do horrible things, and that the price was too great for her cure. Was the horrible thing simply doing what a vampire does, and devour the living? She already did that with . . . with Nix's cats. She . . .

How could she say a human life was worth more than a cat's life? Life is life is life.

That was it, that was the deciding factor. Thinking about poor Sherlock and Doctor Death, and the morning she'd found their bodies, frozen and bloodless, all cramped up with rigor mortis and swarming with blowflies. She was still thralled at that point, and had numbly cleaned them up, and didn't even have a chance to mourn them. They were stolen from her . . . and . . .

No, that was it. She was done protecting Daphne. She deserved the cure, she deserved something to go right in her life. She inhaled, held her breath for a moment, and gathered up her courage. Yes. Okay. She can do this. Already more swimming undersea thoughts meant to drag her under, she pushed her thumb in again, traced the outline of the key and the burnt skin around it, her mind sharp with clear and bright anguish.

And then she stomped over, exhaled, and whacked at the scarecrow with her cane, nearly knocking herself down in the process. Arms out to her side, she righted herself, her balance slowly coming back, and then she stuck her cane in the ground and laughed. That was fun! She paused, and tried to sense if Daphne was peeking in, to see her or control her . . .

But there was nothing, just an abrupt silence. Not even that dizzy feeling, nor the eyes twirling about in her thoughts, nothing. She laughed again, placed her feet squarely apart, and lifted up her cane like a baseball bat. She concentrated, kept her balance as fine as possible, and then swung again! It hit with a delicious thump, and knocked some of the straw out, scattering like feathers through the air. This time she caught her balance even faster than before, placing the cane down right away, and tilting her hips just right to keep from falling over.

Maybe she should do as Mister Brightbones suggested and just burn them . . .

No, that was too risky, look at all the dead leaves on the ground, kindling waiting for the right kind of flame to burn it all down. She liked this forest too much, liked her farmhouse way too much to do something that stupid. She would have to do this the hard way, one sentinel at a time. She hit that same scarecrow one final time, smacking it hard enough that it tumbled over and spilled across the ground.

She felt so alive and awake right now, more so than she had in over a month! She never thought she would be happy to feel her MS all tingly and painful in her limbs once again, but she welcomed it now with open arms. She was herself again, and the only foggy thoughts that still mucked about in her mind were those caused by her disease, and not a vampire taking over her consciousness.

She began to work on the others. There were nine in total, and about halfway through she was completely wiped out and needed a rest. She leaned against a tree, her spine on bark, the autumn leaves gently tumbling around her, as the sounds of wings fluttered in the air. And she heard a cawing, and then another caw responding, a conversation of crows landing in the trees above. She looked up, surrounded by the silhouettes of bare branches and saw just how many crows were there. Too many to feel comfortable, all their eyes watching her like tiny black stones.

Was this the right thing to do? It had felt so right at the time, and yet those birds were so ominous above her head, tiny feathered tombstones. Some had blood on their beaks and fresh entrails dangling down from their recent meals. One had a finger in its bloodied craw, swarming with maggots, a sharp red ring on the center of it. That was a human finger, plump and swollen with the hours of decay.

She caught her breath, tried walking for a bit, just to test out her balance. Sometimes, when she overexerted herself, her MS became worse, and walking turned difficult yet again. It didn't seem to be the case right now, thankfully. She trundled away, back down the stony path to her farmhouse, making certain not to walk too fast or disrupt the birds. As she moved closer, she felt the influence of Daphne fluttering around the outside of her thoughts, a cocoon of comfort nestling in so slow and steady she didn't even realize it until it was almost too late, and she was under her control yet again.

The sun turned sour overhead, blazing hot, and she had one panicked thought, *oh no* and then *run, run, run*. But she couldn't, could she? And Daphne's thoughts started fumbling around in Nix's mind, moving her sense of self away, pushing it into the shadows beyond. She tried hiding it again, the fact that Mister Brightbones came to her, the destruction of the scarecrows, all of it. She put up walls of black static in her mind, calling on the remnants of an empty dream to somehow come and save her, please.

She reached her thumb over to her palm. It took every ounce of strength she had left to do this one, simple action. Her MS weakened her muscles from earlier, and there was an invisible weight trying to push it back, that control Daphne held on her limbs, which was almost worse than the control MS had on her as well. It took all of her strength, absolutely all of it, to push in her thumb, dig it in, harder than ever before this time, like moving through water, through quicksand, through the cotton sludge of dreams . . .

And there, bright pain and her thoughts cleared and she collapsed to her knees, She'd dropped her cane for a moment to push her thumb into her palm, unable to hold it and free her mind from Daphne's control. Because of this, she lost all sense of balance, and tumbled forward when she fell on her knees, the world spinning, mud and leaves clinging to her shirt and pants.

Nix grabbed her cane from the ground, and used it to regain her balance and stood up right, just in time to see the back door swing open and bang against the outer wall in a violent gunshot sound, as Daphne ran screaming from the house, right towards Nix, her eyes wild and cheeks coated with tears. The minute she touched the sunlight her hair caught on fire and her back caught on fire, and the flames spread around her like bright wings, as ashes fluttered in the autumn wind, her burning skin tangled up with the flight of autumn leaves. "How could you do this to me? Don't you know what you've done? You have brought him here, to us!"

And the crows watched overhead, staring down with those black stone eyes.

13

IN Nix's mind she heard Daphne's voice telling her sweet and tangy, molasses words, to come with her, to embrace her and be engulfed in her flames. The thoughts snaked around, tried to force their way in, as Nix pressed her thumb down even harder. Pain, bright, searing, she had to grab the cane again, else fall once more to her knees. "No!" She cried out, "I will not die with you. Get out of my head! Stop controlling me!"

Daphne paused for a brief moment, wavering, as her flames danced around her and ashes scattered from her body in the wind. The look on her face was one of heartbreak and sorrow. "But, Mom, don't you understand . . ."

"I am not your mother! Get out of my head, now! You have no power over me anymore."

"I . . . I don't understand . . ."

The thoughts in her head turned to crackling whispers. "This." Nix held up her hand, showing the key burned onto her palm. And then she pushed in again, and winced at the pain once more. It's odd, but with all the needle jabs and brutal tests through the years from doctor's visits, she'd gotten used to being poked and prodded and stabbed and shocked. It was as if all of those rotten experiences in her life had prepared her for this moment exactly. "With this I can keep you out, and keep myself sane. What were you thinking? That this could go on forever, without me doing anything about it?"

"I'm sorry." Daphne tilted her head down, and looked at the ground, her flames even higher now. "Just let me die here, I can't see him again. You don't understand, if you knew what I'd gone through, you would run and never stop running. Or you would kill yourself, like this, to keep from becoming what he would make of you."

Nix hesitatingly walked forward, keeping her distance from Daphne. Her cane at the ready to lash out and attack if need be. She remembered what Old Wick had told her the other day, the story about the wild mouse and the pet mouse, and she saw now that he was trying to warn her of this very thing. How much did he know? She would have to go and discuss this with him later, after all of this was said and done.

"And what would that be? What would he make me? Something like you? A vampire who was completely healed, and no longer relied on poisonous medications that would kill you just as soon as it would heal you? How dare you keep that to yourself and act like I don't deserve that as well."

"Don't you see what I've become?" Charred bones began to appear under the drifting bits of skin. It smelled awful, a combination of rotting meat and barbecued flesh. "Look at me! I am not cured. I must feed and feed often! Do you understand what it's like to drink death? To feel the last light flutter down your throat and fill you up with ghosts? Fucking awful, Mom, fucking awful, just . . ."

"I don't care! I'll do as you do, feed on animals. How is that any different than eating a chicken or a hamburger? How is it? Tell me, please."

"Because they're not alive and wriggling in your mouth as you drink them in, and you don't feel the moment of their death . . ."

And then she collapsed, twitching to the ground. She made strange moaning, painful noises, and there wasn't much left of her anymore. Her body started to glow a bright green and yellow, with the faces of ghosts appearing in the flame like an optical illusion. This was what it was like to watch a vampire die. Nix thought it would be easier to watch this happen, that she would feel okay with it . . . but . . .

A sorrow. God help her, she wanted to save the girl, to throw a coat on her and take her inside the house to keep her from burning up in the sun. Yes, Daphne got into her mind, and controlled her, and made her into a zombie, yes. But that feeling inside, of what it felt like to mother her, to have her as a daughter . . .

Even if it had been manufactured, it had felt real. Still, now, even here, it felt real. And it wasn't something she couldn't just shrug aside. "Damn you."

She took off her winter coat, and placed it over Daphne's body, blocking out the sun, and putting out the flames as best as she could. She rolled Daphne on the ground, back and forth, making sure the sun did not touch any bare skin and catch on fire yet again. Under the coat she heard ragged sobs.

Dark iron clouds rolled over the sun. They seemed to come out of nowhere, coating the entire sky with shadows. The world dimmed a dark blue, and a frosty wind blew across the forest floor, and Nix felt chilled all over. Goosebumps dotted her arm and her neck, and the fear of an early snow settled into her bones. "We should go inside, the temperature just dropped, and I'm freezing. Last time we had snow this early it was a wet, thick blizzard that closed everything down for miles upon miles."

Daphne pulled the coat back a little and looked up at the sky. She smirked, shook her head and laughed a quick, brief laugh. Snow began to drift in thick, soft flakes down around them. Just one or two at the start, then picking up speed, more and more drifting down. "No, I don't think going inside will do any good." And overhead the crows cawed in the trees, and then took off west, towards the interstate out beyond the woods.

"What do you mean?"

"Because he's already here, in Dark Rivers."

Nix grabbed her shoulders, holding her cane as carefully as she could. She shivered briefly, and wasn't sure if this was the cold or something else. There was a palpable sense of terror in the air, as if every bird and animal in the woods behind them sensed danger, like a forest fire or an earthquake, and then bound past them going out towards the street and the world beyond, the woods tainted with something horrible and dangerous now. It terrified these animals so much that they did not fear the humans, nor the semi-trucks that sped down the backroads, killing all they came across.

"Oh." That was all Nix could say in response. "Oh."

Was this all a mistake? She would find out soon enough. Some part of her was absolutely terrified, but another part of her . . . a much bigger part of her, if she was being honest with herself, was also elated beyond words. The mixture of joy and horror left her breathless, and she smiled beside herself, and did not even try and hide it for a little bit. He was here already, he would be coming to this house soon enough, and she would be healed.

She wouldn't worry about all that stuff Daphne had said earlier, about drinking death, about holding a living creature up to your mouth and consuming them alive until the moment they died in your hands, mouth clasped on cold skin, open wound draining into your throat. That would be something to figure out later. One thing at a time, yes indeed, one thing at a time.

"Can you help me go in . . . it's painful to walk."

Nix helped her up, but then said, "No. I can't, not with my balance . . . even if you just leaned on me, I could fall over and then we would both be hurting."

"Aha. Yeah, I see."

And Nix poised her thumb against her palm again, in preparation for the mind control to start up once more.

"You don't have to do that, you know. Not while I'm like this." And Daphne coughed violently, then winced. "Shit. Ow. While I'm healing I can't do much of anything. And besides, that mind control thing, it's not on purpose. It's just . . . something that naturally happens when I'm around humans and other mammals. The vampire heart sees them as prey, and somehow I can get in their heads, make them do what I want. They bare their throats to me, skin glistening and ready for me to drink them up. I don't know how that is, maybe it's like how catshit can make mice just run up to the cat all fearless and stuff. I dunno. I just know . . . it happens. And I can't control it. And I'm sorry, Mom."

Nix started to walk back to the farmhouse, going even slower than usual, letting Daphne keep pace with her. "You need to stop calling me that."

"I . . . I'll try."

Nix didn't turn around to see if Daphne was following her. She didn't want to look at that burnt face, now see how painful the skin was, or the bits of bone glinting out from under destroyed muscle. She didn't want to see the pitiable look on Daphne's face, or feel sorry for her in any way. Not after what she'd put Nix through, she was lucky she was letting her back into her house. And she definitely wasn't going to bring food for her. There was no way she would be out hunting animals to bring back alive and ready to be slurped up like a glass of water.

Though, it might be good practice. For when she would have to do the same . . .

She smiled again. Any moment now, and he would be here, and it would be so wonderful. She would rip off that dreamcatcher tonight, in hopes that Mister Brightbones would visit her in her dreams once more, and she would learn exactly what was to happen and when. Too bad the day was barely even half over now! And she was too wired to even take a nap. Just look her hands shaking with excitement. She did the right thing, of course she did. This was probably the most important moment of her life.

And in a way, she had Daphne to thank for all of this.

"You know," she said as they walked back, "I might just bring you back something to eat later. Will that help you heal?"

"I guess."

"What do you want?"

"I don't know. Nothing, I guess, though it doesn't matter. I won't die before he gets here."

She opened that door once again, and realized that it was loose and hung from the frame all crooked. Daphne must've broken this earlier when she darted outside. No matter, she would call her handyman later, and he would be here quicker than quick to put the thing back on.

"Nonsense, I'll get you something so you'll have your strength to meet our guest," and Nix wasn't even hiding her joy any longer. Why even pretend? She got what she wanted. And it was amazing how fast it all happened! Those crows must've sent word right away.

"Our guest? Did he come to you in your dreams? Was that dreamcatcher broken . . ."

"Don't you worry about it, dear, don't you worry about it all. Why don't you go and lay down on the couch, and after I rest for a bit myself, I'll go and find you a nice rabbit to feed on. Doesn't that sound lovely?"

The thought of it thrilled her. She would have to get used to it, wouldn't she? Finding the rabbits living and beating, tracking them down, pouncing and feeding on them. Unlike Daphne, she would just stick to rabbits. No cats, no dogs, not her. It wouldn't be easy, and she wasn't even sure she had it in her to kill something living . . .

Daphne stumbled over to the couch, and then plopped face down and groaned out in pain. "Please, just leave me alone for a while. I can't believe you did this to me, not after everything I told you."

Nix sat down on the big overstuffed chair next to the couch, carefully balancing her cane on one of the arms. It fell down, of course, so she bent over, picked it up, balanced it again. This time it stayed put. She smiled to herself and turned to Daphne. She looked horrible, all burnt up. Some of her body was starting to heal now, just a little bit, but not much.

"You haven't told me anything at all! Every time I ask you what he did, or why you feared him so much, you change the subject."

"Fine, okay. Do you want me to tell you what kind of hell you brought to us?"

Nix perked up, leaned in. "Yes, please."

"All right, I'll need that rabbit after all. And you need to make sure they stay alive while you bring it to me, you understand? I'm going to need some energy to tell this one. It's long, it's stressful, and I feel like I'm going to pass right the fuck out at any moment now."

Nix's pulse raced, and she felt both excited and terrified once again. "Okay!"

She was going to go out and do her first hunt. She was really going to do this. She was going to be a vampire. There was no going back now, this was really happening. This was the make-or-break moment of her life, that she knew, a turning point. This was no longer a possibility, it was an actuality. Everything felt even more impossibly real than ever before.

Oh wow. Oh. Oh wow.

14

HOURS and hours she struggled with this task. Catching wild furry animals was hard enough, it was even harder to keep them alive in a sack and not attack each other, or chew holes into the sack, ruining it. She went through two satchels this way, one of them completely ruined before she decided to just stick to rabbits for now, and ignore any other critters. Daphne insisted they had to be mammals, *they need to have that warm blood, so you can taste their death as it enters inside of you. That's when the magic happens.*

There were some moments where she felt something watch her in the trees, and she would look up and see nothing was there, not even a spying crow for Mister Brightbones. Other times, it felt like someone was standing right behind her, or a man-shaped shadow crouched just on the edges of her vision, but when she turned around she saw nothing there at all. Not even a wild animal, let alone some human being stalking her. No way of shaking that feeling, no matter how many times she told herself it was irrational.

So, it felt like no real surprise when she caught sight of Old Wick wandering through her woods, as snow fluttered around him in fluffy, fast-moving flakes. He was coated in them head to toe, as he bent over and inspected the remains of the scarecrows, his hands picking through them like a coroner searching for a cause of death. He gently lifted up the ruined clothing, and traced his fingers over those weird dayglo shapes painted across their chests. He then har-rumphed, talked to himself for a bit, and then leaned back against a tree and sighed.

What was he doing here? He had to know this was her property, small towns talked, and it didn't take long before everyone knew where everyone else lived. Even though he was a newcomer, word got out fast. Was he looking for her? Her pulse quickened, and she moved behind a tree. Had he seen her? No, probably not. He was still leaning against the tree, looking at the scarecrow ruins. She really did a good job bashing those up, and was kind of proud of herself, all things considered.

And then a memory tickled at the edges of her thoughts. Her being in his house, it felt like a dream, or a memory of a stranger implanted in her head. Fuzzy, disorienting, the wax dolls, yes, but the memory was hidden under all of these layers of shadows. It was as if her own mind had buried it deep within the seas of her thoughts, a memory lost for a bit, remembered now in sickening detail.

The house. Him. That wallpaper. Something moved inside of her, and she wanted to scream and run the other way. What had happened there? It felt like something, and yet nothing at the same time, and that made it all the worse. No, she couldn't stay here with him, she couldn't trust him, something happened, horrible in that house, somehow, but she couldn't place her finger on what or why. And then she remembered the figures crawling over the wallpaper, the bitter taste of the tea, and the stories of the cannibal house and the sacrifices between its walls. She had to get out of here, now, run away from him before he saw her . . .

Rabbits or no rabbits, she shouldn't be alone out here in the woods with that man. Before, when she was all numbed and zombified she could resist her intuition telling her to run and never look back. But here and now? Not a chance. Be careful, Nix, as careful as you can. Quiet, too, so you don't draw attention and bring him this way. It wouldn't be easy with those deadleaves and rotten twigs scattered on the ground like sonic landmines. Even harder with her cane, always stumble-tripping and tumbling down. The new snow helped soften the sounds a little, but it would only go so far. She would just have to do what she did earlier, look for the soft spots, the wet spots, where the forest would be quiet beneath her feet. She wished that she was a vampire already. Then she could just hypnotize her prey and be done with it.

She missed her athletic days as a junior in high school. She'd been a gymnast, and the balance bars where her pride and joy. It felt like she was flying, dancing between those bars, flipping over, spinning, and then landing perfectly on two feet. For a moment or two she wasn't on earth anymore, grounded to the world, but instead a creature of the air itself.

And now, thanks to multiple sclerosis, she no longer had any of that prior grace, poise, and balance. Most people couldn't believe her when she told them that. They were like *I don't understand, you can't lose your balance that fast like that. It's an innate thing.*

But that's how MS worked, wasn't it? All at once, a little at a time, thieving every bit of who you were until there was nothing left but this damned disease. But, that didn't have to be the case anymore, did it? No. Hah. She was going to get better. She was going to be a vampire . . .

She was so distracted in her thoughts and reminiscences that she hadn't even noticed Old Wick walking towards her, not until he crunched on a leaf and snapped a twig with his own clumsy feet. He walked with a large, oakwood walking stick. It was carved with tons of little signs and sigils, similar to the ones she'd seen on the scarecrows. What did those even mean? She noticed he wore a necklace of owl bones, similar to the one Daphne had made her wear earlier, before she'd tossed them aside to speak to Mister Brightbones.

For a brief second, she thought she could run, yes, take off and never look back, just darting through the woods along the paths and get out of here. But, no, she would fall for certain. A root, a branch, a spare stone in the pathway, and she would be on her face again, probably cutting her cheek and shattering another tooth. It was too late, anyway, he'd already seen her. If he was dangerous, he would also give chase, and probably get the best of her the moment she fell. Most of the path was dusted with snow, the thick kind of wet clumps that would make it extra slippery and difficult to run away without cracking her head open. She had no idea how she knew he would chase her like that, she only knew in her bones and heart that it would be the case. On all fours, pouncing on her.

"Ho! Ho, Nix, ho! What are you doing out here in these paths? I thought I was the only one who knew about these woods. Lots of strange things happen here, don't they?"

She wanted to tell him that these were her woods, and that he was trespassing. That he had to leave right now, that the cops would be on their way soon enough. But her mouth was dry, and her tongue was a slug in her throat. She couldn't get the words out, some part of her too terrified as to what he was going to do. She rested her thumb over the scar on her palm, fearing that he could do the same kind of mind games as Daphne. Was he a vampire? No, but he felt dangerous just the same. And that memory of his house . . .

"Oh, I just needed to get out for a bit and clear my head, and this is one of my favorite places for that sort of thing. Something just so peaceful about these woods." It wasn't exactly a lie, was it? Those things were mostly true. Well, true enough that they would work in a pinch, without giving anything away.

"Peace, eh? Well, I must say I never liked peace so much. It always felt anxious to me, like being in the eye of a storm." He eyed the small flakes tumbling down to the ground. "Weather man said it's a blizzard tonight and be done in a few days, since it's too early for this kind of thing. Though my bones seem to say it's going to get far worse than that, and I always trust my bones over the weather man any day of the week."

She moved uncomfortably back and forth, shifting the weight from one leg to the other and leaning on her cane. "Oh. Well, good thing we both came out today, huh? Before it got really bad."

"How's that mouse you brought back to your house? I worry she might be hurt, that maybe she broke a bone or two?"

Everything inside screamed now. If only she could run.

"Well, she's fine right now, thank you very much. But I don't see how it's any of your business?"

"It is and it isn't. You still got those wax figures I gave you? The ones for good luck."

She hadn't thought about that in a few days. Not too long ago they'd gone missing, a little after they started making all those weird scratching noises. "Yeah, I think so. I haven't really touched them, so they should still be there."

"Oh, that's good, hm. Yes, it's very good."

"I'm sorry, Mister . . . Wick? Was it?"

"Aha, I guess you heard my nickname. No, it's not Wick, definitely not a mister. But that's a name that will work for now, so go ahead and use it. It means nothing to me, either way. As the bard once said, a rose by any other name would still have thorns."

No, that quote was wrong, she knew that. Was he messing with her? It felt like a threat, the way he said thorns. The word a dagger dripping with poison. She moved one foot back, getting it ready to run. She then stepped backwards, tentatively, then another foot, another. She inhaled deeply, time to run now . . .

And of course, her ankle seized up, and she had to stop. Muscles tightened around her bones, tighter, tighter still, stretched almost to breaking. Stupid spasticity from MS, it always struck her at the worst possible moment. She counted to five, and the muscles relaxed a smidge, the pain loosening a little, but not enough to move an inch just yet.

"I think I should probably head on back to the house, in case it gets as bad as you say."

And the clouds overhead rumbled with thundersnow.

"Of course, don't let me keep you. Do you need a ride back to your house? My car isn't too far from here."

"No, no. That's okay. I think I'll be good on my own."

Old Wick looked over her cane, and stared at her with steel gray eyes. "I see. I'll take my leave of you, then. I'm just glad you've been safe so far, and here's hoping you stay safe."

Nix looked at the ground, closed her eyes, and then inhaled and exhaled a few times, centering herself. She was sure the stress of this moment reacted with her multiple sclerosis, and caused the muscles to tighten and weaken. She had to get back to the house and lock the doors, and soon. There was no telling if the locks would keep Old Wick out, but she had to believe they would. If she didn't . . . what hope did they have? Daphne would have to do without rabbits for now . . .

Wait a minute . . .

"What do you know about Daphne? You keep talking about her like you know her."

Old Wick smiled with tombstone teeth. "Oh, is that your pet vampire's name?"

A chill up her spine. Everything felt electric and terrible.

"Tell me what you know."

"I know you're in a nest of trouble, but don't worry. They're not here for you, you're just collateral damage."

The color drained from Nix's face, and she felt faint. Everything swam around her, as her legs tightened up again, and for once she was grateful for spasticity, it was the only thing that kept her body upright right now. "What are you talking about?"

"Mister Brightbones is on his way to our humble little town, isn't he? I figured as much, the Hallowed House is a beacon for the likes of him. It's why I bought up the cannibal house and turned it on, to get him here."

But, but, Mister Brightbones was coming here for *her* wasn't he? He promised. That's why she removed the scarecrows, so he could see her and come and get her. What was Old Wick talking about? Everything swam and her thoughts ran backwards, and she heard an old male voice whispering in her head. *No! Get the hell out of my thoughts!* She pushed on the scar on her hand, the pain burned like a bright key. It clarified everything, mind sharp and ready to fight.

"Oh, ho, I see you have a nifty little trick up your sleeve. Who showed you how to do that, huh? Let me guess, was it your little guest? Never mind, never mind." He stroked his beard with his free hand, and pulled a loose twig and leaves from some of the curls. "You shouldn't make friends with vampires."

And then he turned around and walked over to the scarecrow, and then abruptly kicked it, and sent the stuffed head flying into the air. Straw scattered everywhere, and fluttered down. The sky darkened a bit more, as the snow started to pick up. It wasn't quite a blizzard yet, but it would be soon. The northern witch wind blew hard against them, chilling her bones, the snow sticking to her hair and her face like bright ice.

"Go, go back to your vampire friend. It's too late to save her now anyway. Too late for either of you, really. I guess I have to thank whoever tore these scarecrows down." And he turned and looked at her, and winked. "Mister Brightbones would have never come this way otherwise. The Haddo House may be a beacon, but these sentinels were well made, powerful things. A good little obfuscation, if there ever was one. A regular work of art." He whistled. "But useless now. It's amazing how things like these are so hard to make, and yet so very easy to tear down."

She walked backwards, steady as she could, her cane keeping her balance right and true. She wanted to turn around, to look and see where she was going so she wouldn't trip and fall, but she couldn't take her eyes off of him, she was afraid that the moment she did he would turn into a wolf and lunge on her and rip her apart like a broken straw doll. She knew that was a dumb thought, and yet . . .

His eyes looked hungry and thin, like the eyes of a wild animal.

"What are you waiting for? Go. Go tend to your dying friend. Nothing will save her now."

She turned, gulped, and moved as fast as she could back to the farmhouse. She stumbled a few times, fell and was coated with mud and snow, and yes, even had to rest for a moment on that cold, icy ground. She lifted herself up using trees and her cane, and tried to keep right on going, never looking back to see if he chased her, hungry and wolven in the darkening forest. Even if she was shaken, even if her mind ached, and her knees were scraped up, and her chest was coated in snow. She would not stop.

And behind her, just out of sight, rabbits hopped out the old burlap sack, running off into the distant trees beyond.

15

THERE were vampire hunters in her living room. Nix stood for a moment in shock. Vampire hunters. In her living room. Unable to move, her cane poised at her side like a weapon, her spine against the archway leading from the kitchen into the living room. She saw them in a brief flash before she hid, and then watched their reflection in the kitchen windows. They looked exactly as Daphne had described them, and yet at the same time they looked even worse, in a horrific way that defied any description. Their skin had a waxy, pale, melted candle look that was soft and unnerving to the eye. Each one was bald, their bodies clothed in a ragged black suit, their heads oddly misshapen and puddling around their shoulders.

Three of them in total, they moved around Daphne's body on the couch. She laid supine, unable to move, her head tilted at an angle, her face pointed directly into the kitchen. Her eyes were vacant, dead eyes. They didn't follow any motion, didn't turn to look at her, they only stared at some distant point, the pupils small dim stars in the sockets of her skull. Her arm draped off the couch onto the floor. It looked like her body had healed itself some while Nix'd been out, the skin growing back over her arms and her face in motley patches.

Now her pants were off, scattered on the floor. One vampire hunter squatted halfway between the couch and the kitchen, his face a spiral of unblinking eyes, staring directly into Daphne, freezing her in place, motionless like a statue. Another vampire hunter paced the room, looking out the windows. His face was a giant, toothy mouth filled with flat teeth that chattered nervously. No other features, just that giant mouth.

The final vampire hunter leaned over her supine body and gently scraped at the burnt flesh of the leg with a long black knife, digging out the muscle and exposing her tibia. Bone thieves, that's what Daphne had called them, and Nix wondered how many bones they'd planned to steal. Would Daphne survive that? She was a vampire, it wouldn't kill her, would it? It would just leave her a boneless puddle of muscle and skin. And that image stung her, tore at Nix. Even after all that Daphne had done to her, she couldn't just take off and leave her here. There was a connection still between them, even if it was the memory of a thrall. She had to save her.

But how?

A vampire hunter reached a long arachnid finger around Daphne's leg bone, and Daphne didn't even flinch, didn't scream out. Nix knew that feeling, that sunken underwater feeling, the feeling she herself had felt so often before the key was burned into her palm.

She didn't even think. Thinking right now would be the enemy of motion. Act. Time to act. Right now. Inhale, go, exhale, run across the living room with wobbly balance, cane in the air, and strike down on the one hypnotizing Daphne! That bastard right there, with the spiral of eyes on his face, fuck him, he's going down. There you go. She fell, tumbled, flat on her face, and the cane sunk in and cobbled away large parts of wax and skull and skin. The body crumpled to the ground as Daphne snapped awake and screamed in pain, kicking the hand away from her bone and knocking the knife across the ground.

Nix's cane was still stuck in the one vampire hunter. She had to pry it loose, stuck so fast, her mouth was dry, everything spun and she had to stand, had to get up. She looked over, saw Daphne leaping over top of her assailant and smashing his waxy body to clumpy bits. What were these things? They were not human vampire hunters, that was for sure, but rather like something made from wax and cloth.

Oh no. She remembered the tiny dolls Old Wick gave her the other day, as she finally pried her cane loose and fell on the floor yet again. Wick had done this, had tricked her into bringing these bastards into her house. How dare he!

A horrible sound, like the wail of an animal caught in a fireplace and burning alive. She turned and looked toward the sound and saw the third vampire hunter bubble into a pool of candlemelt. It was as if a self-destruct button had been pressed, once it was obvious that their mission was a failure. Nix pulled herself up on her cane, her breath heavy in her lungs, the air weighted with the promise of more violence to come.

"We have to go," she said, "Can you walk?"

Daphne stood up, stumbled for a bit, and swore under her breath. "It stings if I put too much weight on this leg. Even vampires have limits, it seems."

Nix laughed at this. "That's one hell of a limit. Being burned alive, and then almost having a bone removed . . ."

"I just need to rest and feed for a bit, then I'll be as right as rain and twice as sunny. Were you able to get those rabbits for me?"

Nix slumped her shoulders. She couldn't tell her about Old Wick, could she? How could she even start to explain that. It felt like this was all her fault. She'd let him into their lives, and brought his stupid vampire hunters here with her. "No, sorry, I, well. I had this bad feeling, like you were in trouble, so I came back."

"Oh. Thank you."

Daphne had this sad, sorrowful look on her face. Her eyes misted a bit, was it pain? Or was she sad about something else? Nix wasn't certain, but that mother feeling took over her again. "I've got a spare cane you could use for now. We should grab that and really get going, since you won't have time to rest or feed yet."

"Are you sure?"

"Yes, of course. Come on, we've wasted enough time as it is. They know where you are now, and I don't think it will take long before this whole place is swarming with more of those bastards."

Daphne sighed, wiped something from her cheeks. Tears? Or something else? And then said in a resigned, almost hopeless voice, "Okay. Let's get out of here."

16

THEY made a great pair right now, didn't they? As they stumbled in that slow drifting snow, and wandered through mud toward Nix's old beat-up Toyota. She'd gotten that at an estate sale a few years ago for practically nothing. It was rusted in some spots, and coughed when it started, but she loved it so. She didn't drive it too much. She hated driving for the most part. The lights were too bright, her peripheral vision too murky. And all the almost accidents had stacked up over the years, making even the smallest drive an act of terror and courage. She really didn't want to drive today, most specifically. It was snowing, she didn't have snow tires on, and even though it was too warm for the ice to come just yet . . .

There was a promise of colder temperatures in the air. Unnatural ones for this early in the year, even this far north in the states. It should be another month, maybe two before this much snow reached them. And yet, here it was, drifting down, making everything treacherous and slippery and biting cold. But they had no choice. They had to go.

"Do you know how to drive?"

Daphne shook her head no. "No one ever had a chance to teach me before I turned, being in and out of chemo so much. My sixteenth birthday just whizzed past me. And after I became a vampire? Well. Getting a driver's license was the least of my worries."

"I guess it's me, then. Get in, let's get out of here."

They pulled open those rusted car doors and heard the sound of air raid sirens in the distance. They were tested every Wednesday around this time, and yet for some reason, they felt particularly ominous today.

"Oh it hurts so much, my skin crawling back, healing. It's just fucking painful and I'm so hungry . . . I need to feed soon. I can feel the world fading around me, like an old photograph losing its colors."

Daphne's voice was so overcome with emotion that her lip trembled and she whimpered a little. It tugged on Nix's heart with notes of guilt and sorrow, and she hated herself for calling up Mister Brightbones in her dream, and putting them all in danger. She knew they had to leave town, to get as far away from here as possible, so Mister Brightbones wouldn't find them. She had to do it.

But wait. Wait. No. These weren't her thoughts at all. Her mind felt distant, jagged, and hard to think for a moment, as Daphne stumbled around in her thoughts, clumsily telling her to leave town, to stay away from Mister Brightbones. Everything felt underwater, muddled up, with only Daphne's voice loud and bright. *Take me away from here, take care of me, let me feed on you, just a little, just until I heal all the way. You're my mom, and good moms feed their children with their bodies . . .*

No. Shit. No. Come on!

Not again!

She dug her nails into the key shaped scar on her palm, as Daphne's voice drifted away in waves of pain. Nix had summoned Mister Brightbones for a reason, and one reason only—so that she would be cured, and return to her old self once again. It wasn't fair that Daphne was healed and not her. They would stay close to town, and she would draw Mister Brightbones back toward them once more, summoning him in her dreams like she'd done the other night. Daphne would just have to deal with it.

She turned on the wiper blades to shed the snow from the window, and then flipped on her headlights and pulled out into the long, dirt driveway leading to the road beyond. Her heart hammered against her ribs, a wild animal trying to escape her chest, as the snow twisted tumble down faster and faster, transforming into the worst blizzard she'd ever seen, all in the blink of an eye.

She gulped and kept on driving. They couldn't go back to her farmhouse. Wick knew where she lived now, and it would only be a matter of time before more vampire hunters found their way back to her home, and attacked them both again and again. The only way out was further in, through the storm, and onto the other side of night.

17

WHITE-KNUCKLED steering wheel, everything blanched of colors, impossible to see beyond those thick flakes. Nix's body frozen in the car, chattering teeth, the heater unable to work. Daphne whimpered in the backseat as skin and muscle grew around the exposed bone, her face pained and growing gaunt. It wouldn't be too long before she had to feed again. Nix didn't like that thought. What would Daphne do when the hunger got too great and the only person to feed on was Nix? Would she rip through the front seat and tear into her, drinking her up?

"Stop looking at me like that. I'm not going to eat you," Daphne said, "I told you I don't eat people."

It was hard for Nix to believe her, after all she'd seen the last few days, and the urge she kept feeling to bare her own neck and feed Daphne with her blood. Would Daphne unknowingly enthrall Nix again, and do it in a way that even her key wouldn't work? And then, she would lean back, neck exposed, and let the teenager drink deep, maybe even let her feed until death, just so she could be healed completely? Maybe Daphne would feel bad about it afterwards, but it was always a possibility that it could happen. Even well-meaning vampires need to feed . . .

No, no. Pay attention to the road, dumbass. Could barely see anything, she had to guess where the edges of the street were, everything a wall of snow twirling in darkness. It shouldn't be this dark so early in the day, it was as thick as night and everything was claustrophobic. She could drive them off the road at any moment, crash into some unseen tree hidden by flurries. In between the snowflakes shadows swirled and moved about in the shape of ghosts. Her peripheral vision was worse than ever before, and now all this stress . . .

Oh no. No. Not now.

The stress aggravated her multiple sclerosis. It wasn't a full-on relapse, no. She didn't get that cold depressive funk she usually got right before one hit her hard. And the inside of her skull didn't tingle, nor did it feel like it was filled with an unseen pressure, like the palm of a hand pressing against her gray matter. This had to be a pseudo-relapse. Before she could even blink, her left arm locked up and she had to let it fall limp and hope she could do well enough with just her right arm driving. That's when the thumb on her right hand started twitching, and her left leg started itching, and then kicking out, like when you get your reflexes tested at the doctor's office.

Shit, the worst possible time for something like this to happen. Daphne started breathing heavily in the backseat, and Nix thought of those nature shows she used to watch as a kid with her grandpa, and that noise . . . it sounded like when a lion was hungry and moving in on some prey. No matter what Daphne said, Nix was prey right now.

Going so slow, no other cars outside. Where were they? It felt like they'd been driving for hours, but it might've just been a few minutes. Were they close to Danny's place? *Something Old*? She hoped so, they could probably find shelter there. Wait. Did she want to bring Daphne inside, to Danny's house, and have her drink him up and leave a shell behind? Like she left all those drained animals before . . .

She flashed her brights in a vain attempt to see if anyone else was out there, driving. No light returned her flashing call. Though, maybe, up ahead, floating amongst the snow, there was a bare outline of amber lanterns and twisted green metal. The old timey styled street lamps in the center of town! They were getting closer, and closer.

And then her tires slipped and slid. Hand on the steering wheel, as the world spun around. She wanted to scream. It felt like it took forever, but it happened maybe in a split second. Daphne screamed in the back seat, a wild and horrible sound as she leapt up. This was it. They were going to die, this was it.

"Slam on the breaks," she hissed in Nix's ear, and then reached over and grabbed the wheel with both her hands. Nix slammed on the breaks, and there was a loud crunching noise, as they spun some more. Since Daphne had the wheel, Nix decided to reach over, and pull up the parking break. They eased to a stop, with the car making a horrible grinding noise, as they pulled right up to the old pharmacy that had been there since the early fifties, the front bumper pushing against the front door, but not breaking it in.

They were okay. Damn, that was close. Nix pulled the key out of the ignition, collapsed forward and sobbed. Her body shook as she sobbed, tiny tremors and shivers moving up her spine and across her body. This wasn't from the cold, even though it was freezing. This wasn't from the sadness, even though she felt something inside of her break and splinter apart. No, this was her multiple sclerosis messing things up yet again.

Daphne coughed, opened the back door and said, "I'm going out hunting wabbits. You stay here so I know where to find you, okay? This shouldn't take too long. After all, the whole town is lousy with them."

Nix nodded and thought *this was it*. She was going to fall asleep here, in the deep frozen cold of an unnatural winter night, and freeze to death. How absurd! She chuckled for a moment, resisting the urge to break down in uncontrollable laughter. She'd never in a million years thought she would die this way. Never, ever.

And she ran through those death scenarios in her mind all the time, ever since she was a kid. It was her way of dealing with the anxieties of the world, picturing how it will all end, the pain of the moment, the nothingness. And for the last ten years or so, she'd always pictured multiple sclerosis as being a large part of her death. Maybe an accident while driving and having a sudden relapse? Maybe falling down the stairs one too many times and hitting your neck just the wrong way. Or maybe your lung muscles just stop working after a while, or your tongue and throat no longer remember how to swallow and you choke on your food. Or maybe, you get a UTI, or an infection of another sort, and all of that immune suppressing medication does what it's supposed to do, and keeps your immune system from fighting. And you die with pneumonia, or a liver infection, or a kidney infection, or a sinus infection that spreads to your brain or blood stream.

There were so many varied, horrible ways for her chronic illness to kill her, and because of that, her actual, real demise had come out of left field. She wasn't prepared to die like this. It seemed ludicrous after all of those preparations, so impossible it never even registered on her radar. Not even after finding Daphne, discovering she was a vampire, all of that.

She laughed some more, cried some more, and then sat back, and waited for Daphne to return all refreshed and fed. Maybe she would freeze to death, maybe not. There were worse ways to go. She knew, she'd run through them all.

18

AN hour and a half, that's how long Daphne was gone. Nix's toes had gone numb waiting, and she'd worried frostbite had set in. She'd pulled blankets and a spare coat out of the trunk, and tried her best to keep as warm as she possibly could. She walked for a bit, here and there, hoping to increase her blood flow, and jostle some heat back into her body. No such luck. Her MS was still being a royal pain in the ass, and therefore walking for too long was pretty much out of the question. She could feel another fall coming on, and decided not to press her luck.

The radio was busted. Her cell signal was moot. No snow plows rushed through the avenues, no people walked around salting or shoveling snow. This whole thing had caught everyone off guard, it seemed, and it kept on going and going and going. It was that wet, miserable kind of snow, the heavy distrustful kind, that takes all of your strength to move it and clear the way. This was what they called a heart attack winter storm, since so many people died trying to clean up after it.

And the irony of ironies was that it wasn't even winter yet. Thanksgiving was barely a month away! She checked on her phone, saw that the battery only had a bar or two left. She shivered now, from cold or MS or who knows what. Did the cause even matter? No. Not now. It was just a fact. She was cold. She shivered. She was in pain. She shivered. She had MS. She shivered. It was now three in the afternoon, and yet it looked like midnight. She had to figure something out, Daphne probably wasn't coming back after all, and she couldn't just wait here for Mister Brightbones to find her. It might be too late when he does. She was tired now, and hungry, and sleep ringed around the edges of her vision. That kind of heavy exhaustion from dealing with every muscle in your body acting up and wearing you out.

She opened the driver's side door, and felt it stick in the new snow. She pushed harder, and harder, the door pushing through and opening wide, finally. There was a triangle cut into the snowpile, one she could stand on for a moment. She wasn't going to try and go anywhere. The footsteps from earlier had already been filled in, and the snow was up to her knees already. Trunching through this would be impossible.

And she saw a shadow move under the streetlamps, not too far away. About two houses down from Danny's store. It seemed to jerk about in its movements, like a marionette cut from its strings. The legs moved in heavy, pounding motions, as it pushed through the snow. She wanted to run. She wanted to scream.

It had a goat's head. She saw it clearly now. At first, it was a shadow of horns and a pointed face. Then, closer, under a different streetlamp, she saw the tufts of fur and the eyes like black stones, and that billy goat gruff of a scruff under the chin. The body was human shaped, and clothed in thick, heavy winter attire. It used a large, knotted staff in its right hand to push its body through the blizzard, as snow matted the fur and the clothing. In its left hand was a small wooden lantern that flickered with an eerie, amber light.

She bit her lip, hard, pain bright and fleeting. It was either that, or she would be screaming now, and clawing her way out of the car, and scrambling out into the blizzard beyond. Panic wouldn't save her, no, it would just draw the goat creature's attention, and then that would be the end of her. Cruel-looking obsidian daggers hung from a frayed rope belt. Everything swooned for a moment, the world tilting sideways. No, you cannot faint here, you cannot. She grabbed a hold of the car door, and dug her fingers into the upholstery. Stay here, stay in this frame of mind, do not collapse. Do not pass out.

The goat took off its head, and that was it, she was about ready to scream and just flail about and let go of this world. She couldn't take any more of this, it was too much. And then, blinking through tears and panic, she saw the shadow of a human head on those shoulders. Danny. That was Danny. The goat's head was just a costume, the whole thing was . . .

Just. A. Costume. Was today the Halloween party at the bookstore? Of course, of course. It was the weekend before Halloween, of course. She didn't blame herself for forgetting, she'd been a little preoccupied.

"Nix? Hey Nix, is that you? I thought I saw an accident out the front window, and figured I would come out to see what's what. I'm sure glad I did."

She waved, shouted back. "Hey, yeah! It's me."

"You weren't trying to come to my party in this mess, were you? Gosh, I hope not, I would hate to have been the cause of this."

He struggled over more of the snow, and eventually made his way over to her open car door. She didn't want to worry him, or let him blame himself for this mess. But she couldn't quite tell him the truth now, could she? No, he would never believe it. She could barely believe it herself.

"Sort of? I was going to get groceries first and then come over, that's why I took the car and didn't just walk down. I'm glad I did! About halfway here the blizzard just dumped on us, and I figured going forward was easier than going back."

"Huh, well, let's get you to my kick ass party and get warmed up. Most of the town is stuck there, and no one's going anywhere. We're having a bit of fun, and telling a few creepy ghost stories, and hey, there's food! You look like you could use some fancy cheeses and dried fruit. What do you say?"

She looked over his shoulder, and only saw more snow piling up and swirling down. More shadows in the shape of ghosts moved behind the flakes. Human, stalking, a negative space come to life. Was there any sign of Daphne whatsoever? No. Nothing at all. She worried that something might've happened to her, felt that mothering instinct again, and then shoved it aside. She couldn't think about that now, her fingers were starting to grow numb, and she was worried that they were turning blue. The numbness could just be multiple sclerosis acting up some more, but she didn't want to risk frostbite either way.

Daphne can survive on her own. After all, she's survived so far, hasn't she? It would be good to get out from under her influence.

"I say okay," Nix said, and used her cane to stand up, her knees wobbly for a moment. "Though you might have to help me walk for a bit, if you don't mind. Snow's not my best friend these days, and ice is even worse."

Danny smiled, placed the goat head back on, and then left his own staff behind, taking her arm with his and guiding them back to his store. He kept the lantern upright, and it gave them light in the areas the streetlamps could not reach.

What about Mister Brightbones? No, never mind him. He probably won't find them right away, anyway. She has time to relax and unwind with good friends and some good food. She'd been through so much lately

She needed this.

19

NIX pushed through the crowd of people, elbowing past various Frankensteins, Cleopatras and Draculas. Never before had she seen Something Old this crowded, and she had to admit it felt a bit claustrophobic and overwhelming. She was glad Danny was next to her, at least for a bit, showing her around the first floor and where all the food was located. "Here's all the good cheeses, as well as some dried fruit, a touch of wine that pairs well with all of that. And if you're feeling less fancy, check out the wing bar over there, and the pizza station to the left. It's got a place where you can put on your own toppings and fire it up in the little stove we got over there."

"Oh, that does sound like fun."

A quick glance around, and she felt so out of place. Everyone else wore a costume of some sort, even the most jaded adults. She hated feeling self-conscious like that, and decided that later on she would go into the bathroom and try and figure out some cheapo costume to throw together with whatever she could find inside. Maybe make herself into a toilet paper mummy? Or just muss up her hair and makeup and go as the best friend in every romcom who cries all the time for no reason? Something like that.

Danny's costume was impressive, but she had no idea what he was supposed to be, so she asked him and hoped it wasn't too rude.

"Oh my god," he laughed, "Are you seriously telling me you've never read the Hellskin novels?"

She felt even more awkward and out of place than she had before. "No?"

"They're only the best thing ever. Come on, I'll give you a copy of the first book from the shelves, gratis. You will absolutely love them,

I know you will! Everyone does. I swear. I'm so surprised you'd never even heard of them yet . . ."

"I guess I missed that day on the internet, when everyone was talking about it."

"That's the thing, it blew up offline, all word of mouth. It's so weird, it's a national best seller, and no one is talking about it anywhere online. Not Goodreads, not Amazon, not Twitter, not even Booktok. Nothing. That sort of thing just doesn't happen anymore, does it? Like it's a unicorn."

"So, who are you from the book? Is the main character some goat person thingy?"

He laughed, and leaned in close so she could hear him over this crowd, his mask still muffling some of what he said, so it was barely audible. "I'm the demon Azlatch, from the fourth book, the Well of Darkness. Some say I'm a portal guardian, but I think he's a portal creator, you know? There is this hell dimension that lives between worlds, right? And the skin between our world and this hell dimension is thin, and easily bruised. When there is a wound deep enough, it becomes a portal from here to there. Azlatch knows the many paths through each dimension, connecting them to every world. He has the map of hell etched into his bones, so he always knows where he was, no matter what. These daggers . . ." he pulled one out from his belt, and held it up for her to see, ". . . are made from the bones of dead angels. Burned and scorched and burned again. They are his tools for opening the doors between worlds, cutting into the skin and wounding it. He was one of the first wound walkers, and one of the last. To see him is to see the pathway to eternity."

"Wow, that sounds . . . kind of nuts. So it's about people going from this world into the hell dimension?"

"Yeah, kind of? And about things from that dimension coming over here . . . it's really complicated. There are sixteen books in the series over all, and who knows when we'll get another one. The author mysteriously disappeared a few years ago, and no one knows what happened to him. Not that it mattered, he was always a recluse anyway. Some of the fandom online thinks that this stuff is too complex and realistic, and he was basing it all on something he really experienced, and he went into the hell dimension one day and never came back."

Nix stared at him for a moment, not sure if she believed that or not. In the past few months she became the mother to a homeless vampire and was visited in her dreams by a creature that could be a demon, or a vampire, or who knows what else, in the shape of a child. The whole hell dimension thing made about as much sense as the rest of it.

He saw the look in her eye and laughed, and gently laid a hand on her shoulder. "Don't look at me like that. I didn't say I believed it! I sure as hell wouldn't be dressing up like a lesser demon from a hell dimension if I did. That would be inviting the wrong kind of attention, you know? I'm just a huge fan, and kind of sad we might never get narrative closure. It's something me and other fans are arguing about on a daily basis, all of the world. Some fans even tried to end it themselves, but they always ended up disappearing after they start. Spooky, right? It just adds to the mystery."

"Wait, I thought you said no one was talking about it online . . ."

"Oh yeah, we don't. Get this! We communicate entirely in zines and through the mail. Isn't that wild? Talk about old school. I'm really surprised none of us have tried to take it online . . . but it seems wrong, you know? To even suggest it. This way, it's our secret, hidden from the rest of the world. Do you want to see the zines and the letters? I got a stack of them in the back office, and it's super cool. You won't even believe some of them, they got all these crazy fan theories."

No, she did not want to see it. She couldn't explain why she didn't want to see it, but her mind revolted at the very idea, her whole body tensing up. It wasn't the MS doing it, that she knew, this felt different. This was fear, and a bright kind of terror she couldn't put into words. So instead, she decided to play it safe and not offend him. He did, after all, just rescue her from probably losing a toe or a finger (or more) to frostbite. "No, that's okay, I don't want to keep you all to myself, I mean . . . you're the host! You should mingle."

He looked around, his eyes barely visible behind the black mesh eyes of the goat skull. "I've been mingling all day, part of me is just pooped out and needs to crash. This party should've been over hours ago . . . and yet, here we are, snowed in. No one able to leave, not even for a moment. I just hope it's not as bad as it was two years ago. You remember that?"

Yeah, she remembered. It was in January, and the blizzard lasted two weeks. Each day several feet of snow dumped down, and by the end of the first week it was over seven feet dropped all together. The snow pile was taller than most people she knew, and every store had been shut down. It was declared a state of emergency, and the National Guard had been called in to help clean people out from underneath all that snow and ice. She remembered thinking at that time that this was the kind of weather that turned people into cannibals. Once they ran out of food, and warmth, and had to search out something to eat in the starving hours.

"I remember, but this one feels different, doesn't it?"

And she meant it. She knew why it felt different, too. The last one was due to global warming messing up the weather patterns. This was due to Mister Brightbones coming to Dark Rivers and looking for her and Daphne. Her heart fluttered for a second, butterfly wings in her chest. *He's on his way, and should be here shortly . . .*

"It does feel different, true. Let's hope it warms up in a day or two and we can all rest easy once again. Until then, I think it might be time for another ghost story."

He walked over to the reception area, where the cash register was, and pulled out a cowbell and rang it. The room quieted down, and Nix grabbed a handful of cheese and dried fruit, and shoved it into her mouth. It tasted wonderful, and she'd had no idea just how starved she was until that exact moment.

"Gather round, oh, ghouls and demons! I think it's time for another chilling tale to get us through this fucked up weather. Who wants to go first?"

A few hands raised in the back, and someone held up a book that was titled *Ghost Stories of Antiquity* and shouted, "Me! Me! Me!"

Danny pointed at the woman holding up the book in the back. It was Anna! She'd come to this party after all. She wore a patchworked dress and had a flute hung around her neck from a leather throng. Around her waist was a ratted rope belt, with rubber rats dangling down across her waist. A female pied piper? Nix felt a combination of terror and joy seeing her here. She loved her friend, but also knew something bad was going to happen here. The way Old Wick was acting, the little vampire hunters he was placing all over the place. Nix wanted to wave hi, but decided maybe not, not yet.

"All right, Anna! Read us some M.R. James! Make sure you pick a good one."

"They're all good ones, though, aren't they?"

20

AFTER the third ghost story, the crowd began to disperse and meander through the store once again. They chatted with each other in a dull roar and noshed on the last of the food. Nix decided that she needed some alone time—the crowd was getting to be a bit too much—and went off into a small corner of the anthropology section to hide. No one would find her here, nothing stopped a party like dusty old bones and dead civilizations. The problem was, someone else was already there, the person she least wanted to see, and actually hoped against hope that he wouldn't even be here. Hell, until just now, she hadn't encountered him at the party at all.

And yet, there he was, Old Wick, looking very suspicious, in the very same corner she was planning on hiding for some peace and quiet for a few moments. He hovered on the comfy old chair that was placed right next to the book shelves, the one she planned on sitting down in and pulling a book out and pretending to read while the party died down for the evening. Frustrated, she went to turn around, to find some other place to hide out, when she saw him placing tiny wax dolls on the shelves near one of the books and stopped, frozen in her path. The vampire hunters.

Run, go, she should just find a way and get out of here . . . though where would she go? back in the frozen wastes outside? Maybe to Anna's bakery, that might be a good idea. Anna wasn't even here tonight, she hadn't seen her, so she was probably still working late into the night. they could hang out together, maybe spend the night baking as well as she could. She was just glad that unlike others with MS, the cold didn't seem to affect her in much the same way the heat or stress did.

She turned, walked away . . .

And he harrumphed and grabbed her shoulder. "Nixie, just the woman I was looking for! I wanted to apologize to you, it seems my mouse traps didn't work."

Frozen still for a moment, she swallowed, then gently turned around. How many of those had he placed throughout this whole place? Was this a trap? Mister Brightbones coming here might be a bad idea. Hell, what if Daphne stumbled in here looking for her? This would be bad, so very bad.

"That's okay," she said, "I think you were wrong about the mice being in my place, anyway. I have two cats, you know. They tend to take care of any mice that came my way."

She wasn't going to give him the joy of seeing her squirm.

"Ah, from what I've seen, that mouse is big enough to eat a cat or two. Would be a shame if anything happened to your poor little pussies."

Her skin crawled at those words, dripping with vile insinuation. It brought back the memory of Sherlock and Mister Death, her poor cats, whom she hadn't seen in so long. . . she had . . . she just pushed it to the background of her mind. And here he was, that disgusting old toad of a man with a ridiculous beard, smelling like pipe smoke and bringing those bad thoughts back up again.

She coughed, nervously in her hand, and tried to wiggle out of this conversation. "If you'll excuse me, I have to get back to Danny, I think I'd forgotten something . . ."

"Oh, I'm sure you have," he dug his hand in deeper onto her shoulder blade, "You have left something outside in the snow, haven't you? Well, I wouldn't worry about that anymore, if I were you. Things like that have a way of taking care of themselves, yes they do."

She calmly placed her other hand over top of his, tried to gently lift it away and said, "Excuse me, I really must be . . ."

But no, she couldn't budge his fingers. Her multiple sclerosis made her hands so weak, she dropped things so often, and right now it was like trying to push a block of stone through sand.

"You know, those mice are the least of your troubles. A big old rat has found its way to Dark Rivers, yes indeed. The rat may live with mice, and dress up with mice, but he's a rat nonetheless. A rat that eats everything he comes into contact with, the kind that ate their way out of the royalty's stomachs during the French Revolution. Big, ugly, hungry, walking about in the shape of a mouse. But don't you worry, I have a plan. I made a rat cage, just for him. I built it out of mouse bones."

He hissed those last words out from behind closed lips, and then let go of her shoulder, patting it and straightening out her shirt. Nausea roiled around in her stomach, and she had to sit down, goosebumps dotting her arms and the room tilting sideways yet again. Was this vertigo? She hadn't had that since her second relapse, and really hoped it wasn't coming back, not now. No. It couldn't be. She sat down in that chair, and the world straightened up again. She hoped never to see Old Wick ever again, but knew in her heart of hearts she would never be so lucky.

"Take care," he said, as he turned to walk away. "And keep that cane close. I bet it would work as a weapon in a pinch if need be, just after all I've seen you do with it. And I have a feeling you're going to need one soon enough."

There was no way she was going to watch him walk away. She turned her head, glanced in the other direction. That sick feeling in her stomach subsided for a bit, and she realized that what he said wasn't a warning to her about what he was going to do. There was too much concern in his voice at that last little speech he gave, like he was more worried about something else coming after her. Something else coming after all of them.

Mister Brightbones, of course.

A soft shiver, head to toe. The promise of being healed, and the horrific cost. She looked at the chair. No way in hell she was going to sit on that, not after Old Wick. Something about him oozed menace, even when he was giving her advice on how to keep herself safe. She felt like a pawn, moved about just for his amusement. She pushed the chair aside, and turned around. So much for solitude amongst the crowd. She looked at the creepy vampire hunter dolls, reached out and touched them. Remembered what they did, how they attacked her and Daphne not too long ago, and her stomach lurched. Who was the good guy here, who was the bad guy? Mister Brightbones wanted to cure her, but if Daphne was to be believed . . .

And Old Wick wanted to save her from the vampires, or so he said. But his methods, oh his methods were the most horrible thing she'd ever experienced. And even though Daphne had hypnotized her and dug under her skin, changing her and controlling her, she still felt something like love. Not exactly the motherly love Daphne wanted, but more like an older sister.

She snatched up the vampire hunter dolls, and they squirmed and felt alive and squishy in her hands. It made her retch in the darkness, and she almost dropped them. They were sharp and soft at the same time, like a mouth filled with tongues and teeth, as she put them into her pockets and left them there. What was she going to do with them? She wasn't sure, but she knew leaving them here would be dangerous. Too many people. If the vampires came, the hunters wouldn't protect them exactly, that she knew. They would tear through the humans to take the bones of the vampires. Awful. She would dispose of them outside, at some point. Maybe push them deep into the snow, far away from the hunting dark.

She waited until he was gone and merged back in with the crowd, and then found her way back around to the food. She grabbed some more cheeses, a bacon-wrapped mushroom, and a bit more wine. Fuck it. She was going to fill up as much as she could and then figure out what to do next. In the distance she heard the results of the costume party, and to no one's surprise, Danny won. His costume really was the most elaborate, beautiful thing she had ever seen. It looked more like a movie prop designed by the Jim Henson company, and less like something you could throw together from a Spirit Halloween store.

She clapped with the rest of them, smiled briefly with a mouth full of brie. Danny rang the bell yet again, and called all attention his way once more. "A little bit ago we all got that same emergency alert on their phones, I take it?"

Nix did not, her phone's battery was completely dead now, and she hadn't had a chance to even think about charging it yet.

"So, we're all supposed to shelter in place and wait this snowstorm out, not even driving or walking, it's too dangerous. They said they can't even get the snow plows out to plow it."

She could tell that he expected everyone to cheer and holler and be excited. Instead, a lone whoop! Whoop! Rang out, and some murmured confusion and nothing more.

"I know, it's kind of a bummer, and I'm sorry about that. We've got a lot of blankets and pillows here, but some of us might have to share. Sorry about that. I do have quite a bit of food that should

keep us going for the next few days, and since we're all in this together, I'm not charging anyone for anything. Of course, once we're
all rescued, the prices will be back in place. But for now, don't fret
about food or drink. Just make sure you are respectful of each other's
needs as well as your own, and be kind to each other."

A few people shouted, "Hear hear!" and Nix smiled. She guessed
if she was going to be trapped somewhere during a storm that this
was as a good as place as any. Then she thought again about Mister
Brightbones, and the vampires, and how quickly they would probably devour everyone here and she was sick to her stomach yet again.

What had she done? This whole thing was a huge mistake. Nothing was worth that, nothing. She'd lived with multiple sclerosis for
this long, she figured she could live with it for a bit longer, if need be.
Sure, she would be blind and wheel chair bound soon if they didn't
find a medication that worked for her brand of MS. But that was a
far more conscionable price to pay compared to the alternative. She
pictured for a moment a different life, a new life for herself. Watching them all die, bleeding out, and her drinking her friends to death.
Their bodies shivering, their eyes distant and grey as the life drains
out of them. Her own body healing at the cost of their death, and she
felt sick to her stomach, No, no, this wasn't right.

She just couldn't live with herself if everyone here died because
of her own need to be whole and well again. Dancing was not worth
this. Daphne was right, and even worse, Old Wick was right. And
yet, she didn't trust that terrible old man. Even if he knew the dan-
gers of Mister Brightbones, he made her so uneasy, and his vampire
hunters freaked her out something fierce. The memory of them in
her house, attacking her and Daphne was still raw and fresh and
bright in her mind. He had used her, yes, to get to Daphne. And now
he's leaving all those little vampire hunter dolls all over the bookstore? What does he know, what is he planning? He must be using
all of them, somehow, to lure the vampires here.

Maybe she could have both. Maybe she could lure Mister Brightbones away from this place and still become a vampire, no need for
bloodshed. She knew in her bones that this was wrong, that it would
never be that simple. That pain was always the price for magic, and
this kind of magic would require so much pain.

A big burly man named Zeke, who owned the camping store down the street raised his hand and nodded. Danny laughed, said, "Go ahead and speak, were not in kindergarten."

"We've got quite a lot of tents and blankets and coats over there just sitting in my store doing nothing. Big heavy sleeping bags that could keep us warm if the electricity or heating goes out. I know we're not supposed to go out, but it's not too far away, and I think this might be worth our trouble."

Danny nodded. "You know what, I think you're right on that. We're not going to let you go alone, right? Let's get a small party together and head down there, after all there is safety in numbers, and we need to keep warm. I doubt any of us brought any winter coats this early in the year, it was just sixty degrees yesterday. So we should layer up as best as we can, and head on out. Who here wants to join us?"

A couple of people raised their hands, including Old Wick. She saw the look in his eyes, a glimmer of maniacal glee, like a kid the night before their birthday. What terrible gift awaited them outside? She couldn't let them go out there without her, she didn't trust Old Wick at all, and knew that he led them directly into the mouth of a lion. A sense of dread rolled around in the pit of her stomach. This was it, this was the point of no return. Her hands trembled a little, and she knew it wasn't from multiple sclerosis this time, but instead nerves. Raw biting nerves, and that fear of the horrors ahead swimming around in her mind.

She raised her hand, against every nerve in her body screaming no, no, no, stop! She had to do it. She just had to. Damn her conscience for being so right all the time. If they were going to die, she had to be there, to try and stop it as best as she could. She couldn't let them go out there with Mister Brightbones waiting for them. She couldn't let Old Wick lead them right into danger. What game was he playing? She only wished she knew.

21

THE cold was still brutal outside, the wind biting, as the flurries stung their eyes. Nix kept blinking the snow away, as she pulled her coat tighter over her shoulders, trying to keep the warmth in her bones as best as she could. Still dark sky getting darker now toward the evening. The world was haunted with ice and lampposts and shadows. She chuckled for a moment when she realized that this was the time for her usual evening constitutional. Good thing she got a walk in after all.

She was glad she brought a winter coat with her, and only hoped that Daphne wasn't frozen solid right now. She didn't want to stumble on her corpse while they made their way across the street to get supplies.

Did vampires even get cold? She had no clue. Daphne seemed cold all the time for the most part, maybe she warmed up after feeding? She had to stop thinking about this, and pay attention. She was straggling a bit behind, the blizzard blinding her again, the shapes of the people in front of her just a blur of shadows. Shit. She had to keep up, it didn't matter if vampires froze to death. She sure as hell could, and definitely didn't want to.

She tried moving a little faster, her legs seizing up and her muscles tightening into a thick rope, as the cane slipped some on the snow. She had to stop for a moment, catch her balance, just so she wouldn't tumble over into the large snow drifts. The cold was so brutal, even under all these layers. "Guys," she couldn't help herself, she had to go at even pace and she couldn't keep up. "Guys, wait up, please!"

Breathing heavily now, bent over for a second. Heart racing, she felt her ankle seize up a little, and her left eye blurring and losing color. *Not now, not now,* she really hoped this wasn't a full-on relapse. *Please be a pseudo-relapse, and please, let it be nothing too serious, something that would pass.*

There was no way to get her to a hospital now to get the high dose of steroids that would calm this down. She was screwed, especially if she couldn't walk without tumbling over. Her hand gripped her cane, terrified. The shadows seemed to stop. *Please, hear me, please.* "Guys, I need some help!"

The streetlamps flickered overhead, their amber glow slowly going in and out, in and out. The artificial darkness grew like bat wings over the sky, a mixture of storm clouds and shadows over the sun itself. She knew this was all Mister Brightbones work – it had to be -- so the vampires could walk around in the daylight, of course.

She was about ready to call out again, when she saw a shadow racing back to her through the flurry of snow, barely visible in that flickering streetlamp light, strobing the shadow's movements as it ran closer and closer, making the whole thing feel unreal and like a dream. The particles of snow moving with the strobing light, dancing around the body as it grew closer and closer, becoming more distinct with each moment.

Oh no, oh hell and brimstone, not him. Of all the people to come here and help me out, not him.

He carried a walking stick in the crook of his arm as he ran down, his beard tangled up with ice and snow. Old Wick. Anyone else but him, she wanted to just turn around and run away, but she couldn't, not without risking a fall and being buried in this blizzard. She would freeze to death if that happened, she knew she would

But Daphne was still out there and Mister Brightbones was on his way to Dark Rivers, if he wasn't already here. And that was all her fault. God, guilt was such a stupid motivator, wasn't it? Nothing good ever came from it, and yet here she was, letting her guilt get herself into trouble yet again.

A chill up her spine, and not one from the cold, as Old Wick grew closer and closer, waving to her and smiling his sneaky, underhanded smile. This was going to be it, wasn't it? She was going to get her fool self killed, and the irony of it all was that it wasn't from multiple sclerosis. There was a bitter comfort in that one, a very bitter comfort indeed.

"You need some help there, little lady?" His voice was so patronizing, it oozed false concern and comfort. She could never ever trust him. Never in a million years.

Nix nodded and grunted yeah.

"I told them I got you. Told them not to worry none at all, that Old Wick would make sure you got there a-okay," and he smiled when he said this, all teeth bared and ready to bite down. So much threat in that smile, so many horrible things unsaid. "Danny wanted to just turn around, take you back himself while the rest of us went to the sports store, but I was having none of it."

And he stood in front of her now, all the snow whipping about him, that strobing light turning his features into a skull stacked on a bone thin body. He wasn't even out of breath from running down here, and that struck her as unnerving. At his age, in his shape, he should at least be a little weary. And yet, here he was, at the peak of health. And here she was, thirty years or so younger than him, about ready to collapse.

The gods of this world were cruel and horrible things.

"I convinced him to let me come and get you. I'm very good at that sort of thing, you know. Convincing people."

And she felt his eyes sparkle at her through the snow, and knew that he was trying to get under her skin again, like the way Daphne used to. She reached over, dug her thumb into the key-shaped scar on her palm. The pain was bright and her leg buckled, turned to jelly, and she fell on the snow. He reached out, grabbed her, and she pushed him away. "Leave me be," she yelled at him. They weren't too far from the bookstore, maybe she could make it back without much trouble.

"You think you can keep that up," he hissed, "Using your little charm like that? You think that's going to keep me out of your head? Each time you use it," he spat the words like venom. "You wear yourself down and your little illness gets worse and worse. How much longer can you handle it, how much longer before you feel the multiple sclerosis take over completely and destroy you?"

She pushed him back, her arm muscles so weak, like pushing an anvil through sand. He sparkled his eyes at her again, and like the tea and the yellow wallpaper of his house she felt herself spinning, unable to grasp onto anything. She reached down, to push her thumb against the scar again.

Yes, it might make her illness worse, but she didn't care at all. She would rather that than let him inside her head again.

And before she could do it, her action was interrupted by a group of shadows pushing through the wall of snow, shouting and laughing. Danny and the rest of them, spinning their weak flashlights in the sleet like errant lanterns in the night. Fairy lights in the shape of cellphones.

"Hey, you two, come on! It shouldn't be taking us this long to just cross the street, even in this mess of a blizzard. Come on! Or should we help you get back to the bookstore first, and then go the rest of the way ourselves?"

Old Wick stared at her, glared at her, eyes all daggers and shadow. A warning.

"It's okay," Nix said, even thought it wasn't even a little bit okay. "I've been through worse than this. I can make it, if someone can help me walk a bit, since my cane keeps slipping."

Danny frowned. "Are you sure?"

"I can help her no problem. Isn't that right, Nix?"

And she gritted her teeth so hard her cheeks hurt. "Yes," she said, "Yes he can."

And that was that. They were going to walk the rest of the way across the street arm and arm, her and that horrible Old Wick. And there really wasn't much she could do about it.

She only hoped that her pseudo-relapse would go away the minute they got into the warm store and she could walk by herself again. At least her cane would be more useful there, and maybe she could even get something that would be more helpful walking in the snow or the ice.

She knew that they made cane tips that had spikes for walking on ice or snow. She had a feeling they probably wouldn't have them at this store, but she had to hope.

She had to hope.

22

IT should not have taken them this long to cross the street and get to the sports store. What had normally taken them only a few moments on a day of light traffic had almost taken them an hour. The wind pushed against them, an icy wave of frost biting their skin. Nix thought a few times of turning back around, but Old Wick held her close to him, pushing her onward and keeping her upright. He didn't seem to need his own walking stick, and he refused to let her use her cane, and instead propped her up the entire time. His skin felt cold, icy cold, clasped against hers. He did not wear a winter coat either, like the others, but instead braved the elements all raw and brutal, smiling as they went.

All the while, she kept noticing that sparkle in his eyes, flashing like silver or copper, tiny coins planted into his skull, For a moment she circled her thumb across the scar on her palm, feeling the jagged edges, and thinking for a moment of pressing down. But no, she realized, he wasn't casting this mental net on her, no, he was doing it to the others. To Danny, to Zeke, to Anna and the rest that had come with them to get supplies. She felt these controlling thoughts like sharp whispers in her head, and knew that he was trying to do something, but what? What? That she couldn't tell.

She moved her thumb back, decided not to press down. He didn't want her, and it would be a waste of her strength to try and stop him. She had to conserve it now, the brutal cold making her multiple sclerosis act up more and more, and then more she regretted coming out here, now, to this. The way her arches tore on her left foot with each step, the way her muscles tightened so that her foot was almost like a claw, grasping down, her vision blurring more and more.

She had to save it. To make sure she could use her strength when they needed it most.

To trick Old Wick, somehow. To separate him from the rest, so that he would be too far away to control them with his slick, mesmerizing stare. Maybe they could get lost in the storm, and she could make sure he never got back out. And then the others would all be safe, wouldn't they?

After all, Mister Brightbones was only coming for her. Surely, he would leave if they didn't find her.

Oh, you fool, she thought, *they will devour everyone here and leave this town a ragged empty shell. Even if they don't find you. You were just a pretense for a location, that was all.*

And yet, that was all Daphne, wasn't it? Mister Brightbones promised her a cure. And so far, he had kept his promises, and made no threats against her. Hell, he'd helped her, and given her this scar to keep her head on straight and safe. Old Wick, on the other hand, well. He was full of manipulations and horrible half truth. He brought murder to her house, and tried to skin Daphne alive for her bones.

She knew what she had to do.

The building was in front of them now. A long row house, where the entire first floor was the sports store. The large windows glared out, covered in fingers of ice and large tufts of snow. Beyond shadows moved in the darkness, the lights off and the doors locked. And yet there were movements, creeping along the edges, making rattling sounds in the distance. Like bones dragged along concrete, and the sound of it set her teeth on edge, and Nix wanted to run and run now. Something waited for them beyond the doors. She felt it now, a heavy looming presence, and her insides felt so cold all of a sudden, like her guts matched the storm outside.

They walked towards the front door, the blizzard blinding them for a brief moment. She wondered why no one else seemed to hear those sounds, why no one else seemed to be freaked out about those sounds, or from the shadows moving in the darkness beyond the windows. The wind whipped again for a moment, and then calmed, just for a second, just long enough for them to huddle under the awning together, as Zeke reached into his coat pockets and searched around for the keys.

Wick let go of her hand and sniffed the air. A strange, almost primal gesture, like a predator hunting his prey. Nix moved away from him, stood back, unnerved by the calm moment of this storm, the snow drifting slowly, sadly around them. No longer a freakish blizzard, yet still colder than it had been in October in years, almost decades now. She felt like she was holding her breath for this moment, waiting for either the sky to break and let the sun back through, bringing day back with it, or for the storm to pick up again and coat them in frost and snow once more.

And then Old Wick pounced forward, grabbed Zeke's hand. "Hold on a moment there, hold on."

And Zeke reared back for a moment like he was going to punch old Wick, and Nix held tight onto her cane and kept herself upright and balanced. Falling now would be bad. If she did, and the snow picked up again she would be buried, she knew it. Maybe they would help dig her out, or maybe not. The way Old Wick controlled them now, forced them to do whatever he saw fit? Well, she was sure he would just leave her there to freeze to death and not care at all, as long as that suited his plans.

And Old Wick's eyes sparkled, those strange coins glowing in the dark of the streetlamps. "Now, now, that won't be necessary, will it? Look, look Zeke. Don't you see, someone's in your store."

"Oh," and he stepped back, and looked at the windows and gasped. "How did they get in there? I locked it up tight, set the alarms, no one should've gotten in without me knowing."

Danny shook his head and sighed. "Guess this mission was a bust. Sorry, Zeke. We should probably head back and have everyone bunker down for safety, don't you think?"

"No, I don't think. We need to call the cops, we need to get someone here, we need to get them out of my store!"

And Old Wick smiled, and at the sight of it Nix shivered and was covered in goosebumps. Not from the cold, but from some old terrifying sensation she couldn't place. Like the feeling of waking up from a nightmare when you're young and confused and you're not sure if it's still happening, and that terrible sensation sticks with you, clinging to your bones.

That's how his smile felt to her, like a nightmare of a scared child. And Zeke seemed to melt under this smile, his own eyes sparkling, a reflection of Old Wick's eerie, controlling glare.

"Listen here Zeke, it's brutal out there right now. I know we don't want to cross that street again, and it all seems pointless. And I know you want to keep your store safe from thieves and vandals, yes. But that's not what this is."

"No?"

And now Danny came over and said, "It's not?"

"No, no, it's not. This is something our friend Nix needs to check out herself, isn't that right? This is an old acquaintance of hers, one that's come to pay a visit."

Nix did not think she could get any colder than she was a few moments ago, but here she was proven wrong. Even though the wind was quiet and near dead, and even though the snow was soft and floating and no longer blinding and brutal, she felt it. She felt that cold crawl into her, dig under her skin. It moved into her heart, as it radiated out through her veins and into her bones. And she wanted to scream, this fear so great. He meant Mister Brightbones. How did he know?

And now Danny, and Zeke, and Anna, and all the rest spoke in muted, mummified tones. Like the words of a somnambulist tumbling out of their lips. "Nix? What is he talking about? Nix? What is going on? Nix?"

And Nix didn't know what to say.

"Well, am I right? I can smell him here, and he smells like death. And it looks like he brought some friends with him, including that little mouse of yours."

And the others in their loose party stared numbly on, like they were sleepwalking and stumbling through a dream, and only Nix and Old Wick were real.

"I don't know what you're talking about . . ."

And his eyes flashed at her, and she reached over and pressed her thumb against the key-shaped scar. And quicker, quick, viper quick, he lashed out and grabbed her wrist with his hand, and then pushed his own thumb into her scar. The pain was sharp and hissing, the skin pinching and moving, and for a moment she thought he was going to pull her scar back open. And for a moment, she thought she was going to pass out.

"Oh, no you don't, Nix, my dear. This pain is my pain now, you understand me? So I'm going to use it as my own and put a stop to this. You summoned that Mister Brightbones, and that's all well and good. And now I want you and Anna to go inside there and meet him for me. And this is important, you understand me? This is important," and he pushed down even harder, her eyes pinching shut from the pain, as he dug around the scar, like he was fishing for the nerves that would hurt the most. "You will bring him back to the bookstore when you're done, you understand? Now come on, say it. Tell me what you're going to do."

Pain so overwhelming she couldn't think. "Bring him back to the bookstore."

"That's right, my dear. I may seem old, but I've got some strength in me yet. Strength enough to break you and shatter your limbs across the wastelands of the world. You understand me? Say yes."

And she nodded, the pain keeping her drifting and unreal. He let go of her palm and she grabbed it quickly, trying to ease the burning sensation as best as she could, but unable to even dim it even a little bit. Motherfucker, that hurt so much. And now she could feel his words worming around in her head, his sick commandment that she had to obey.

"Now, Zeke, right? You open that door up and let the girls go on through. They got work here to do that doesn't involve us. We're going to head back to the bookstore, and when people ask what happened we're just going to tell them we couldn't get into the store, it was too snowed in. And Anna and Nix here decided to go check up on her bakery. All right? That's the truth as you know it, the complete and utter truth."

And Danny and Zeke and the rest all nodded. A sinking feeling crawled into Nix, her thoughts still blinded dumb by the pain in her palm. She had wanted to meet Mister Brightbones and have him cure her, yes. And she did want Old Wick gone and out of her sight. And yet, was she really getting what she wanted? There was something horrible just on the horizon, some terrible revelation that the pain crowded out of her head. Anna was coming with her, but for what? And why did she have to bring Mister Brightbones back to the bookstore? She felt like she was going to throw up, dizzy and numb and vomitsick. Her multiple sclerosis combined with the pain, giving her a throbbing brain fog she couldn't think around.

Old Wick was up to something, she knew it.

He was using all of them. But for what?

For what.

And then the door swung open, the darkness waited patiently for them beyond.

23

DARKNESS changed the sporting goods store. What was once a familiar place she'd stopped into from time to time now became estranged and changed. Like a strange dream version of itself, remembered on waking with heart palpitations and a cold sweat. The bones of the place were the same, and yet somehow that was a cold comfort. It made the familiar just strange enough it unsettled. The shadows growing and shrinking from the lamplights outside and their flickering glow. The snow beating against the outside windows, picking up once again. And outside, a crackle and roar of thunder, with a bright flash of lightning and then darkness again.

Something moved among the shadows, voices whispered, and there was a sucking noise and then laughter.

Anna was silent, numb, next to her. She played with her hair, twirled it around her fingertips. Her eyes were glassy, and her bulky winter coat barely concealed the pied piper costume she wore underneath, the rubber rats swinging just under the coattails.

"Nix, this isn't cool. I'm scared."

Nix nodded and grabbed her hand. "I'm not going to lie, I'm pretty damned scared too."

"I thought it was your friend that was here, that's what that guy said. He said it was your friend and we had to go meet him and talk to him."

She heard the sounds of talking, though it was hard making out what they were saying. The echoes of the building betrayed any coherent words, the way they bounced about with the heating going full tilt in the freezing cold.

"Yeah," Nix said, trying hard to hear where the words were coming from, so she could better grasp where the vampires were in this place. "He's right—it is my friend. And that's precisely why I'm so scared right now."

"Your friend is scary?"

"I don't know, and that's what scares me, if that makes sense."

And Anna laughed a nervous laugh and smiled briefly. "Yeah, I guess in some weird way it does make sense."

And Nix wished they were just back in her bakery, shooting the shit and talking the hours away. Like they did so many times over the last few months, when she would make the hike downtown and hang out during the day, just to run some errands or get away from the influence of Daphne. That would be so nice, so much better than this cold, haunted hour. Where vampires waited for them in the dark, vampires she had brought here, vampires who could cure her. Her mind was still heavy with brain fog and pain, and she knew there was a hesitation about joining them, about being cured.

But she couldn't remember what. She just felt a pull over towards them (she sensed them now, over there, by the camping section, where they had tents and hunting gear), a soft gentle pulling of her blood, like ocean waves toward the beach, pulling her toward them. A soft ache, there, like a thorn in her heart.

She would go towards them.

But Old Wick is planning something horrible, isn't she? And wasn't this what he wanted?

The ache and the pain and the pull grew more, and more, high tide in the rhythm of her heart. She reached down, tried to place her thumb against the scar, but it was no use. It gave her pain, yes, but it was so painful already it didn't matter, and it got lost amongst the noise of her sorrow. Old Wick had hijacked her spell and her scar, he had taken it over and left her with nothing but echoes inside of her head. His echoes.

And now, the voice of Mister Brightbones. High, childlike, a choir of a voice with the shadow of age behind it. *Oh, there you are, Nix. We've been looking for you, my sweet child. You should join us now, back in the shadows of the store. I want to give you my beautiful gift, the one I promised you if you brought me here, brought me to Daphne. She's here, you've done your part, now let me do mine.*

And he said that last word mine with such viciousness it shocked her back for a brief moment. Everything felt charged with violence.

This was it, this was the moment of truth.

And bring that tasty treat with you, please. She has a part to play in our little drama as well.

She wanted to say no, but she couldn't. There was no resisting it, no turning off the thoughts in her own head. All moments of her life led her here, to this moment. That was it, no going back now, the point of no return. It felt destined, pre-ordained, something that could not be stopped. Her future as a vampire like a train running her down.

No, no, no. She couldn't do this to Anna, she couldn't take her there, with her. She's not chronically ill, she's not disabled or dying, they won't turn her or cure her. This world in the shadows was not for her, no. They would feed on her, and that would be it.

"Nix, it's okay. I'm not scared anymore."

And Anna was smiling a sad, melancholy smile. The kind of smile that carried a touch of sadness in its shadow. "Let's go back there and meet your friend, he's showing me such beautiful images in my head."

And Anna cried a small tear running down her cheek, her smile even wider than ever before. Almost impossibly wide, and she closed her eyes, the smile so bright, the tears streaming down.

"They are such beautiful, beautiful things. Oh, Nix, I am so tired. Did I ever tell you how tired I am?"

Nix held her hand and didn't move, and tried to keep Anna from walking forward, holding her back a little bit. "No, I don't think so? It's okay. If you're tired, we can go back to the bookstore and you can rest."

"No, you don't understand, I'm not tired like that, you know? I mean I'm tired in my bones, in my heart and in my muscles. I'm tired and worn down from every single day, every single day of my life adding up over the years. I just need to rest, rest for a long time. And not sleep, because my dreams have been so exhausting lately, too. But a long, silent empty rest. Without sound, without light, without dreaming."

And then she paused, opened her eyes, bright in the shadows and the darkness, the lamplight illuminating around her like a thick halo. Nix felt the whole world drop from her, an ominous future staring at her directly in the eye, inevitable, happening right now in front of her, unable to turn away.

"And all those beautiful pictures your friend is playing in my head, they feel so right, so comfortable. Please, take me to him, please. So I can rest, please. I'm not scared anymore, I promise."

And Nix felt her heart pound pound and her undertow blood pulling harder now, and she found herself walking forward, leading Anna back to the darker corners of the sporting goods store, where Mister Brightbones waited for them like a candle, flickering.

24

THEY moved arm and arm into the shadows back beyond the street lamps, with Anna quivering next to her, like a leaf about ready to tumble down from a dead oak tree. A flickering glow called to them from the far edges, the light of Mister Brightbones. It hurt a little to look at it, but not much, just a soft headache ringing around the edges of their vision. Nix held onto her tightly, her thoughts like moving through mud and fuzz, what everyone on the multiple sclerosis Discord channel called brain fog. It was like thinking through sludge, all of her thoughts a mile away.

She knew she should be terrified, that she should be concerned for Anna, for herself. But she couldn't remember why, couldn't even think of the vampires slaughtering everyone. All she could think of was the pull of her blood, and that Mister Brightbones offered her a cure. A cure. All other thoughts and memories drifted away, slowly away. She tried to latch onto them, tried to remember what or how or why.

But her mind stumbled, fell. And so she led Anna back, nervous and sick to her stomach, her skin breaking out in hives, and she had no idea why. Other than the cold, other than her MS acting up and getting worse. There was always fear when that happened, yes. But now it was more so than ever before. A fear deep in the core of her body. Fog seemed to crawl through the sporting goods store, knee deep, rolling in waves of grey and silver. Where had it come from? It's hard to tell, but it pushed her as well, tidal, moving with the motions of her blood, leading her back, back, toward that flickering amber glow, toward the vampire encampment beyond.

Closer, closer. The air thickened, the fog grew and expanded. The light danced in that fog, briefly, up ahead. There were other lights, portable electric lanterns scattered and placed on different shelves and across the floor, creating a constellation of cold blue illumination. Nix's heart beat faster, faster, a wild animal beating against her ribs. Her mouth was dry, her hands cold and clammy. Closer, closer, Anna holding on tighter now, trembling even more so than before, it was almost as bad as when Nix's multiple sclerosis worked itself up into a frenzy.

And there they crouched, fog swirling around them, coiled bodies waiting for them to arrive. The vampires. The ones she'd called toward them. Her blood ached with their promises, pulling her closer. They were mostly shapes, outlined shadows by the lantern lights. All except for Mister Brightbones, there, in the center of it all. Mister Brightbones.

The child from her dreams, yet somehow the face was older, and riddled with cancer across his face and around his eyes, where a dirty a blindfold laid stretched across, barely containing it. His smile was both kind and wicked at the same time. His clothes filthy, ragged, threadbare, close to falling apart at the slightest touch. His hair golden curls, and his nails long and sharp.

Around him danced a sunspot afterimage of a skeleton, glowing and flickering with amber light. It hurt to look at it, much like it hurt to look at the sun, burning itself into your corneas. But also, it made her headache more pronounced, like a small sliver of pain digging underneath her thoughts. Shit, oh shit almighty. Nix wanted to vomit. She almost retched for a moment, almost. The smell of rot and death heavy in the air.

"Welcome," he said with a voice of candy, all sugar-dripping sweet. "I've been looking for you, yes I have. I see you brought us a present? Good, good, you'll need to feed once I've given you my gift, it's the only way. You'll need to feed and feed true, all the way down, digging deep until she gives up her ghost. And then you have to drink even more, drink that ghost up until it's gone. That's where the magic is, yes indeed, that's what cures you. If you don't do that right away, you'll be a wight. And oh, Nix, my child, you do not want to be a wight."

Anna? She was supposed to feed on Anna afterwards? Why couldn't she eat something else, like a rabbit or a fox or a squirrel?

Or a complete stranger, someone she didn't even know? Why did it have to be Anna?

And thoughts drifted toward her through the brain fog, the panic memory that they will devour everyone at the bookstore. That she regretted bringing him here, and the death he'll leave in his wake. And Old Wick wanted her to do that, to bring him there, to take him . . .

Oh, sick to her stomach, mind aching, trying to think, to concentrate, to remember. To stay herself, to stay sane, what was Old Wick playing at? Did he want to sacrifice everyone in town? Why?

And then her brain fuzzed up again, her panic thoughts melting into background noise and rich undertow fuzz. Drowned out by the beating of her own heart, by the rich tidal music of her blood.

And Anna whimpered next to her, a soft mewling sound, shivering. "Please," she said, "Please take me closer to him," her voice so kitten quiet, Nix was unsure anyone else could hear her.

The other vampire shadows shuffled in closer, closing the circle slowly, slowly. Nix counted about nine or ten of them, roughly. Ragged, unkempt, blood splattered, their teeth gleaming yellow daggers all sharp in the shadowlights. She spied Daphne there, in the corner, looking sad and distraught. More waif thin than ever before, her eyes like stones placed in her skull, her clothes loose and the color leeched from her cheek. She felt her hunger even from back here. Oh, poor Daphne, what did they do to you?

And then a crawling fear, under her skin, around her bones. Oh Nix, what will they do to *you*?

And she noticed stranger figures in the shadows, a group of men and women shuffling about, the smell of rot wafting off of them and carried with the fog, making her gag. That hot summer garbage smell. A buzzing of flies, rich in the air, and she saw them swarm around these figures. Their greyish blue motley skin, patches of pale and tan. Their eyes half rotten and torn out of their heads. One of them was munching on an arm, a human arm, gnawing deep into the bone, attached to some corpse hidden in fog and shadow.

Were these the wights Mister Brightbones spoke of? That she would turn into if she didn't feed on Anna until death after he gives her his gift?

Oh god, oh damn, oh no, oh no. What had she done? What terrible thing had she done to bring him here?

He floated forward, stretched out his hand, the long nails beckoning her, gently pulling on her blood, closer, closer. "Come now, my child. Be not afraid. Do as I say and all will be fine, my greatest gift will be yours and you will be healed. Imagine, that pesky multiple sclerosis gone, no more suffering, no more foul medication that is worse than the disease itself. Just peace and eternity."

She felt it, that need to go toward him, to let him drink from her. That same overwhelming urge that she felt around Daphne, and that sad part of her that needed to die rising up in the brain fog. That inherit death drive in all living things, rising up, rising to the surface. Let him drink, it said. Let him do it.

Anna faded into the background, she didn't see her any more, her form a fuzzy shadow and nothing else. The vampires faded, the wights, everything. Her fears fading, fading.

"Come closer, here, let me feed. And remember, remember the key I gave you," and he held up his palm, reminding her of her key-shaped scar, "I never take what isn't wanted. Press against it now if you wish it to stop, and we won't feed on you, nor Anna. The others, well, they're fair game. The hunt is the hunt, after all. But I can promise that much."

And Nix stared numbly down at her palm, felt the crest of the key-shaped scar with her fingertips. It was numb and it throbbed, but she knew it wouldn't work anymore. Old Wick hijacked her scar, hijacked her magic with his own. Now when she pressed even lightly against it, she only heard his voice in her head, instructing her to bring Mister Brightbones back to the bookstore.

She moved her thumb back, and numbly walked forward. Yes, yes, this is what she wants, isn't it? Wouldn't it be worth the price she had to pay? Yes, yes. And look at Anna, eager-eyed and thirsty for her own death. Yes. She would be doing her a favor, isn't that what friends are for? And Anna would be helping her, curing her. Wasn't that so beautiful?

So very, very, beautiful.

Nix leaned her neck forward, and was dizzy and the world dimmed around her as she felt a row of jagged teeth bite down and tear through her skin, her blood rushing out of her, happy to find a new home.

25

NIX could actually feel her blood leaving her body, in a way that was difficult or impossible to explain. She'd had blood taken billions of times, and it never really felt like this. When blood left the body, it felt a little wet on the outside, but you couldn't feel it actually flowing outwards, pushing toward the exit wound like a river. But she felt that now, her blood roaring through her, fighting to get out, to leave her body. She felt his tongue licking it, pulling her blood closer, closer to him.

It wasn't painful, not exactly, no. Pain was the wrong word for what she felt. Her neck ached at the wound, but it was a distant throbbing ache. The blood rushing through her was a thundercurrent, a roaring of ventricles, but it didn't hurt as it swam out of her body. It just left her feeling hollowed out, drained, like the life force itself flowed out of her. It was similar somehow to how multiple sclerosis made her feel, so it was something she was almost used to at this point. The weakened muscle aches, the head throbbing, the eyes bright with pain, as she watched Mister Brightbones feed against her.

His true form floating about, flickering. That skeleton-shaped sunspot, aching. She closed her eyes a little, a little more, fading into shadows, sinking into nothingness. Just letting herself be hollow now, all empty and deflated. She still saw that sunspot skeleton, even after she closed her eyes. Like staring at the noonday sun or a bright halogen light, it stayed onward, burned into retinas. Maybe it will always be there, forever and ever. Always the skeleton image of Mister Brightbones, right there, in her eyesight, never leaving her, not even in thick restless sleep.

She felt herself drifting now, a dim pale shadow stretching over her vision. She opened her eyes for a brief moment as the lips left her neck, and she realized that the whole world was in sepia tone, and she was so weak. So horribly weak. A throbbing shadow crawled across her sight, and everything dimmed more and more. She saw a void, a terrifying darkness, coming right toward them. She shuddered and gasped at the sight of it, barely clinging onto the last threads of her life. Who is this who is coming?

"What, what do you see? Tell us what you see?"

And she whispered, muttered, "A great empty void, something devouring the entire world. It scares me shitless, and it's coming for us, it's coming right for us . . ."

The void was on the edge of reality flickering, pulsating, something in the corner of the universe itself. Not quite crossed over yet, yet waiting, a haunted presence. And she could feel its terrible hunger, it called to her, and her bones ached for it, wanted it to annihilate her completely. She wanted it and that made her tremble all over in a sharp, distinct fear. To see her own death drive laid bare before her. What a terrible thing. She shivered and moaned, and Mister Brightbones wiped his mouth.

"You lie. There is no void here, no child of the abyss. You fucking lie. Maybe I should stop now, and deny you any food at all, let you be a half thing, a wight, a ghoul. Doomed to wander after us, cleaning up our mess and eating the dead we leave behind. How do you like that?"

She ached all over and started to weep, but her eyes were too dry and nothing came out. All moisture sucked from her body, pulled out of her with her blood. His face was a smear of gore over her, and the sunspot skeleton laughed maniacally and she wanted to crawl away from here and die. But she couldn't die now, could she? Not in the normal mortal ways. Already he'd changed her. Already he'd cursed her with his cure.

Oh god, oh god, she should've listened to Daphne.

And it was Daphne now who saved her. Standing up frail in the dark and hungry, the halogen lights like a halo around her body. "You will do no such thing. You taunted her with a cure, how dare you leave her to rot like this without taking her the extra mile. Who cares what she saw? Void or no void, you promised."

Mister Brightbones grumbled and sighed and said nothing. The sunspot skeleton stopped laughing and seemed instead to wane and flicker with raw hunger.

"Speak true, child. What did you see that scared you so. Describe it, describe it, do it."

"The voi . . ."

A finger to her lips, it smelled like her own, blood, coppery and raw and salty, "Dig deeper. Deeper. What did you see?"

She shivered again, the world dimming and dimming some more, all colors drained, the fuzzy edges of reality now a vignette around her. She couldn't see it anymore, but she sensed it, slouching in the shadows like a giant black lion, with shadows for eyes and fire for teeth. The hunger was palpable, and all consuming, not being able to see it, but instead *feeling* it. Sensing it in the core of everything.

She felt faint, swooned a little, rocking on her body, as the world spun and she want spastic. Every limb tightening, the muscles pulled like a rope under her skin. This wasn't multiple sclerosis; this was something else. She was dying, and in that horrible moment she screamed as her body thrashed uncontrollably. And the vampires came from the shadows, came out, held her down, Faceless things in the dark, all meat for the worm beyond. The great worm that was the void.

And Mister Brightbones leaned over her, hungry and flickering. "Tell me what you see and I'll feed the rest of it, pushing you further now, further and closer to death, right up to the edge of that dark kingdom beyond. You'll be able to touch it, you'll be so close. Give me this, and I'll let you feed on your friend there, feed until death, and be cured. Go on, tell me, or I'll leave you like this. Pain, suffering, misery, broken even more than you'd been in life, and constantly hungry, always hungry, unable to eat anything but the corpses of fellow humans."

She coughed out the words, her voice all ragged and burning. "I can't see it now, but I can sense it everywhere. the void. But that's not the right word for it, it's hungry and it's waiting, it is both nothing and something at the say time. And it finds us horrible and disgusting, and wants to devour us. It wants to be alone in the universe, and it finds human life, all life, revolting."

And she spoke the truth, she felt it everywhere, the disgust at life, the hunger, and need to devour it and destroy it. And that need to be alone, truly alone, and content with itself. The nothing that was something. The hunger that was everything.

"I hope for your sake you're wrong, and this is just some foul hallucination."

And then he leant down, and fed some more, draining the last of her life from her body, as the world drifted away, and reality flickered . . .

And then she was someplace else.

It took a moment to regain her bearings, everything seemed familiar, but also somehow distant. Then she saw the wallpaper, and realized exactly where she was, and why it took a while to recognize it. This was the Hollow House, the Hallowed House, the House of Bones. And this area, here, this long hallway of a room covered in that creepy wallpaper? This was where she appeared in her dreams, each and every time. And yet, right now it felt different.

In her dreams it was all pristine and well kept up, the walls scrubbed, the cobwebs dusted away, and no rot or ruin of any sort. But now, right here, mold and fungus dotted the walls as spiders crawled through the shadows, leaving wispy webs behind like veils of silk. How did Nix get here? Was she dead? Was this all part of what it meant to become a vampire, and she would no longer be in her body, but something else would, a demonic form wearing her skin and always hungry? And she would be trapped here forever, outside of her body? Was this the cure Mister Brightbones had promised her? Oh, how horrible.

A voice behind her, so old and familiar it broke her heart. She never thought she'd hear that voice again outside of a dream or a rough memory in her head. It felt more real than a dream, more haunted than her memories. A voice that was strained now, and all hollowed out, and sounded like her aunt had swallowed coals and burned her throat with smoke. "Nixie Nix, my sweet niece, I need to show you. Here, come and see . . ."

She did not turn around at first. She was afraid that if she did, it would be something else there, one of those hunting leviathans in the shape of her aunt, wearing her ghost like a cheap Halloween costume. The skin slack and loose around the edges, and instead of eyes and a mouth there would be empty voids from beyond the edge of time.

26

NIX followed her aunt through the Hollow House, wondering if this was a dream or real, and if it was neither at the same time. How many times had she walked these halls every night in sleep? She was really here, wasn't she? Not physically, but then again, she was barely physical anymore, either.

"Come and see, come and see, come and see." Her aunt's voice rasped, rattled, and sounded like she spoke backwards, but was completely understandable at the same time.

"What happened to your voice . . ."

"Feed, don't feed on flesh, feed on blood. Can't undo what you've done, but live. Live. Feed. On blood. Live. I warned you. Now you must feed. Feed to survive. Feed on blood, feed on death. Not on rot, not on corpsemeat. Blood. Fresh and burning. Death. Bright and turning. It is sad you must feed on your friend, but you have to. You need to."

Little black flies fluttered around her body, taking nips at her, and she kept swatting and pushed them away. "Soul gnats," she said in that uncertain voice of hers, as Nix followed further into the unseen portions of the house, "They want to take me. To the burnt place. Can't have me. I am me, and I am mine."

And they turned another corner, walked down further steps, rickety noisy things. Cobwebs stretched across the ceiling, with the corpses of starved spiders scattered throughout their sticky fibers. Oh god, Nix hoped they wouldn't have to remember the way they went. What with all the twists and turns and dead ends, she was already lost in this familiar place. And what was she going to show her? What was so important for Nix to see? They went up a long hallway and it felt like they were going back in time somehow. Paint and wallpaper peeled back and recreated itself again and again. Pictures hung and then unhung and then disappeared from the walls to be replaced with the handprints of messy children. Were they walking backwards through time? Or were these the sentient loops that Old Wick talked about, the ghosts replaying their last days over and over again as the house fed on their suffering?

Children, yes, the sound of children playing filled the halls as their ghosts ran past them, laughing like tiny birds. A chill ran over Nix's entire body, goosebumps prickling on her arms, as a few ran right through her. She knew something terrible was happening up ahead. Something she did not want to see, but knew that she had to, in the end. The secret of the Cannibal House.

"Hurry, hurry, we must hurry. You fade now, need to feed soon. Come and see."

And her aunt pointed ahead, to a large arched doorway that led into what looked like a greenhouse beyond. Small trees and tall overgrown plants crept along the walls and pathways. Vines hung down from the glass dome ceiling like eager gallows. There were corpses everywhere, with some of the bodies still just barely alive, and Old Wick (now younger, yes, young Wick, with a dashing pince-nez and disarming black eyes, he wore a nice suit with a cravat around his neck and a knife in his hand) walked through the bodies. He found one of the living still, reached out, pulled back their hair and slit their throat. As he did it, he chanted something under his breath, something like "oh, dark between stars, show me the door," and then "oh, stars between the dark, show me the one I seek," and then "this world deserves nothing, and shall receive nothing."

Nothing. Nothing. The void at the center of the universe, the start of the Big Bang, the devouring heart of black holes, the great weight of nothingness and the slouching figure that walks toward them all. She saw it, flickering behind his eyes. A beast cut out of night, a leviathan of stars, and immediately fear set into her body, and curled up around her stomach all icy and hot. She wanted to run from that and keep on running. It was the unmaking thing, the one that came to reclaim the bits and pieces that exploded out from the heart of the universe. She wanted to curl up in a ball and cry . . .

"It can't see us. Watch. History first, so you understand. Watch."

The kids were even ghosts back then, Nix realized that now. There was only one child that was alive, and they were playing with her to protect her. She would be the one child that survived all of this, the cannibalism, the ritual, Old Wick himself. She did the math in her head, and realized that Old Wick looked about forty or forty-five years old here, so that meant he had to be ninety now? That didn't seem right, Old Wick looked more like he was in his late fifties now, tops. Maybe early sixties?

"Just how old is Old Wick?"

"Ageless. Three hundred and seventy-five here. He went by Haddo. Oliver Haddo."

It must be hard for her aunt to talk across the dimensions like that and speak to the living. She talked so hesitatingly, moved so sluggishly, like every single movement or word out of her mouth was a struggle that drained her of energy. Nix was sad for a moment, and thought back to the nights when they would stay up late, talking into the wee hours, when dawn would break. And they would yawn, and make some coffee, and talk some more. Back then, when she was alive, her aunt spoke quick and rapid, with the words tumbling over each other and punctuated by short bursts of laughter. Seeing her like this now, struggling to communicate, it made her want to give her a hug and hold her for a bit.

Now wasn't the time, though. She watched as the last living adult was killed. Now it was just Wick and that last living child running through the halls and playing tag, completely oblivious to everything else that was going on around her. That poor kid, Nix thought.

"Did we go back in time to save her?"

"No. Just watch."

And the kid stopped playing all of a sudden and stood frozen in the dark. Nix hadn't noticed before now, but the child was covered in scars from head to toe, like someone had cut her apart and then put her back together again, poorly. What happened to you, little girl? What happened that was so horrible . . .

And the child's eyes changed. They turned golden and bright and something was different about her movements. She stopped right then, right at the moment of the last death, and then tilted her head to look up at the constellations beyond the ceiling. She stood there, watching, as the ghosts around her dissipated, no longer playing. The child ghosts seemed terrified of the living girl, and for a moment Nix felt terrified, too. Her blood ran cold for a second. She knew those eyes, that manner of walking. She'd seen him in her dreams so many times.

The voice that came out of the girl was so familiar. Mister Brightbones.

"What am I doing here, in this child? You, there, mortal. Did you summon me?"

Young Wick looked frustrated and angry. "No, I did not summon you, who the hell are you? And where is the one I actually called? Fucking hell. They must've done it wrong, I got sloppy letting those amateurs think they were the ones in charge, last time I'm going to do that."

The girl walked slow through the corpses, toward where Young Wick knelt over his last kill, the final bit of blood dripping from the still-pink neck. Even though she knew this was not real, that this happened in the past, quite a long time ago, Nix felt her stomach grumble at the slaughterhouse smell of the room. It wanted blood, but the blood was lifeless, so worthless. Another hunger as well, that charnel feed for the flesh of the raw dead. No, she must resist, she couldn't eat here anyway, this was a place of echoes, wasn't it? She would only eat the memory of corpse meat, not the real thing. Oh god, oh god, she was turning into a wight, wasn't she? A horrible ghoul of a thing.

RESIST.

The girl spoke with Mister Brightbones's voice and it was disturbingly angelic. "Who did you summon?"

Young Wick looked away and said, "No one." And then he started walking forward, a glare in his eye, his fingers twisting about in some strange sign language. Index and pointer up, then thumb bent over, then thumbs on either side of the temples, then two fingers pressed against his heart, twisting. Mister Brightbones laughed.

"This body is my body now, spells like that won't work I'm afraid. I take it you're trying to summon the Child of the Abyss, yes? He won't come for you." The little girl stopped walking and cocked her head to one side. "How funny that you thought some maggot such as yourself could even attempt such a thing! And look at all these people, dead. What a waste. What a complete and utter waste. I could've saved them, you know, saved them all from death with a single kiss. What did you give them? Nothing. No, wait, scratch that, not even nothing. Nothing didn't even show up for you."

Young Wick grinned, and Nix knew something bad was going to happen. He put both his arms down at his side and shrugged. "He won't come for me, is that it? Well, I have a feeling he'll come for you." Wick then rolled up his sleeves and revealed complicated geometric tattoos that glowed faintly in the dim dying light of the evening sun. "If I can summon you, even on accident, it means I can bind you just as well."

The girl frowned and clapped her hands. "I'm done playing with you, this silly little game tires me." She spat on her palm, rubbed it together, and then closed her eyes. Her lips moved, and Nix heard this barely audible whispering sound of dead leaves rustling on an autumn night.

Young Wick collapsed to the ground, writhed in pain, his screams echoing the screams of all they'd witnessed earlier. Nix looked at her aunt and said, "Why are you showing me this? I can't stop this, this was in the past."

"Watch," her aunt said. "Watch, understand. Then you must stop."

Young Wick lifted his head up, the blood in the room a pungent odor of decay, his left eye clenched shut, his arms twisted about in catatonic spasms. He spat blood out of his mouth on the floor. "You may be done with me," he growled, "But I am not done with you. I will find you. I will trap you. And you will be my bait for the cancer that eats the heart of the universe."

And then everything swam for a moment, flickered, as the room changed, floated through the years, a small vessel on the waves of time.

27

ONION-SKINNED, the years moved past, layered over each other as Nix watched. It was like seeing a sped-up film of each decade dancing around her, the seasons whirring past, the sky changing so quickly, as she watched. She felt dizzy, and wanted to make it stop or slow down. But her aunt stood there, silent, still. Watch, watch, wait and watch. You must see the history of the house. The truth it needs to show you.

Young Wick aging as he builds his vampire hunters. So many failed variations, their bodies piles of melted wax, bone, and raw animal blood. Sigils stretched across the floor, written in salt, and chalk, and more blood. And then they get up, moving, those vampire hunters. Eureka! He'd finally figured out how to do it, to get them to move and to hunt. Weak at first, moving like a jerky marionette, or like infants just learning to walk for the first time. Unsteady, animatronic, yet filled with some sick mockery of life. They went out, and started to collect bones.

The years sped on, even faster and faster, whirring, vertigo, Nix wanted to sit down, but there was no place to sit. Time was unmoored, and here she was in a rough approximation of reality, spinning by in her spirit form. Maybe she should go back to her body . . .

What body?

She flickered for a moment, was in the bookstore again. Real for a moment. Blood pumping through her veins, her lungs filling with air. Feel that? Solid ground beneath her feet! She was hungry, starved. The smell of rot sang to her . . .

And then she flickered again, was back with her aunt.

"No you don't. Stay. Watch. Watch to understand. So you can survive."

The memories of the house continued on, sentient loops playing its twisted history for her as she watched. Vampire hunters would leave, come back bringing bone after bone. So many vampires over the years. How many did it take? They would bring them in burlap sacks, stained with filth and viscera, dump them out into a yellowed pile. All brittle and clanking as they fell and tumbled out. And Young Wick (getting older now) would go through each pile, pull just one or two out, and toss the rest into the flames. A howl in the bones, as the last spirits of the undead burned away with them in a puff of shadows. More and more and more over the years. A vampire genocide.

All for what purpose?

One bone, two bone, three bone, four. As the years sped onto decades, time unlooping and repeating, she watched as the bones stacked up, higher, higher. Held together by twine and sigils and a strange silence. A cage. He was building a cage out of vampire bones. The world seemed to grow distant, echoing again, the call of her meat to become real once more . . .

She fought it, as best as she could, she had to see what happened. She had to understand.

Watch, watch. Her aunt said. There is so much at stake here.

Now Young Wick became Middle-Aged Wick became Old Wick once more. His beard seemed to grow in real time, as the vampire hunters brought more bones, and he traveled across the world. What was he doing out there? Building more houses, of course. The Coffin House, the House of Sky and Shadow, the Unspooling House, the Sleeping House, the Shadow House and the Graveyard House. More houses, each of them with terrible secrets. But this house, this one was the most important one, wasn't it? The key to all of his Great Work. The Cannibal House.

Snow drifted outside, thunder in the sky, as the last bone was laid upon the cage. It clicked shut snapped into place, the world no longer running by in high speed, no longer a sentient loop or a memory, now a reality. Now modern day, present day, the current time. And when it finally snapped right there, something howled in the shadows and shook the bones of the house.

A clicking sound, a flickering in the dark. Wailing. From all those cannibal and bacchanal hours. Where the ghosts sacrificed themselves, to feed this house, to turn to this very moment.

And Old Wick smiled as he howled in the darkness, and the world shivered, as if cold. And Old Wick smiled again, and his teeth shone like a waxing crescent moon.

"I've played the long game, you old rat bastard, and now here I am, with a cage I built from your children's bones. This is the kind of thing you won't ever be able to escape, oh no. And that will be catnip for your brother, the Child of the Abyss, the void from the beginning and end of time, and he will come here, unable to resist this, and I will catch him and bind him. And then this world will be good and fucked. And I will remake it in my image, just you watch. It will be perfect, and a better world. A world without all this bullshit suffering, this empty hollow existence. I will give it *meaning*."

And then Nix flickered once more, but she couldn't fight it, the pull of flesh and bone and muscles was just too strong. And she smelled it, all coppery and rich, pulling her further into the shadows. Blood. Warm and inviting. Blood.

Feed, her aunt had said. Feed on blood. Feed on death. Not on corpsemeat. Survive. Prevent this all from ending in a whisper of nothingness. The void is already on its way here, you saw it in the eyes of death, you saw it coming for this world. It knows Old Wick is calling it here. All it needs is for the trap to be set, and Mister Brightbones to be in that cage, pulling him to Wick. You must stop it. You must stop this all from happening. Feed. Feed on blood, not on death. Feed. Survive. And save this meager world from emptiness.

28

NIX felt a woosh of flesh and bone and blood stitching itself around her consciousness, pulling her back into the real. First lungs slowly inhaling, exhaling. That low death rattle of one so close to the edge of dying. Her vision slowly returning to the real world, her eyes dimming, her muscles weak and flexing around bone. Everything hurt, that near death ache as the nerves fire off their last impulses before going quiet and then nothing, nothing anymore but silence and the soft slow march of death.

She returned to her body, yes, she returned to her body as it was failing her for one last final time. Her multiple sclerosis firing off in a grand finale fireworks of white blood cells attacking her dying nerves. Everything dimming, mind, body, everything. The blurry thoughts of brain fog, wrapping around her, increasing that dizzy burning near-death sensation.

And then blood. Oh that thick rich pungent smell of blood calling her back to the living. She heard that heartbeating in her dull muted eardrums, the thumthump of the living calling out to the dying. Everything tinted a feverish red now, like an October moon coating the world in a blood red light. And the center of that light, the lamp that was illuminating her whole world right now?

There, right there, leaning over towards her, a bright heart lamp calling out to her, pulling her forward. Dizzy and numb, Nix's thoughts struggled to cohere. Was this multiple sclerosis? Was this brain death? Was this something else?

She couldn't tell, all those thoughts wrapped in cotton. All that was left was this need, this burning hot need inside of her, drawing her further and further on, keeping her alive in this moment, the hunger driving her, oh god the hunger. And yet, it wasn't quite a hunger, was it?

No, it was a thirst. That intense thirsty feeling of someone so dehydrated their very tears were dust, and every inch of her body ached for a single drop of water.

Just a drop, just a drop of that water, that red water that flows through the rivers of our hearts, just a drip drop would be enough to keep her, to keep her here, to keep her alive.

Feed. Feed on blood. Feed.

Her aunt's voice so strong in her head, echoing around the dark corners of her mind. *Feed*, feed on blood. Feed. And live. Live to stop this all from happening.

She shivered from head to toe. *Yes, Aunt Doreen*, she thought. *Yes, I shall feed.*

After all, I am so thirsty, so very very thirsty.

And the figure, that red thumping lantern figure, all the blood flowing through it so bright and beautiful, it leaned against her. And she heard Anna's voice (was that Anna? How could that be Anna?) So sharp and clear, like a thunderbolt in her bones.

"Nix, Nix my love. You're like a sister to me, my love. Please, I need you to help me."

And Nix leaned in, closer. That smell of blood overpowering, the red heartlight eclipsing her vision, leaving only sharp shadows in its wake. She had no idea how beautiful it would be to feed. Daphne never mentioned this to her. Oh how horribly beautiful.

"Please, Nix, we are so close, I know you'll understand this, you'll understand it more than anyone else in my whole life. After all our conversations, I feel so close to you, and I know, I know you'll get this."

And whisper, so wet and sharp in her ear, like a knife fresh from the kill. "Living is so exhausting. Every day, in and out, the same repetitive tasks over and over again, the same repetitive day, over and over again. Waking, sleeping, waking again. The bills drowning me, Every day baking muffins and bread and making coffee that barely anyone eats or drinks, just to throw it out at the end of the day. Such a small, small town, no one has the money or the time for my food, and so every day I bake and I destroy, I bake and I destroy."

And then the humming red outline leaned in closer, so thirsty, could taste it in the air, that hot blood stink. "I'm so exhausted, every day a Sisyphean task without end. I want it to end, I want to just stop it all and sleep, sleep so long and empty. Please, Nix, please, give this to me. I know you can do it, I can sense it in you, the power to give me what I need."

And Nix responded, her voice so parched her words like sandpaper, her lungs so close to death, they wheezed and rattled, so slight, so low. "I am so thirsty for your death."

Where did those words come from? An aching chasm inside of her, boiling about, taking over her thoughts. If she was rational, if she wasn't so close to death, if her multiple sclerosis wasn't fogging up her thoughts, if Wick's spell over her wasn't so strong and vibrating, maybe, yes, maybe she would see the horror of this situation and stop herself, just stop herself. It wasn't worth being cured, wasn't worth saving the world.

But none of those things were true. Her key-shaped scar throbbed, but it was hijacked now and pressing it would do no such thing. Her dying mind swirled into shadows, and her multiple sclerosis clouded everything except that need, that overpowering need to drink, to drink and be satiated.

She leaned in some more. And in the distance Daphne screamed out no, screamed out, you don't have to do this, Nix, don't, stop, don't!

But it was like she was far away, down some distant dark tunnel, where the words get lost in the echoes and thunder of trains roaring overhead. Nix felt the pull of sadness for a brief, shining moment, where she pulled back just a little, a tiny bit, not much . . .

And then a hand flashed in the dim blood light. Mister Brightbones? Maybe. Or maybe one of the other vampires? Maybe. In the hand was a straight razor, catching the light, as a neck opened up, and blood spilled, a river in her mouth. She couldn't help herself, drowning in the glory of it all, her lips now on the open wound, sucking on the raw ragged skin.

"There," a calm voice said with a heavy Virginian accent, "Your teeth haven't come in yet, so you need a little help opening this one up."

And oh, her thirst didn't slake when the blood roared down her throat, almost choking her at first, her mind so empty, it almost forgot how to swallow properly. No, her thirst grew, spreading through her body, roaring in her veins, as the blood flooded inside of her. She felt her muscles growing stronger, she felt her eyesight sharpening, and her breathing no longer ragged and shallow, but instead heavy and full. The breath of the living, the blood of the living. She weas dizzy with the beauty of it, the taste of it, and this sparkling feeling moving through her own body now. Like the blood inside of her was electric and singing, singing so beautifully as it flowed through her.

And she saw Anna's heart now, felt it like a rabbit beneath the skin. She wanted to chase the rabbit, and with each gulp and sip and slurp, the rabbit tried to run further and further away, quickly dancing into the field beyond. But no, little rabbit heart, you can't escape from Nix. Nix was the great heart hunter, the blood-drenched vampire queen.

Further and further she followed it, pulling deeper, as Anna moaned against her, a pleasurable sound that gave her goosebumps all over, as Anna shuddered, head to toe, tiny pleasurable spasms, an orgasm of blood beneath her. Death, death was coming.

"You must feed all the way, feed until death."

Mister Brightbones voice fluttering over them, like a bat wing of birds. She knew the truth of it. And for a moment, yes, for a moment, she realized what she was doing.

Oh, Anna, oh now. What was she doing? Oh poor Anna. She doesn't deserve this, she deserves to live. It was a moment of weakness, wasn't it? We all get so tired of living. But that doesn't mean the answer was death, was it?

Daphne was sobbing and screaming behind her, and she watched the shadows of other vampires try to silence her, to muffle her. What was she doing? She had to stop this, she had to.

And yet, that rabbit heart stuttered a little, stumbled. And that spurned her on, so close now, the death so close. Her body was stronger now, she wrapped herself around Anna, felt warm flesh to warm flesh, as the wind roared outside and beat against the walls of the sporting goods store.

"Oh Nix, I see it. Do you see it? It's so horribly beautiful! And it's coming this way, and it's so hungry, so hungry and beautiful and oh. Oh. I'm weeping now, so beautiful. Do you see it? A lion made of nothingness. A void in the dark so hungry it wants to eat everything." And then she started laughing maniacally. And for a moment Nix saw it too, and remembered, and almost stopped feeding, almost.

The Child of the Abyss, there it was, in the shadows on the wall, in the darkness between heartbeats. Always hungry, always despising all of humanity. She almost stopped, almost. When Mister Bright-bones (or maybe someone else?) pushed her head against that open wound, and she pushed on deeper, and deeper, that rabbit heart stumbling some more, and some more, and then slowing down, and finally, finally, it collapsed, no more.

The heart light dimmed and then went out, and Nix leaned back, smiling at the haunted world. Anna was still in her arms, no longer twitching or moving, her body ice cold and her features slack and wooden. Mouth agape, eyes wide open, the pupils dilated so that it looked like two black holes were placed in her face.

And she felt something she hadn't felt in forever. Her feet, there, beneath her legs, no longer numb from multiple sclerosis. The colors of the room brightened, reds far more bright and visceral than ever before, as her optic neuritis slid away into nothingness. Her limbs felt like her limbs again, no longer a tightness of muscles, or a weakness of hand strength. She was, oh, she was cured.

She was fucking *cured*!

And she laughed, holding the bloody corpse of one of her best friends, no longer thirsty. Just pleasantly alive, and not fully realizing the horror that had happened here. Not yet, anyway.

That would come later.

29

THE world felt bright, on some weird ontological level, in a way Nix couldn't explain. Yes, her multiple sclerosis was healed, reversing her optic neuritis abruptly, which lightened the world a little. Before, everything was desaturated, and now it all seemed more vivid and intense. But it was more than that, like her eyes could see deeper into the darkness, The shadows now mere grey shambling colors, no longer pitch black and impossible to see. Even the slightest light burst in front of her eyes, almost blinding and beautiful, but still enough to see.

No wonder the other vampires hated the sun so much. Not only did it burn them, but it blinded them, too. And now, yes, now the camper lanterns and the light of Mister Brightbones's glowing skeleton was enough to see everything. More than enough, actually.

What had been a cluster of vampire shadows before were now a clear ragtag group of strangers. Lips blood red, skin pallid and corpselike, with blue veins like visible maps dwelling just below the surface.

It was odd, she felt like she could tell the era where they'd been turned just by the clothes on their back. She guessed it was like seeing old middle-aged men and women who still dressed up in the rebel clothes of their youth. Except these vampires never actually aged, frozen in their moment of becoming, unable to move on and embrace the modern world both mentally and physically.

Bellbottoms and fringe jackets on some, ripped jeans and neon hair on others. Flannels over t-shirts, and a pair of lone goth girls dressed up in all black Victorian finery. Not like people actually from that era, but instead that early aughts goth fashion that mimicked it with elaborate dresses and memento mori makeup and jewelry.

A mullet over there, next to a Cindi Lauper lookalike with fingerless gloves and spikey hair. And in the center of it all was that odd child of her dreams, blindfolded, with cancer crawling across his face, and a sheepish grin. He had blood splashed all over his oversized salvation army clothes, from when he slit Anna's throat for Nix to drink.

Don't think about that, though. Don't think about what just happened, now that your mind is clear and your thoughts are sharp. Don't look over at the ghouls eating Anna's corpse, bones and all, to get rid of all evidence. Ignore the smacking and clacking sounds, of bones breaking and marrow being sucked dry. Ignore them fighting over the intestines like raw dogs.

Ignore, ignore, ignore. She had to do it to stay sane. Her stomach felt squirmy and wrong, the blood pumping through her now all hot and sticky under the skin. Like a furnace, heating her from the inside out. That was her blood, Anna's blood . . .

No don't think about it. Thinking about it makes you itch, right, Nix? So just don't think about it. Think about Daphne, there, oh Daphne. She's refusing to look at her, instead glancing everywhere else. She was sick again, needing to feed again. She looked corpse cold, and her body emaciated from the bloodhunger. She saw it then, a glance of panic in her eyes. Nix had a feeling if Daphne didn't eat soon, that cancer would come back and all those years she'd been frozen would come back and age her, and then that would be it. She would be a corpse.

And she was in chains. Cold iron chains, from the looks of it. Her wrists manacled, with a chain between them leading up to another manacle across her neck. It seemed to burn the skin where it touched, blistering and gnarly and red. Why wasn't Daphne looking at her?

She must hate her for what she'd done. Bringing Mister Brightbones here, and then feeding. Feeding on her one true friend. Hadn't Daphne warned her? Hadn't she told her about drinking her own parents to death?

Was this cure worth it? She wished it was so. But it was hard to justify it. She heard that smacking and growling of the ghouls and the wights, those foul, stinking half vampires, feeding on Anna's corpse, and thinking she didn't deserve this. Anna did not deserve this.

But, Nix reasoned, *I don't deserve multiple sclerosis, either. Nor type 2 diabetes. Sometimes shit gets doled out, and that's how the universe works.* It was a shameless justification, but she was still angry deep down inside about her diagnosis, even though it's been over a decade since she'd found out. Every single relapse (and there had been many, with several years it happening every other week like clockwork, in and out of the hospital) brought back that sharp pain of just how fucking unfair it all was, how wild and angry it made her.

And now she used that pain to justify what she'd done to Anna. She tried to make it into an act of god, somehow. But it wasn't, she was no god. It was an act of cruelty, plain and simple, but she wouldn't think about that, not now, not right now, not at all.

It felt like an eternity of silence in her thoughts. An eternity of smacking devouring sounds. But, it had only been mere microseconds, barely any time at all. It was like those times she took acid in high school, and time seemed to dilate and change, become strange, stretching out. So when Mister Brightbones actually spoke, she jumped a little, the noise deafening, and snapping her out of this internal reverie.

"Welcome," he said, "Beyond the veil of blood. Here, everything is so much brighter, so much lighter, so much more *delicious.* We haven't just healed your illness, we have healed that cursed, wretched part of you called *humanity.* You're above it now, above them now. You are vampire."

Nix leaned back, against one of the shelves lined with camping equipment, and felt that Old Wick trying to get back into her thoughts again, rummaging around in her head. That commandment, to take them all back to the bookstore, she remembered it, pulling on her mind, pulling on her bones.

But, hah, yes, she could resist it so easily. It had no power over her at all anymore. It was like a balloon, floating away from her, not of her concern at all anymore. And that made her smile, oh yes, smile with blood on your teeth, blood on her breath, smile. She was a vampire now, one who had just fed. She didn't need the scar on her hand, not anymore, she was stronger than that. Maybe, even yes, stronger than him?

Or was that the blood thinking for her? She felt a million times better, and that gave her this sense of invincibility. And she knew that was a false thing indeed. Oh yes, Nix could still remember those pains, the trouble walking. It was still there, in the corner of her mind, and hadn't faded away just yet.

She'd been in remission before. A relapse was always possible.

And then Mister Brightbones walked forward, more and more, closer and closer. He spoke like he heard her thoughts, and who knows, maybe he did? She sure hoped not, though. "You poor thing," he said, "So used to medications and cures that never really work. Always wondering when this remission will end, and when another relapse will hit you and be the one that takes you down and burns you out for good. But this is different, it is, it's so different. All you need to do is feed. Not all the time, just when you're hungry and your blood is running low, feed, feed until death, and then you'll never go back to your old life. Never, ever go into a relapse ever again."

Nix nodded in the shadows, as Mister Brightbones's skeletal lights danced around her, making the darkness flicker and grow like candle shadows. And then she realized what she had done, for a brief terrible moment, that taste of her best friend's blood on her tongue. Oh no. She remembered what she had seen, near death and when she was feeding. That horrible, hungry, emptiness. Crouched there in the corners of reality, waiting to feed. It struck at the core of her, shivered her to the bone. She wanted to cry, she wanted to sob and bleed out all of Anna's blood in her tears. Maybe that would bring her back to life? Maybe it wasn't too late?

No, she'd drank her friend's death. That was what was keeping her alive. And then she remembered her aunt, her promise, and knew that shit was about to get real.

And then the vampire hunters in her pocket started to squirm and wiggle. She had forgotten all about them, how she had taken them from the bookstore after Old Wick had set them aside. She meant to throw them in the snow, in the darkness, maybe bury them in the ground. But she had forgotten about it completely.

And here they were, waking up in her pockets. And here she was, a vampire. Oh god oh no oh shit.

30

THEY wiggled and squirmed in her pockets and her mind was caught in a panic. Should she throw them out now? But then it would be a bloodbath, a slaughter, and they would blame her. Even if the majority of vampires survived, they would treat her like a spy, like someone who had brought vampire hunters into their midst.

But that's what she was, wasn't she? She still felt Old Wick's commandment in the back of her head, to bring them to the bookstore. She could resist it, easily, now with her vampire mind, but it was still there worming around, trying to take over her thoughts and control her. The scar even burned and throbbed, whispering his painful commands into her body. Did he know that she took the vampire hunters out of there and planned on disposing of them? Did he find out?

She felt the new blood rushing in her body, it felt electric and sparkly, like it was alive and lightning coated. Anna's blood, so powerful, so strong. She heard her whispers in her head now, too, those dying words. The void, everywhere, that void, watching. That void.

She had to stop it. But how?

She felt the vampire hunters growing a little in her pocket, expanding just a tiny bit, their sharp teeth gnawing close to her skin like tiny needles. She wanted to scream and jump and run around.

Mister Brightbones was still talking, and she hadn't been paying attention to him at all. Instead, she was panicking inside, and she reached her hands inside her pockets, felt them alive and squirming and biting against the palms of her hands. She was going to scream and throw them. She had to. She had to do it.

"We need to feed," Mister Brightbones said, "And this town feels so empty. Do you know where everyone is, Nix? Can you show us where they are all hiding? Oh, don't worry, don't be afraid."

And he slid forward, gliding across the floor like he did in her dreams. It was exactly like he was floating, his feet dragging a little behind him, his arms outstretched and his long fingers outstretched, making long shadows in the dark. His true form flickered around him, that sunspot skeleton. It didn't hurt her head any longer, like it did before she fed and became one of them. Now it filled with bright light and this powerful, ecstatic feeling. Manic, that's the word for it, seeing his true form now filled her with this overwhelming mania.

"What do you mean," she said, hoping he didn't see the vampire hunters squirming in her pockets. "I don't feel afraid at all. I feel so powerful!"

He smiled and his teeth were like gravestones lining the inside of his mouth. "Good, good. So you won't mind us feeding on all these little friends of yours? You're not going to be like Daphne and regret it and try and run away from us?"

Daphne rattled her chains in the back, her mouth hanging wide open, her eyes wide. She quivered, shock and horror, her eyes crying small tears of blood. "No, Nix, don't do this, it doesn't have to be this way."

"These people didn't care about you at all, did they? No, not even a little bit. They saw you as a burden, as someone that had to care for, like a little China doll, set to smash at the smallest tremor. They called you cripple, they insulted your cane, made fun of the way you walked, resented you for your weakness. They didn't want to care for you, and resented you for needing them. Isn't that right?"

The mania grew stronger and stronger in Nix, like a rising tide of blood and fire. She smiled now, a jack o' lantern smile, a little unhinged with her own sense of power. She knew, on one level, that he was wrong. That she was fiercely independent and never required help from anyone else.

And yet, on another level he touched on fears that were threaded deep down inside of her. Fears she never mentioned to anyone else, not even Anna, or Daphne, or her aunt when she was still alive.

Fears that ran like a crack through her heart. And one small touch was all that it would take, one small phrase and the crack would splinter out, open up, and crumble everything inside of her.

Mister Brightbones's words were like fingers pushing against this crack and prying it apart. She gulped.

"No, I mean, you're right . . ."

Was he? Poor Anna never thought that. Or did she? Did she just put up with Nix, acted like a friend because of her condition, and not wanting to be seen like an evil person ignoring a cripple? Her blood still tasted sweet on her lips, and thrummed alive in her veins.

Are you forgetting your true mission? Why I brought you back?

Aunt Doreen's voice in her head, yes. Oh yes. Thank you for reminding me. There is something more important here. She can't lead them back there, she can't let the vampire hunters take over, she definitely can't let Mister Brightbones get into that cage that Old Wick built for him. It would lure the void closer, closer. And Old Wick would get what he wanted, a world all his own, devoured by shadows.

She had to lead them astray, and somehow get rid of the vampire hunters. They squirmed, grew a little more, a little more. Now there were the size of apples in her pockets, their sharp teeth whirling and gnawing and looking for an escape.

"All right," Nix said, and tried to hide the lie behind her eyes, away from Brightbones's prying fingers. "If you all need to feed, I know exactly where we can go. There was a Halloween party going on at the edge of town, that's where everyone's at. We'd come here to get some supplies, and ended up splitting up. Either they're back already or are all walking back and we can ambush them on the way."

And Nix tried to steel up her gaze, hardening her thoughts to seem like she was really being this tough, that she really didn't care about her friends. That she wasn't about ready to lead them all astray, losing them in the winter darkness.

It was necessary, though. She had to keep them away from the bookstore, away from the Cannibal House, and most importantly, away from Old Wick, his vampire hunters, and that cage he had lying in wait.

Daphne cried out "No, Nix! It doesn't have to be this way."

But Nix tried her best to ignore her. She couldn't let Daphne know her true thoughts, it would ruin everything. Mister Brightbones would be able to tell right away that she was lying then, and it would all be over.

I'm so sorry Daphne. She hated lying to her. Yes, she wasn't her real daughter, but there was a kinship there, deep down. Something that brought them together, and she hated betraying that trust.

And Mister Brightbones grinned, still not seeing the strange creatures moving in her pockets. She had to do something about them soon enough, else they would all be fucked six ways to Sunday. But not yet, not just yet.

"Let's go," she said, "I'll show you the way."

And Nix started walking towards the entrance, her face shining with still wet blood, the air so crisp and bright. She hoped that they wouldn't run into Danny and all of them. She hoped that they had made it back to the bookstore already, and they wouldn't cross paths at all.

And if they did? Well, she would release the vampire hunters right away. The ensuing chaos might just be enough to get them all out of here and away from Old Wick and the rest.

The door banged against the wall, the blizzard roaring outside. Mister Brightbones smiled behind her, and whispered, "Do not be afraid, this is my blizzard. It's so we could hide and hunt the humans without them knowing, and allow us to walk around in daylight without burning up. Trust me, it will part for us."

And Nix nodded and gulped. She had a thought, then. It might just work. God, she sure hoped it worked. "I'll let you go first then," she said, "To make sure it parts. These kind of blizzards always freak me out."

"Ah, I see. Even cured it's hard to get rid of that fear. I see you're still holding onto that cane, even though you don't need it anymore. It's hard to just let it go and be okay, it's hard to not worry about the disability coming back, especially during this kind of storm. I understand, we'll go first, if you'll tell us the way."

Nix nodded. God, please don't look at my pockets, they're getting even bigger now, angrier now. They want to hunt, they need to hunt.

"Take a left out of here and we'll just follow the street towards the edge of Main. You'll see my car there and Anna's bakery," a soft sad ache in her heart, Anna, whose blood was still there, warm and sticky inside of her, "That's where the party is."

Hopefully that will buy her enough time to figure something out, some way to get them out of Dark Rivers and away from Old Wick.

Mister Brightbones nodded, and the vampires walked past her, moving out the front door to the harsh winters beyond. Daphne gave her this pained, sad look of betrayal, one that cut Nix right to her bones. But she had to ignore it, had to wait until they were completely outside.

And then she quickly threw those little vampire hunters (now double in size from before) as far into the store as possible. It felt good to be able to throw again, to move her arms again without clumsily dropping everything from muscle weakness. She felt so good walking again, her legs moving silk and smooth like a well-oiled machine. No more muscle pain, no more hip pain, none of that. She smiled, and in a moment of brief madness where she'd accepted her new life as being cured, she laughed and tossed her cane across the store floor, watching it scatter in the shadows. And now she wanted to dance, to run, to test her new body to the best of its abilities. Oh god, how she missed running! Oh god, how she missed dancing!

But she couldn't sit there and relish in it, no.

She had to get moving, before the vampire hunters grew and came after them. She walked outside, framed by the broken doors, the blizzard obscuring everything around them.

31

THE snow seemed to dance around Mister Brightbones in a weird funnel of white. As the rest of the gang of vampires moved around him, restless, following the path forward. Nix right next to him now, pointing the way to Anna's bakery, the dim streetlamps flickering soft halos in the dark. It was difficult to tell what time it was. Had it grown late? Is this actually night now? Or were the storm clouds still blocking out the sun with their heavy darkness?

Nix had no idea, and it was disorienting. Much like the blizzard, and how it made the world strange and unfamiliar. She had to constantly re-group her thoughts, and try and see in her mind's eye how the world used to look, so she wouldn't get lost.

They were in the middle of the street, snow-covered cars lining either side, like metallic beasts buried in shallow white graves. The cold felt so odd to her right now, Anna's blood burning through her body like a roaring furnace, and the snow icy against her skin, like sharp prickles of frost.

"I don't see any lights on," the Cindy Lauper-dressed vampire to her left said, "And damn I am getting hungry. We should bleed the new girl, feed off that blood she's got inside of her."

Another vampire to the right, dressed in old school goth fashion, replete with a trench coat and a fishnet shirt, said in a soft baritone, "You know that's not how it works, Suzie Sue. It won't do a damn thing for us secondhand like that."

"Just because it didn't work in the past doesn't mean it won't work *now*, will it? That death is still fresh in her body, still clinging to the blood. I bet it would keep at least two of us going for a little bit."

"Not enough, though," Mister Brightbones said, his sunspot skeleton floating around his body, the blizzard like a veil of snow occulting him. "I told you this before, back when you tried to feed on each other and we were hard up and trapped in the Alleghenies, remember?"

"Oh right," Cindy Lauper vampire said, "Back when those vampire hunters had us cornered up there, picking us off one at a time. If wasn't for that snitch bitch," and she spat at Daphne, "We could've been just fine."

Daphne rattled her chains, whimpered. "I told you, I didn't do anything of the sort. I left you guys because I couldn't take it anymore, I had to be on my own. It was too much death, just way too much. But I would never sell you out to that asshole, I would never . . ."

Nix ran her hand through her hair, nervous for a moment. They were coming up on Anna's Bakery soon enough. It would be the moment of truth, and then they would know she lied to them. Would they put her in chains too, just like they put Daphne? Oh, it was too much. This was all too much.

"She didn't snitch on you," Nix spoke calmly, even though she was trembling inside. "When she was at our place the vampire hunters came after her, I had to fight them off and we barely escaped with our lives. Old Wick isn't working with her, he wants her dead too."

"Likely story," the old goth said, and began to wheeze and cough as he talked, his voice sounding rougher, heavier. "Are we getting there soon? I don't smell any blood on the air, I can't sense any heat of living things. And there are no lights anywhere, and we need to feed. We need to! I can feel my COPD coming back fierce. It's making it hard to breathe."

Nix shrugged, though no one could really see it. She lifted her head up, and listened with her new ears, hoping to hear something they couldn't hear. A voice talking far away, the roar of blood in someone's veins. Any sign of life whatsoever, anything to keep this charade going a little more.

Something moved behind them. A scratching scraping noise, like someone dragging metal on cement. Scrrrrrape, scrrrrape, scraape. Her whole body felt tense, the new blood moving even faster and faster inside of her, taking her mania up a notch. She felt electric, keyed up, everything alive and burning.

"I, I don't know where everyone is anymore, I just know that we were supposed to meet back at the Bakery after getting supplies."

Scraaaape, scraaape, scraaape. Why wasn't anyone saying anything about that noise? How could she be the only one hearing it? Was it because she just fed? That sluggish dead heart now beat faster and faster with Anna's blood, and she worried that she might burn through it so quickly now, her heart beating too fast. Like a blur of butterfly wings in her chest, beating so fast.

Mister Brightbones stopped for a moment, looking behind them. He had to hear this sound, why wasn't he saying anything? Why was no one else hearing it but her? It was so loud, it set her teeth on edge. So horrible. It made her cringe, nails on chalkboard. As it got closer and closer, and she noticed that there were two sounds now, two scraping noises deadened by the snow and wind. "You said they went out with you, correct? Maybe they're still out there, stuck in the blizzard. Maybe that's why they haven't returned to the bakery just yet."

Nix stepped back from the sound, tried not to show how nervous and terrified she was, and instead leaned into his explanation. "Yes, and so we should wait for them when we get there. I'm sure that's we're they'll come back, absolutely positive of it, I promise you."

Tall shadows moved in the darkness behind them. They had to see it, they had to! Lumbering shapes, almost as tall as a building, about one story, maybe one and a half. And they swung something back and forth, dragging it on the ground, like a giant pendulum of wood and steel. She wanted to scream and keep running, and get the hell away from here. Those were the vampire hunters, they had to be them, they had to. They had grown so quickly and followed them, and she should've known that was going to happen.

They had been made of wax, yes? She should've melted them when she had the chance. But with what fire? She had no lighter, she didn't smoke. Maybe at the sporting goods store, a camping lighter, one of those long thin ones for starting campfires?

No, it didn't matter. That was the past, and now she was stuck in this horrible present. She would die here. This would be the end of her. Now, now, that she was finally cured and ready to live a mostly normal life. Now that she was an actual murderer, who fed on the blood on her best friend. Now was the moment of reckoning, of death. It was all for nothing, the murder, the vampirism, her taking in Daphne and calling on Mister Brightbones. She should've known better. There was no cure, only death. And here it was, the proof of it all, how cursed she had been her whole life. Nix did not deserve to be whole and healed again. Not with the price Anna paid, it was too high, too steep. Death was all that mattered for her now. Death, death, death, She deserved it for what she did.

She should've been stronger.

"Damn these cancerous eyes," Mister Brightbones said, "Damn this bullshit. I can sense something with my second sight, yes, something back there, behind us. But it's not them is it? Not the people we can feed on. I know you can see it, Nix, I can sense it in your fear, it is seeping off of you in waves. Tell us what you see, and what terrifies you so."

And Nix spoke calmly, almost a whisper, her words barely leaving her lips. "Vampire hunters."

And Mister Brightbones started to laugh.

"You have every right to be afraid my child. Every fucking right to be afraid. And if we survive this, oh yes, if we live through this? I am going to make you pay. Even if you're not leading us into a trap, this is still all your fault. And for that, oh yes, you shall pay."

The scraping closer and closer now, and then an arc of glaring light in the shadows. A moon shaped blade, a scythe as tall as the Vampire Hunters themselves, swooping through the air, aimed right at Nix. She wanted to say *how is this my fault*? But she couldn't, because she knew it was true. She just didn't know how Mister Brightbones knew. And yet, somehow, he knew.

She wasn't going to survive this, was she?

32

ANNA'S blood thundered through Nix's veins, hot and fast with fear, her dead heart pumping, her mind racing, her thoughts tumbling over one another, unable to escape the panic of her skull. Run, don't run, scream, don't scream, fight back, don't fight back, do something, anything, just something to survive. As the massive scythes flew through the air, slicing into the vampires, cutting them in half as their bodies writhed, still living torsos, the legs kicking in the air. She'd dodged out of the way, just barely, just barely, and caught sight of Daphne stumble running, her chains jingle jangling, musical in the snow shadows. Panic, bright surreal panic, wondering if they would survive this, if either of them would survive this. This, this, this chaos of the moment.

Her new vampire eyes watched in awe as the hunters, giant, massive things with multiple spidery arms, pulled the bones out of the crawling, writhing, vampires, all in one quick yank, and then draping them around their bodies in a spiral of skeletons. The motion smooth, unsettling, the sound of skin ripping and the splash of entrails across the snow, leaving only their conscious minds inside the hollowed-out puddles of flesh, as the vampires grasped and reached out, squirming like maggots, begging for life. Begging for Mister Brightbones to come and save them.

And where was Mister Brightbones? Nix couldn't tell in the chaos. Some of the vampires were still all in one piece and not deboned just yet, and they were darting around, screaming, trying to survive, much like Daphne. And Nix stood there, stunned, terrified, uncertain as she watched the horror unfold around her. Unable to think, unable to figure out what to do, frozen in the moment.

Until a pain burst out from the key-shaped burn in her hand, accompanied by sharp foreign thoughts impeding on her mind. It was Old Wick in her head, his words echoing like it came down a long distant tunnel, but there it was, speaking to her. Trying to control her, but unable to, now that she was a vampire full of fresh blood. Anna's blood. Poor Anna.

"How dare you disobey me. I gave you an order, I did it for your own good. Where are these vampires? Why haven't you delivered me Mister Brightbones? Oh child, I was trying to protect you, to save you from them and their terrible desires. Now I see you are not worth my time. You too shall die and die horribly. Such a pity, you held so much promise."

Child, child, child. What was with her and Mister Brightbones calling her child all the time? The blood burned hot and bright now, a flame in her chest, her heart a roaring light of anger and frustration. She was no child, if anything, they were the children.

Age didn't matter for such things. She wasn't some ancient demon or some undying old wizard set out to destroy the world like either of them. But she had seen far more, felt far more pain and sorrow than either of them could ever imagine. Mister Brightbones may be in a boy who was dying of cancer, but he was not that boy, did not understand the pain of being chronically ill or disabled. Neither of them could come close to understanding that.

No way she was a child. And once you took her age into effect, for a human? She was no spring chicken, either. *Though she wasn't human anymore now, was she? She was a vampire.*

Still, still, all she had experienced, all she had lived through. How dare they treat her like this? How dare they act like she was a pawn in their sick twisted games?

She was no pawn. Her aunt Doreen was right, she must stop this in any way possible. Not just stop Old Wick, or Oliver Haddo, or whatever his name was, but she had to stop Mister Brightbones, too.

Yes, she was cured. But the cruelty he demanded for such a cure, the blood sacrifice? Daphne was right. Oh damn, oh hell, Daphne was right. She heard her chains rattling behind her, and decided she had to save her, had to save them both, and then stop all this from happening. She had to find Old Wick and burn down his house, to keep the cage from trapping Mister Brightbones and bringing the Child of the Abyss even closer.

But will that stop it? You felt it when you fed on Anna, Nix. You felt it so strong and bright and hungry. The emptiness will devour you, will devour you all.

"Bring him to me, child. Let the vampire hunters take him and the bones they harvest to the Cannibal House on the hill. Do it for me, child. I know you kidnapped my vampire hunters and brought them there. I can see through their eyes you know, and now they will do my bidding. Help them help me, and all will be redeemed. I promise you a quick and painless death, which is more than you deserve. You could have been my acolyte, child. You could have been an undying god of a new world."

Her scar ached again, and she realized they were connected through it. That when he took over her hex, he tied the two of them together, across space and time. Her vampire heart burned some more, anger so bright, so powerful. Maybe she should see if that connection worked both ways?

Scythes swung through the air, but she ignored them. Giant pendulums, like the one in Poe's story, but she ignored them. She couldn't let anything distract her, not even Daphne calling out, calling her name in a panic. She couldn't let them destroy her concentration, not if she was going to do this. Not if she was going to stop him.

She harnessed that fire in Anna's blood, roaring through her body, tainted with the anger of her own death. Focused on it, brought it to a blaze inside of her. And then she reached over, and pushed her fingers deep into the scar.

Her fingers dug around inside, pushing into the dead skin, feeling the pain overwhelm her, the pain of magic, the fire of Anna's blood, the anger, such bright horrible anger, as she dug around, pulled on the skin, dug under muscle, dug into the vampire blood, letting it drip out, and felt the connection with Old Wick, felt it there, like a silver thread between them.

And then she burned it. A tugging, like something yanking on her bones, and that pain again, but it was nowhere near as bad as the pain of multiple sclerosis, a pain that was a memory now, a memory fading slowly with the moments, and being replaced with a new pain. This pain.

The pain she caused him. Caused Old Wick. She heard him scream in her head, ragged and raw and then silent. And she smiled.

And the vampire hunters collapsed in a thunder of wax and bones.

33

EVERYTHING was chaos. The still-living vampires ran and scattered faster than she could keep track, as they disappeared into the snow drifts and the shadows beyond. The cowards, Nix thought. Did they not see what she was capable of doing? How she stopped them right in their tracks?

Hunched over, her body felt so hot now, so burning up feverish hot. Anna's blood was nuclear under her skin, yes, keeping that corpse body warm and toasty and not ice cold. Was it normal for the blood to be burning this hot?

Did she even care? No, her mind manic now with the power. She did that, she connected right to Old Wick and messed him up enough that it killed those vampire hunters.

What else could this blood do, now that it powered her vampire heart? She could destroy Mister Brightbones herself, yes. Gleeful, her mind bright and filled with a manic joy. That would end that! No bait for the void with him being dead, erased from this world!

A whisper in her thoughts, distant, like the wings of a moth fluttering against a window pane. That better not be Old Wick trying to get back in! If so, she would definitely give him another taste of her powers and see if he liked that. The whisper now louder, louder. Wait, no.

It was her Aunt Doreen's raspy, stuttering voice. That ghost voice that spoke to her in the shadows between worlds, when she was near death and dying, right before she drank the blood and was reborn with a vampire heart filled with Anna's blood. What did she want now? Couldn't she see she was busy, trying to do the very thing she'd asked Nix to do?

No, no, that isn't the way. Even without a body, he can be trapped. In fact. In fact. It would be easier. Like catching a butterfly in a net.

Nix closed her eyes, breathed out slowly, trying to calm the fire in her heart. Anger now at her aunt, anger that wouldn't do a damned thing. What if she let it all out? Pointed it at her aunt's ghost? Would it burn her away, wipe her out into nothingness?

The thought terrified her. And what terrified her even more was how badly she wanted to do it, to see her powers unleashed, to feel the bright joy in her veins when she destroyed even death itself, banishing a ghost into a void. No, no, she couldn't do that.

Laughter in her head. *Go ahead and try. I would welcome oblivion now. Everyone wants to live forever. Until they do. Until they do.*

And then, soft, a shadow beneath her thoughts. *He's had other bodies than this. A girl, the one I showed you? He was banished from it, and sent adrift. More vulnerable then, almost captured twice until he found this one. Poor boy. Poor trapped boy.*

She opened her eyes. The chaos had died down. Most of the other vampires had fled, except a small handful that still clung around the snow shadows, weeping blood over their friends. The bodies undying still, reaching out, grasping, puddles of meat and skin, all boneless agony. She felt herself weep a little at the sight of them, her blood mania sliding away for a little bit.

Where was Daphne? Was she still okay?

Ah, over there, right there, moving towards the crumpled vampire hunters' limbs. They were scattered about their massive corpses like spiders with their legs pulled off. Her chains rattling still, as she made sure the vampire hunters really were dead after all.

Go to her. Go to her and help her. Then find Old Wick and stop him. Stop him.

"How?" And Nix realized she'd said this out loud, but didn't care. Even when the other vampires turned to her look at her, even the crawling boneless ones, with their writhing muscles oozing them further, like slime oozing along a wall. But she didn't care, now was not the time to be self conscious. Now was the time to be in the moment, a time for action, for survival. She had work to do.

Her thoughts were clear now, sharp. No longer tinged with mania, and it was a relief. Thank god.

You cannot kill him. You must behead him and bury the head. It's the only way.

And in her heart Nix knew this to be true. That the blood of Old Wick was bad blood, the kind of blood that would devour a vampire from the inside out. The poisonous blood of an undying magus. No way to kill him with her teeth or tongue, no way to drink him to death. And bullets, yes, she could feel it in her bones, bullets and knives and the rest wouldn't do it. Her aunt was right, beheading was the only way.

How the fuck was she going to do that?

She probed her mind, tried to get her aunt to give her a clue, to give her a way to get this task done. A machete? An axe? What the hell would even do that? She'd seen it in movies, and it always looks so easy. And yet, she had this feeling, in her gut, in her deep-down root of her soul, that it would definitely not be that easy. Bones were hard to cut. They had to be.

She probed again, asked again. And all she got back in response from her aunt was silence. A deafening, horrible silence that crept inside of her and took root in her body. The silence like the void itself, the void coming to devour them all.

Nothing. She would have to figure this out herself, damnit. She opened her eyes, looked around at the carnage again, and started moving toward Daphne. She still didn't see Mister Brightbones anywhere, and didn't really care at the moment. There were more important things to worry about. She walked over to the vampire hunters' corpses, ignoring the few survivors that stuck around, not caring at all what they thought, and walked right up to Daphne.

She turned, looked at Nix, and smiled. "You did this, didn't you?"

Nix couldn't help herself, she laughed. "How did you know that?"

"I saw the look in your eyes when it happened. This crazed manic look, and then you dripped blood over the snow from your palms. How did you even do it?"

Nix leaned in, shook her head slightly. She knew that time was of the essence, she saw the void in everything, saw it getting closer and closer. If she killed Mister Brightbones and trashed the cage it would go away, that she knew. He was the one bringing it in, bringing it closer. He was the one to destroy them all.

"It doesn't matter," she finally said, her voice hoarse. She felt the blood slowing in her veins. Was it burning up already? Was she almost out of it so soon? Maybe she'd done too much, burned up too much of Anna's blood by attacking Old Wick. It was worth it, though. So worth it.

"It does matter, though! If we can stop them, we can survive! Those damned things have been hunting us and murdering us so much."

But she couldn't tell Daphne about her connection to Old Wick. She knew that the other vampires would hear her, that Mister Brightbones would hear her, too, and think her a spy for that creepy old bastard.

"I don't know," she finally said. "I just focused on them, and focused on the fire in Anna's blood, and then they collapsed."

Daphne nodded. "I see."

But she could tell she didn't see. And that was okay, she would keep her in the dark for now. After all, Daphne had kept her in the dark for all sorts of things. Things that might've changed the course of events, maybe. Or maybe not.

The skeletal lights of Mister Brightbones flickered, as he rose between cars covered in mountains of snow, and walked toward them, his dirty blindfold pointed right at them. His sunspot skeleton made Nix's head hurt again, like it was trying to poke around inside her, to figure out how she destroyed the vampire hunters. Thankfully, she kept him out, kept her secrets to herself.

"I think you owe us all a few explanations."

And behind him the other vampires started moving toward them, following Mister Brightbones. The ones with their bones picking up the fleshy puddles of the boneless and carrying them towards Nix and Daphne, their toothless lips crying out in pain.

She didn't have time for this. They had to stop Old Wick. She realized then that she had to go back to the bookstore where he was after all. Damn him all to hell. And if she did that, she would have to ditch Mister Brightbones somehow. But how? If he followed her to the bookstore, she risked him getting captured and put in that cage before she could stop Old Wick. And if that happened? Well, then the void would come to earth, and Old Wick would get what he wanted.

A world devoured, and a new one put in its place, with him as god. But how would she ditch Mister Brightbones? How could she set this right?

34

A ring of vampires encircled her in the snowbank, with Daphne stumbling and clanking behind them. A ring of vampires with Mister Brightbones flickering at the lead, snow a flurry around their bodies, turning the rest of the world into a blur of blizzard and shadows. Only a few streetlamps remained, and they flickered and sparked and then went silent, no longer shedding their dim halo glow. The sun was a frozen shadow, hidden behind a wall of dark, ominous clouds, shutting out all daylight. The only illumination came from Mister Brightbones, and his flickering skeletal afterglow, casting strange shadows across the mounds of snow. She felt trapped, disoriented, knowing that she was by Anna's bakery, and yet not knowing it at the same time.

Like she knew it on a logical, rational level, and yet on some other primal level she was confused and had no idea where she was, her mind trapped and lost in the strangeness of her world. The snow changing everything, the shadows changing everything, until only there was the vampire lights and nothing more.

Nix clutched her palm, bloodied between her fingertips. She felt her dead heart quicken with Anna's blood, and worried now that she would burn through it quicker than quick, and be left only with the dust in her veins. And then after that? Her multiple sclerosis would return until she fed again.

It seemed to her that Daphne's blood always lasted longer, even when it was just small animals like squirrels and rabbits and mice. Did Nix burn blood faster because of her anxiety, and her body pumping the blood at high speed? Or was it because of the vampire hunters, and her own little trick to get them to stop?

Either way, she had to conserve it now, yes, she had to slow that ragged rapid heartbeat and get it under control. She felt the blood thick and sluggish now, murmuring through her veins, and knew it was not much longer at all. *Okay, come on*, she thought, *slow down, slow down.*

If she still breathed, she would also slow down her breath, to give her heart less reasons to pump so rapidly. But no, she had no breath, her lungs empty rattling things, and she only inhaled to get enough air to speak. Amazing how quickly her body adapted to this afterlife, like it knew on some instinctive level that breathing was pointless except for talking, and knew exactly what to do.

Yeah, yeah, she thought. I'm nature's vampiric miracle. She had to stop thinking about this and start acting. Start moving towards a solution.

"I saw you, I did, you knelt over in pain, your mind concentrating on something. I saw that new blood burn up hot and fast, and then those vampire hunters collapsed. So tell us child, tell us all what we need to hear. How did you do that?"

She gulped involuntarily. It felt dry and strange in her throat. She felt hot again, her heart trying to beat and burn a little faster. No, no, stay calm, she thought. We got this, we got this.

But do you? Do you really?

"I don't know what I did, I was acting mostly on instinct," yes, yes, mostly a lie with the core of the truth. Hopefully it's enough of a core that they can't smell the lie inside. So far, so good, Mister Brightbones wasn't saying anything either way, he just looked at her quizzically.

"Continue, child. I'm sure there is more to it than that."

Of course, of course. "I was terrified," more cores of more truth, "And I felt Anna burning up inside of me."

"Anna?" he asked, with a sharp lilt to his words.

Daphne spoke up, calmly, "The woman you had her murder."

Nix felt a shiver of shame at the truth of it, but decided to push it aside. Now was not the time for grief or guilt. Now was the time to survive.

"Yes, she owned the bakery, it was her blood I drank up, her blood burning away inside me now. It's so hot, fiery with her anger, and I remembered what you said about pain powering magic. I had no idea why I did it, but I pressed against the key," and she held up her hand, showing the scar that Mister Brightbones gave her, "And then channeled that burning blood and all that pain into my heart. And then I used it, like a whip, and lashed out. I, I, I . . ."

She fell for a second, on her knees, dizzy. Oh shit. She had to slow her heart rate down, slow it down so more. It was so hot and so fast, and it would be gone so quickly if she didn't just slow it down, slow it down right now.

Come on, come on. All concentration on that heart muscle, on changing the rhythm and the flow of her own body. Keep it in sync now, with the rhythm of the universe, with the tidal patterns of the moon. Slow, slow. Waves go in, waves go out, come on now.

They're waiting for you to speak again. She touched her forehead, it was wet. Oh shit. Her hand came away bloody. She was sweating blood, oh shit. She had to stop this. She had to. There was only so much blood left in her body before she was dry and she had to feed again.

"I didn't expect it to work," blood in her eyes now, staining her vision a lurid blood red. Even the light of Mister Brightbones was now so red, such a deep, brutal hue. "I thought I was just going to have this pain and fire inside of me and that was it, the vampire hunters would get me and kill me and I would be done for. We would all be done for. But somehow, against all odds, I was able to use that pain and that fire to knock them down."

She panted and wiped more blood from her eyes and from her forehead and she felt faint and dizzy. So much blood just leaking out of her, this was going to be it. She was going to be drained dry before she even knew it. What a waste. Poor Anna, her blood gone so quickly, because Nix was so shitty at being a vampire.

Mister Brightbones cocked his head, his skull shadow following his movements. He looked suspicious, like he wasn't sure he wanted to believe anything she said. His eyes questioning her, but his lips saying, "Interesting. We'll have to discuss more of this later, I think. The scar shouldn't have done what you said it would do, but maybe the pain and blood fire acted as a catalyst to something else, some horrible thing you carry inside of you, like a maggot in your heart."

He bought it? Oh damn, he bought it! She felt a bit more manic and gleeful once more, felt her heart starting to thump faster, her bloody sweat pouring down faster now, faster. Oh shit, oh shit. She licked her lips, tried to open her mouth, to lick it back inside of her.

But that's not how any of this works, is it?

"But first, we need to find us some blood to drink, and finish a few things here," Mister Brightbones said, as he walked to the circle of vampires, turning his back on Nix. She felt the cold burn against her hot vampire flesh and the hunger began to gnaw inside of her once again. How much longer before she would have to feed? How much longer before her multiple sclerosis came back?

The thought terrified her. As Mister Brightbones walked amongst the vampires, and found the ones without bones, their bodies slumped over arms, oozing puddles of flesh. Their eyes rolling, their mouths making gross gurgling noises as they tried to speak, but could not. Oh, oh, how horrible. Nix shivered, and thought of turning her head, just so she wouldn't see them anymore, but stopped. Stopped. She felt like she had to witness this.

Why? She couldn't tell you. But somehow, someway, she felt it was important.

As Mister Brightbones walked up to each and every one of them, and gently kissed them on the forehead. And each time he did, the bodies went completely slack and motionless, as a bright light flickered and grew and then shrunk again, scattering the shadows amongst the darkness.

And when he was done, he looked at them and said, "No need to bury them, my children. Leave them here for the sun to wipe away from the earth."

Nix wobbled a bit, weak in the knees. A moment of horror in her mind, that her multiple sclerosis was back, oh god, oh no. But that wasn't it, was it? It was the sheer absolute terror and fear of the moment crawling into her thoughts and running around in her mind. Of knowing that the same thing could've easily happened to her, if she hadn't been able to stop this, and that Old Wick would certainly not spare her, especially not now. This was her future if she didn't stop him. Just like the future of the world would be swallowed up by that great void. The void that was coming for them all.

35

AFTER a moment of silence for the fallen, Mister Brightbones turned to Nix. Jelly legged, her mind whirring, and that thirst starting to burn through her. This was the last of Anna's blood, she could feel it. It was like her insides were drying up, like when you're trying to suck out the last of the milkshake at the bottom of the glass, the straw sucking and sucking, making that horrible slurping noise, just to get the little bit that still remained.

That's how she felt right now, right at this exact same second. *Slurp, slurp, slurp,* the straw of her heart sucking om the last little bit of Anna's burning blood. Her body ached so much.

"You know where the humans went, don't you." Mister Brightbones pointed a finger directly at her, the bandage on his eyes slipping a little, and revealing the pure white eyes beneath. The finger had a long, crooked nail, and looked more like a talon than the finger of a cancer patient.

She gasped and tried to think of something, anything to say. The bookstore. A dangerous thing, taking him right to Old Wick. And yet, she had to get back to him, to stop him, to behead him like Aunt Doreen said. She smiled now, bloody sweat still running down her face and almost blinding her, turning the whole world a hash ochre tint.

"I think so, maybe. I remember them saying that I should meet them back at the bookstore if things went to shit. I think things probably went to shit, and that's why they're not at Anna's Bakery."

Oh god the lie upon lie upon lie. She hoped she could keep all these straight, and she hoped that she said it in a way that was completely believable. She used to be a total shit at lying, but she sure hoped that being a vampire somehow changed that. Maybe that could be one of her other vampiric super powers . . . lying and not getting caught. She almost laughed at the thought, it was so absurd. And yet, that's what this whole situation was, wasn't it? Completely absurd.

Please, please, believe her. Let this be her new super power. Please, please.

Mister Brightbones stumbled forward, his gait strange and twisted, like he was walking through mud and was about ready to fall head first into the dirt. And yet, he righted and caught himself each time, as if his stumbling was an act of ballet, a sort of graceful ungraceful movement. It reminded her of how she moved not too long ago, when her multiple sclerosis was going strong and she needed the cane so badly.

And that fear came back. The blood was slurping sludgy almost empty inside of her, almost entirely burnt up. There was a scorched taste on her tongue, and she could feel her muscles seizing for a second, just a brief second, and then relaxing again. Oh shit, oh shit, she wasn't ready to go back to that. After all she'd been through, and with everything still yet to come.

"You best not being lying to us child, " he wheezed, and smiled. "I can see such things."

And closer, closer, he stumbled, the circle of vampires eclipsed her, moving in while Mister Brightbones moved forward, tightening and closing around her. The skeleton light sharp and bright, cutting through the blizzard that seemed to pick up strength with every ticking second, growing more and more fierce. More fierce than any blizzard she'd ever experienced in Dark Rivers, even during regular winter weather.

He pulled off his ragged blindfold from his eye, and let it droop from his hand. The wights amongst the vampires clattered their teeth when he did this, like cicadas in the summer heat.

Two holes where his eyes once were, ringed with cancerous lumps creeping across the cheeks and eyelids. And behind that eyeless darkness flickered a sick, golden light. It matched the amber glow of his skeleton light, piercing the shadows and wafting from his head like glowing smoke.

"Go ahead and tell me these things again, and I will see what is truth, child."

The chattering teeth grew louder and louder as he stepped right up to Nix, his face looking up into hers. Weak in the knees, her mind dizzy with Mister Brightbones peeking into her mind, tiny psychic fingers poking into her thoughts. She felt him reaching around in there, and while she knew she was speaking the truth about the bookstore, it was all wrapped up in lie upon lie that would unravel with the lightest thread.

She focused her thoughts, laser sharp, on the bookstore and nothing else. She didn't think about the key-shaped scar, didn't think about Old Wick corrupting it. It was hard, because thinking about not thinking is like a whisper of the thought, echoing in her mind. Focus instead only on the bookstore, and the memories of all the people there . . .

Shit. Including old Wick. Shit. Including him placing the vampire hunters on the shelf. She was trying to block it, to keep Mister Brightbones from seeing this memory completely, but it was too late. Shit.

Mister Brightbones roared, his head tilting back, the sound a mixture of anger and terror and deep in the bone hatred. "Oliver Haddo is here? He's here and you saw him? And you're leading me toward him? I saw those vampire hunters in your memory! You must be working for him. You foolish child. He's the reason my brother is out there, the child of the abyss, looking for me, looking to devour everything. Don't you know he finds living things disgusting abominations of the void? A corruption of the universe? You are maggots to him, crawling across the rotting skin of the world."

Nix reached over to the scar, tried to put her thumb against it. Pain in her bones and her heart, but the fire in Anna's blood was dying off, burnt away. Like scorched oil, thick and sludgy in her veins. She felt her muscles twitch and tighten, her left eye blurring and losing color and vibrancy. Her left arm started spasming, and when she tried to step back, away from Mister Brightbones, she felt the arches on her left foot tear painfully. The muscle had stretched so tight from multiple sclerosis that moving it even a little bit tore it, and down she went.

Shit. What a lousy cure that was, it burned away so quickly. She felt tears in her eyes, not again, she couldn't go back to that again, the hunger bright with her new teeth elongating, sharper. Everything was red from her sweat, now drying and caked against her face. She wiped her eyes, no, she can't cry, not in front of them. But it was hard not to. Not because of what he was saying, but because of the small gift of freedom. Of being well for a short amount of time. She'd been sick and disabled for so long, she forgot what it was like to not be in pain. She forgot what it had been like to see clearly and in full color, to walk and run and dance without a cane.

Oh shit, she'd thrown her cane away. Why had she thrown her cane away? She thought it would be like Daphne, who could feed on something as small as a squirrel or a rabbit and be good for a day or two. And yet, here she was, drunk on an entire person, and burning through it so quickly.

She stepped back again, her left ankle twisting under the spasticity of her muscles, and almost stumbling, falling, as he stepped closer, closer, bright eyes burning in the night. His skeletal lights dancing around his body, a kaleidoscope of bones, as he stood over her tumbling body.

The circle of vampires closed around them, as he put his blindfold back on.

"I saw the vampire hunters in your memory," his words like stones, dropping into the dust. "You are leading us toward them, aren't you? Taking us to our death. All for that bastard Oliver Haddo. What have you done, child? Why would you do this to us after I healed you?"

She realized he did not put two and two together, that the vampire hunters in her memory were the same that attacked them. That he did not see her taking them, bringing them here, and stopping them. Probably for the better, yes, then he would definitely think she was spying against them.

Her heart was sluggish with the last of Anna's blood, her limbs growing colder and colder. She shivered, and didn't know if it was from the cold, or multiple sclerosis, or the promise of violence that hung in the air.

"I cannot trust you any longer. Like Daphne before you, you have corrupted our gifts and betrayed us. Bring out the chains, my children. Bring out the chains, we have another to leave for the sun when we are done here."

36

OH shit, they were going to do her up like Daphne! Chain her body and soul. She'd fallen to the ground and now scrambled to try and get up, but her body betrayed her every step of the way. Her multiple sclerosis making her arms weak and unable to hold her weight, making her wrist spasm and lock up so when she put her weight on it, she stumbled fell even further, scrambling along the snow and street, scraping the palm of her hand and her knees. She whimpered, tried to move back, as the hissing wights moved forward, chains in their hands dragging along the ground.

"Cold steel to bind the vampires in place," Mister Brightbones said, "You won't be able to communicate with that bastard Oliver Haddo any longer, my child. You'll be muzzled up nice and neat and silent. Even if I let you drink someone else, your powers will be muted until I remove those chains. And only I have the key."

She held up the palm of her hand. Sharp pain and ribbons of flesh dangled down. The little bit of Anna's blood that was left oozed out in a thick gooey mess. No longer the strong, burning blood. Instead a coagulated sludge, drip, drip, dripping down. One, two, three. Soon she will be empty, and she knew her multiple sclerosis was going to relapse the moment it was, and it would be a doozy.

She could tell, right away. It was like a storm under her skin, the clouds thick and heavy with lightning. She let out a soft mewling sound, scurrying back as best as she can. Tick tick tick, her symptoms will return. Tock tock tock, new symptoms on top of old, a blind fury of a relapse. It's how it always was before, wasn't it?

The medications would never work. She was going from relapse to relapse, with only a week or two of remission in between. They constantly had her on high dose steroids, draining the calcium from her bones and turning her into a bloated, emotional wreck with a bright red face. And finally, finally, finally it seemed she had found a way to put it behind her, even if it was only between feedings!

But here it was, back and strong and fierce. And Mister Brightbones probably wouldn't let her feed again, not after he put her in chains. She didn't want to do that, didn't want them to tie her down and take this away from her.

She needed to feed again, her hunger so strong, it was a burning ache in her chest, like she swallowed hot coals, and the only way she could relieve it was if she sucked something dry of all of its vital fluids, and then drank in its death. Oh to taste the last dying moments again, like a star on her tongue, exploding in her heart. She licked her lips just thinking about it, moving backwards as the wights moved closer.

If only she could drink those wights! Suck them down and leave them to rot in the snow. But they were already dry husks without any blood, on the half life between living and undead. She heard it when they walked towards her, shuffling the way some elderly patients shuffle. Their hearts sounded like dead leaves rustling. And she knew if it weren't for her multiple sclerosis coming back, she could easily outrun them.

Was that why Mister Brightbones targeted the sick and dying and disabled? Not because he wanted to cure them, but because they were easier for him to control and corral into what he wanted? And what did he want?

She scrambled back some more, her raw palm burning on the snowy ground, leaving a mess of black ichor and dried coagulated blood behind her. She felt herself grow pale and wan with each unticking of the clock, each second moving closer and closer to the big one. Oh shit. She felt it now, felt it coming on.

How bad would this one be? Her worst of the worst had her falling down stairs and falling on sidewalks and her whole body going into intense seizures, the entire left side of her body locking up in rigid spasms. She knew others who went completely blind in both eyes for weeks, and others still that ended up in small comas, waiting for their brains to heal themselves and the white blood cells to no longer attack them.

No god, no, please don't be like that. All would be lost then, and she would have let her aunt down, and the whole world would be fucked.

Hissing and closer and closer, rattling those chains closer and closer, time felt like an infinite spiral as her body betrayed her over and over and over again. She let out a quick brief gasp and fell to the ground, her arms in a rigid spastic cramp, like claws, the pain so intense tears came to her eyes. Her back writhing and moving without her command, like a snake in the snow moving back and forth. And she tried to mentally will her body to stop, but it couldn't stop. Her eyes blurred and blurred some more until everything was just grey color blobs. Shadows and brief outlines of shapes and nothing more.

Oh shit. Oh fuck. Oh shit. A full body relapse had only happened once before, her second year of multiple sclerosis. It was super rare, usually it only affected one side of her body, and that was usually the left side. Sometimes, rarely, it would affect the right side and not the left.

But only once before had it been like this, affecting both sides of her body at once. She screamed and her words were gargled and raw. A large shadow, looming over her. The clink of metal, burning her skin. That cold iron was a fire against her flesh and she hated it. If she had control of her limbs she would push back, crawl away. But everything was so rigid, so stuck in place, her spine twitching, all she could do was lie still and take the pain.

As the shadows tried to move her arms and legs. The spasm was too strong, her body, too rigid. It would be impossible to do it without breaking her bones, but they didn't know that. They couldn't know that, unless someone else also had multiple sclerosis, or if they had seizures, or something like that? Maybe they did.

But they tried to bend to breaking and she cried out, her voice hoarse, her lungs unable to fill all the way for speaking. Blood spattered against her lips, and she felt the cold iron biting down. Was this even necessary? She couldn't move at all, even without the cold iron chains, her body was completely seized up.

Down, down, hoarse voice wheezing, down in that snow, in that ground. Still unable to move. Her jaw locking now, unable to talk. She'd never had a relapse this bad, never ever. This would be the one that does it, this would be the one that killed her.

"Our sicknesses are always worse after we die. Such is the curse of unlife, my child. But that will be no excuse. You either follow us, crawling and broken in the dirt, or you die when the clouds eventually part and I let the sun in to kill you. Your choice."

She laid there, unable to do anything. Blind, frozen, her body rigid cramps completely. Her heart fluttered in her chest, barely able to move with the little bits of blood still left in her veins. Both death and multiple sclerosis slowly eating away at her, until she would be no more. "I can't move," Nix gasped, barely able to fill her air with lungs to speak. She didn't have to breathe, thankfully, but she still required air for words. And her multiple sclerosis was not helping with this at all. If she was alive and undead this might've been the death of her. Unable to inhale, unable to breathe.

"Fine," Mister Brightbones said, "So be it. You will be here my child until I let the sun come out and kiss your skin. And then, well. Then you will die. I tried to cure you, tried to help you, but all you do is betray me at every turn."

The shadows moved around her, drifted away from her. All except for one, one that cried out with Daphen's voice, "No! No! You can't just leave her to die like this. Not after you made her what she is! You can't just do that."

And the vampires' shadows stopped for a moment, as Mister Brightbones laughed and said, "I think you should stay with her child, it is only fitting. To have our betrayers die together like this, all alone and without any hope. No blood to revitalize you, like you said. They're all elsewhere, in this bookstore, waiting. And you will never get to them, not like this. You will die, my children. You will die."

And then the shadows dispersed, leaving them in the dark alone, Daphne moving closer to Nix, her chains rattling in the silent darkness.

37

HOLDING each other, there in the artificial night, knowing that at any point Mister Brightbones could have the storm dissipate and day would come, the sun bright and burning on their bones. Daphne held her close, and kept saying, "I'm so sorry mom, I'm so sorry."

And Nix rankled each time she said it. Yes, yes, there was a connection there, something close to maternal, yes. But she also knew that those feelings might be chemical, might be manipulation from Daphne's vampire essence. Even though she was a vampire now, too, she remembered how she felt before, remembered the fugue state and how she did everything for Daphne.

And yet, even remembering all of that, and feeling bitter and hateful, she still felt this connection. This need to care for her. Maybe "Mom" was less the truth of it, maybe something closer to a little sister? That seemed more right. There was a connection there, even when the vampire hypnotism was gone.

Unless her being drained of blood and life returned her back into that state where she was suspectable to such things? Oh god. Oh. She hoped not.

Not even sure her key tattoo would work now, after what Old Wick did to her.

Oh fuck. Oh damn. Old Wick.

She tried to move, tried to push herself up, but the relapse was still going strong, making her limbs rigid and tight and painful. She tried to speak, again, sucking in air to push words out of her lips. Painful, so tight, the air barely moving. A rattle in her dead vampire lungs, but she could do it, she could barely talk, but she could do it.

"Fuck. Need blood."

Daphne's shadow squeezed her tight, her chains rattling as she did it. "I know, we both do."

"No. Can't stop Old Wick like this."

Shit, shit, shit. It hurt so much to talk, it took practically all of her energy. What did her grandma used to say when she was fighting off the Big C? Oh, right. She didn't have enough spoons for this shit. That memory would've made her laugh and smile at any other time, but not now. Not today, not this time.

There was too much riding on the line.

"No." Inhale now, as deep as can be. "Need to stop Old Wick. Can't like this. Need to."

Gasp, shit, pain. Her ribs and lungs burning like skin scraped across cement. Hurt so much but she had to push through it, push through and say this. "Stop Old Wick before."

Come on, come on, inhale deep, just push through the pain. Become the fire, become the burninghurt, let it wash over you in a river of flame. "Before Brightbones gets there."

And then she couldn't help it, everything tensed up at once and she screamed. The dead shouldn't breathe, the dead shouldn't talk, and yet here she was, dead and talking. Her relapse impacting all of it, making everything a million times worse. Mister Brightbones was right, being dead made her illness into a monster. One far worse than ever before.

She wished she would've known about that. Daphne tried to warn her, but failed at explaining just what it meant when she said this wasn't a cure, this was a curse.

Oh god, oh fuck, it was more than a curse. It was doom itself.

"Wait," Daphne said, and her voice sounded nervous, her shadow shivering. "What do you mean? What does Old Wick have to do with any of this?"

Before Nix could respond, she felt a throbbing on her palm, and looked down. That key-shaped scar ached so much right now, like a toothache under her flesh. She wanted to pull the scar out, rip it from her skin to stop it from hurting so much. She wondered, briefly, if it was Old Wick trying to connect with her again. But her vampire powers definitely put her in the upper hand again, even here, with her powers fading and broken and her skin all wrinkled and deflated. Like the blood was air in a balloon, with her skin hanging in loose, limp rags from her body.

The ache punctured her thoughts, dizzying. Images of Mister Brightbones, and the words *betrayal, betrayal, betrayal* whispering about in her thoughts like an echo chamber. So, they were connected still as well, weren't they? Her and Mister Brightbones, connected through that scar, through her vampire powers. He taunted her, and yet, yet . . .

It gave her an idea. It probably wouldn't work, would it? No, it was insane to even think it. And yet, and yet.

The snow lessened around them a little, and then a little more. The blizzard slowly easing back, like a wave of winter receding. Parts of the clouds seemed to part, and Nix felt panic. Her heart wheezed and rustled like a dead leaf, and she knew that if she was still alive (or filled with the death of another) it would be racing and terrified.

"Nix, Nix! Tell me, what does Old Wick have to do with any of this?"

Nix was now dizzy and her vision swam, and then the world seemed to vignette around the edges, like the lens of an old silver nitrate camera. She had to act now. Right now. Blood was just about gone, and the sun was coming out, fuck, the sun was coming out.

"No time," her breath ragged, could barely fill her lungs above a whisper. Curse these vampire lungs, curse this vampire heart. She reached over, placed her hand against Daphne's lock, right against the keyhole.

The scar was Mister Brightbones key. They were still connected. Oh damn oh shit oh damn this had to work. Please work, please.

Nothing. Nothing. Shit, nothing. She pushed against it harder, clank, cold iron burning against her palm, That throbbing toothache of a scar pulsing and she focused on that pain. Oh yes, her blood was almost all gone, her mind shutting down, her multiple sclerosis rearing itself up and taking a bite out of her once more, yes. But she knew that was power, yes, power in that pain. She remembered Mister Brightbones telling her all magic required pain. And holy shit, was she ever in pain.

Just funnel it through that scar, funnel it through that connection between her, Mister Brightbones, and that key that caused the scar. Please let the connections be enough, let this pain be enough. There was so much of it, and she was so weak now, the whole world dimming out grey, like a silent whisper. All the colors bleached out, and that vignette getting smaller and smaller, closing in.

Like the circle of vampires earlier. Like the vampire hunters around Daphne earlier. Choking on her sobs, pressing harder against it, eyes closed, pain so bright and strong, her body like a weak pile of bones. Arms so weak. Was this multiple sclerosis? Or just the rot of her dead body catching up to her finally? So weak, she can't keep her hand there, she would have to drop it . . .

Click.

Nix laughed as the chains fell from Daphne in a chorus of jangling metal. She felt herself swoon, and realized that she couldn't see at all, just all blackness, even though her eyes were open. Oh shit, this was it, this was going to be the end of her. She grabbed Daphne, pulled in as much air into those rotting, rattling lungs as she could muster, and said, "Get me blood. Now."

And the world tilted on its axis and she got a mouthful of snow, as the darkness took her yet again. Eyes wide open and staring into the vast emptiness that was her world now.

38

WAS this death? Nix wasn't so certain. It didn't feel like any idea of death she ever entertained through her rough and spotty life. Sure, her ideas on the afterlife were simple ones. Either she stopped existing or went to some other place. Like, a different world beyond this world, something good or bad or in between.

But this wasn't any of those things, not really. If there was nothing after all this, she wouldn't have a consciousness, would she? It would be nothing at all, her mind a quiet hum in the center of the universe. Without a body to generate that kind of conscious thought, it should be gone entirely. Nothing at all.

And yet, here she was, thinking. Her thoughts untethered, floating. Not quite a dream like state, though not exactly fully conscious either. She existed in between, in a liminal place, on the threshold.

That was it, maybe this nothingness, this floating thought existence was just the threshold between states, that twilight of the dying hours. Not quite dead yet, but almost there. Past the body's rot and struggles, and existing now in that momentary breath between this existence and whatever laid next.

Which could still be nothingness, couldn't it? Or being born again in some new body, or going to some paradise or purgatory or hell. Either way, this felt unlike anything she expected at all. Just her thoughts, running around in a void. Existing where nothing existed. That felt wrong, maybe this whole thing was wrong.

Or maybe being a vampire screwed it all up. She became an abomination, a thing neither living nor dead, so she would be denied either now. No afterlife, no unlife, just her thoughts, suspended in the void like fruit in gelatin. What a horrible thing that would be, to entertain herself for eternities, an infinite of the mind unwinding on itself. Oh shit, she would go insane, there was no way around it. Being dead like this would drive her insane.

She thought of her aunt, and wondered how she was able to take on a body, take on a form, come and talk to her like she did. Show her the past and the future. What did her aunt have that she did not? She said she practiced occult stuff, stuff so powerful it would make other magi jealous as all hell. If only she would have taught her some of her tricks, taught her anything at all. Maybe that was the games they played when she was a kid? Training her for a future where occult powers would be necessary?

She had no clue. If that were the case, it didn't come in handy at all. Her mind had forgotten such things with age, like most child-hood games. Wiped away with the hours of drudgery and boredom that adult life required of you. Even if you were disabled, and now a vampire. That drudgery was still there.

Maybe she could reach out to her aunt? Yes. Maybe that was it. She could reach out to her, or maybe to Mister Brightbones or Old Wick, and see if they could . . .

No, not them. Either one of them would destroy her now, she was almost a hundred percent certain of that.

No, she would have to see if she could reach her aunt. After all, her aunt came to her the last time she was dead, right? Dead or near death and waiting for her vampire cure to waken her and give her new life. So all she had to do was reach out, reach out with dreaming tentacles . . .

Aunt Doreen, come on, Aunt Doreen, where are you? Come on, see me, feel me, hear me, touch me. Reach out to me, I know you're out there . . . please help me stick around long enough to stop all of this. It can't be the end yet, it shouldn't be the end yet.

She could feel her body still. What was this? She hadn't felt it a second ago, and yet now she could feel it. It was hard to explain, a little like when you first start waking up. And you're sliding out of dream, and slipping back into the meat of your body. Your limbs become a part of you once more, you're conscious of them existing. All that muscle and bone and sinew. She could feel them in a very painfully real way. Her spasms were still going strong, her hands and her arms the worst of it, the muscles tight ropes, pulled so painfully tight.

And she felt something wet against her lips, against her chin. Was she drooling? Wait, no. No, wait, that wasn't it, it wasn't it at all, was it? No, wait, no. It was salty, yes, and sharp, like licking a battery. It tingled on her tongue and she felt something ignite inside of her, like a sparkler lit and throwing off light.

And Daphne's voice now, whispering in her air, the sound of snow hitting her skin like thunder. "Drink, come on, Mom! Drink drink drink. You can't do this, you can't let them take you! The sun is coming out now, we've got to hurry up, and I can't do any of this alone. I need you, Mom, I need you to drink."

Something squirmed against her neck, she felt it kick and move and then woosh, a gush of blood, this river in her throat and she felt it now, warming her up all nice and toasty. The heat spreading out from her lips and her guts out to her limbs, fighting back that numb empty feeling and letting her flex, letting her move once again. But it wasn't enough, not enough to finish it up.

She needed more. She needed, yes, she needed that rabbit heart, right there. That rabbit heart running in her veins, that soft death that waited on the other side. Felt it quiver and beat, push further, greedy on the lips, greedy in her tongue. push harder. It squirmed against her face, against her body, she felt it now, it was bigger than an animal, yes. But it wasn't a human, was it? It felt so small, but not small enough to be a rabbit or a squirrel or cat or dog. And it leaned against her now, no longer squirming. It wanted to die, she could tell, and she needed it to die.

She saw its death, that heart beat dwindling, a rabbit still trying to hop away from her, but she almost had it, she was right on it. The creature in her arms sighed, and then started sobbing, and she heard a voice, so quiet and young and soft. Oh shit. A little girl? Daphne brought her a little girl? Oh no. Why would she do that? Why wouldn't she bring her a rabbit or a squirrel? Anything but this, anything but this child in her arms.

She opened her eyes, brief and bright. They weren't in the street anymore, they were under the awning of a store, the clouds parting, revealing low slow rays of sunlight. Still half dark and half light, the overcast clouds making the world dim but not dark. The snow no longer falling, and starting to melt into brief puddles around them. Oh shit.

And it was a little girl in her arms, so small. Blue jeans and pig-tails and her skin pale now, so pale against Nix's body. No, no, no. Anna was bad enough, but this? This?

And she heard Daphne, sad and morose. "If you want to keep going you have to finish her. I'm so sorry, Nix. But this is what we are now, and if you need to stop Old Wick, you need to finish her. I can't do it alone, and neither can you, so you need to do this for me, for us. Please, mom. Please!"

And Nix knew that she was right. She knew what she had to do, oh god. She knew it then and there. She bent down, and finished her meal.

39

THE dead body of the little girl fell slump from her arms onto the pavement. And Nix did not want to look down, did not want to see her shriveled up, wrinkled body, discarded like a cicada shell on the ground. All hollowed out, the blood thick and rushing in her veins, a whispering in her heart. What was this? She could hear that little girl whispering in her blood, babbling. She didn't want to look down, didn't want to see it . . .

And yet, she couldn't resist. The blood sparkling in her veins, a roaring furnace filled with that idle childish chatter. Mister Brightbones was walking right into Old Wick's trap, and it was all her fault. She had to get to old Wick and behead the bastard before he used Brightbones as bait for the Child of the Abyss. She shivered, kicked the corpse of the child so it was face down, her chains tight and restrictive.

But her muscles, yes, her muscles were strong and newborn and no longer spastic with multiple sclerosis. Her eyesight rushed back in a wave of color and shapes, and everything became more real and physical, in a way she couldn't explain. It was more than her multiple sclerosis going to sleep inside of her bones, it was more than just a simple cure. It was that blood mania gain, hot and terrible in her heart. She realized it and saw it and yet fell prey to it again. Yes, this mania was a *good* thing, wasn't it? Hell, it was a *great* thing right now, a necessary thing for what they had to do. What she had to do.

She was going to have to walk into the lion's den and behead that lion, and then stand up all bloodied and roar into the void. Show that Child of the Abyss who was boss and scare it away from this world, never to come back. Hell, she could probably even kill Mister

Brightbones like this, couldn't she? This kind of madness, this kind of vampire strength? Yes, yes! In fact, this was stronger than it was before, with Anna's blood.

At least, it felt that way, anyway. Was it because she was fully transformed now, a complete vampire, no longer moving from dead to undead but entirely crossed over? Or could it be young blood, so young, licked her lips now, so thirsty for more of that. Oh, no, don't think about that, don't go down that route. You're not a monster Nix, no, you're not a monster.

She turned away from the corpse, the chains pressing against her skin with every movement, and she felt it sapping her, the blood under her skin fighting against the power of cold iron, trying to sap her strength. Shit, she was going to burn through this so fast.

Daphne stared at her, just a little to her left, staring at her in horror. Even though she was the one who did this to her, she was the one who brought her a *child* for heaven's sake. How dare she look at her like that? Like she was the monster, after everything Daphne did?

No, don't point this fury and rage at Daphne. You have to point it at Old Wick, at Mister Brightbones.

"Are you full now?"

"I guess, I'm feeling a lot better . . . did you get anything to eat?"

Daphne nodded, but didn't say what or who she ate. But Nix could tell by the haunted, hollow look in her eyes that it was probably another child. This one's sister, or brother, probably. Oh Daphne, oh, what did you do?

What was necessary. Nix understood that. Necessary. But still horrible.

"Good, I guess," And then she looked out at the sun, saw it stretched across the sky. It would probably be another hour or two before it was dusk, she knew that. Now that the artificial night from the storm clouds was gone, they were bare and vulnerable to the sun and what it could do to vampires. She knew, she watched it happen with Daphne. And yet, she still had to check. Still had to try it out.

She reached her hand, the chains jangling and restricting and burning in their own way. She had to shuffle walk shuffle forward past her binds, just to stretch out her hand, stretch it out and . . .

Oh shit fucking hell damn motherfucking shit.

A spark of flame and she felt it in her *bones* holy shit, how did she feel that in her bones? She stared at it, the pain only slightly worse than spasticity pain she'd felt only recently. Stared at it in awe. This shouldn't be happening, and yet, here it was, happening. She caught on fire, and she felt it burning away some of the blood, just like the chains. Shit, shit, shit. She shouldn't waste it like that, waste that poor girl's blood like that. She shouldn't let her sacrifice be in vain.

After all, that was what it was, right? The girl sacrificed herself so Nix could save the world. It made sense, and she should honor that sacrifice by not wasting it anymore. She waved her hand, and it took forever to get that flame to die off in the shadows of the awning. Ow, ow, ow, the hand burned black. It's going to use more blood now to heal it, damnit. Why did she do that?

"Are you done playing around now? I thought you said we had a mission to do, that there wasn't any time to mess around and here you are doing this, Mom. Messing around when we should be going."

Nix nodded, the chains hurting her neck and her shoulders. Ow. She had to get this off. "You're right. But how are going to cross the street and get to the bookstore like this?"

Daphne looked behind them, at the sports store they'd been at earlier. Where Nix had devoured Anna, and set her whole second life in motion. Daphne pointed at the umbrellas in the window display and nodded, briefly. "With those."

"Okay, if you think they'll work," but Nix wasn't so sure. How would that cover them entirely with shade? Even if they each carried one, the shadows would have bare spots where the light could drift through, and then they would be screwed blue and tattooed.

"Let me just get these chains off so I stop wasting this blood and we can get going."

And she leaned over, concentrated that pain and mania all in one spot, directly onto that key-shaped scar on the palm of her hand, and pressed it down, tightly. It took a few moments, and she thought she heard her blood screaming, and burning up so brightly, and she tried not to use too much of it . . .

She didn't want to feed again. Not like that. The chains fell and she felt a little emptier now, a little more hollow. Oh shit. A lot of blood used up in that little act.

"Come on, let's hurry now, Mom," Daphne said, "Even in the shadows our blood burns quicker in the day."

Shit, of course it does. Of course. She flinched at hearing *Mom*, but decided it wasn't worth mentioning now. She could call her whatever, it didn't matter. What mattered was cleaning up this mess that she made. All because she was trying to stop Old Wick from doing what he was doing. Like a proper Greek tragedy, it all happened anyway, no matter how hard she tried to stop it. In fact, her stopping it made it happen all the quicker.

40

BLACK umbrellas like parasols blocked the sun from their bodies as much as possible, as they walked down the street toward the bookstore. So much snow had fallen in such a short amount of time, climbing up over their heads like tiny snow mountains. Even though the blizzard was magically produced, the ice and snow stuck around still, while the air was warming up and the sun had come back out.

It made traversing the sidewalk and the street damn near impossible. When it was still icy cold with new snow falling, you could walk on top of the six feet of snow or so beneath your feet. But now that it was melting it became more unstable, more dangerous, toppling and mushy and like walking through hills of sand.

Add in the sun still draining their blood away faster than they would like, even still here, under their umbrellas, and the whole mission felt doomed and sluggish. She wanted to just run down the street to the bookstore, and then run across the street, but no. No.

That was not going to happen. It was slow sluggish movement, while the world slowly came to life again around them. They watched as the few people who weren't celebrating Halloween at the bookstore stumbled out of their storefronts, houses, and apartments, and began to shovel the heavy, wet mess. Nix remembered a few years ago, when they got seven feet of snow in two days. Rough blizzard that one was, and shoveling was heavy and wet, much like this. Each time she raised the shovel it felt like a small child was sitting on it.

At the time she called that demon snow. Satan's dandruff. But there was nothing supernatural about that snow. Just screwed up weather patterns brought on by climate change. This snow, on the other hand, this vampire snow? It really, truly was demonic in origin. If she hadn't felt so overwhelmed she would've found it funny.

But not now, no. Not now. She led the way to the bookstore, mostly because Daphne didn't really have an idea of where they were, not really. She hadn't grown up in Dark Rivers like Nix. She hadn't experienced the time that airplane crashed in the center of town twenty odd years ago, or when the university caught ablaze and had to be shut down. What a nightmare that was, she remembered it all too clearly. She was just twenty herself back then, but too proud to go to college. She was better than it, smarter than it, she would blaze her own path into the world.

You could still see the ruins of it a little outside of town. She used to go there and wander the old burnt-out shell. She couldn't tell you why she did it, she just found it comforting, somehow. Later on, they had plans and funding for the city to demolish it, but it never actually happened. They were too busy rebuilding the town square, the tragedy of the fires and the plane crash still too raw and brutal in people's minds for them to just bulldoze it.

Even though they were planning to eventually put a memorial up in its place, which would've been nice.

They trudged further on. Nix felt something humming in her heart and her blood, and realized she could hear the heartbeat of every single person who had come outside to shovel. She could hear the rhythm of the blood rushing through the veins of children out now playing in the snowbound street. There were no cars out on the road driving, they were still buried under snow. And there was no way you could drive on the roads. The snowplows had not come out yet, and even if they had, it might be impossible for even them to maneuver about and remove the insane piles of snow.

That last time, when there was seven feet in two days? The city had to call on the national guard to dig them out.

She tried to ignore the sounds of blood around her, and that pang she felt in her heart and her bones, that hunger pain making her want to feed. Even though she had some blood in her still, the hunger was strong.

"Resist it," Daphne said. "You should have enough for awhile now, even in the sun. Unless you burn it up doing something stupid, and I know you're not stupid, Mom."

She flinched again at that word, *Mom*, and the terrible memories it brought up. Of her being entranced, under Daphne's thrall.

She shook that horrible memory away, now wasn't the time for that. "Why's that?" she asked, "There was less blood in that child than in Anna."

She shivered at the terrible memory. How quickly she'd sucked the little girl dry, and how fast she felt her death enter her heart. The death somehow felt bigger than Anna's, in a way she couldn't explain.

"True, the child has less blood, but they have more death inside of them, and death is what powers us, it's what he heals us. Her life was taken so soon and quick, which meant you got to drink up all the years ahead of her, all the promises the future held. They're inside you now, Mom. That's what keeps us going, what we burn up when we do our work. The blood is the vessel, but the death and all the years they had ahead of them? That's what we feed on. The promise of what's to come. And she had so much life ahead of her, making her death so much bigger, so much more potent. I'm not a ghoul, I promise. I chose that child for a reason."

Nix nodded, and she felt it, she understood it now, and that terrified her even more. They were ghouls though, weren't they? Not like the wights, who ate the corpses of the dead, bones and all. But in the truest sense of the word, the way they fed on the living, preyed on them, all for their own selfish cure. Not caring who they hurt, how sick it made them, just so they prolonged their own suffering for a little bit longer. One hundred precent ghoulish.

"You still haven't told me yet, Mom," Daphne said, catching up to her now, the two of them walking side by side. It was hard to hear Daphne over the roar of blood around them, the sound so loud and tantalizing. But she concentrated, she listened and tried to tune the other stuff out. "Why do you have to stop Old Wick? And what does Mister Brightbones have to do with any of that?"

And Nix stopped for a moment. The umbrella barely blocked out the sun, the shadow covering most of her body. But if she moved it just a little bit this way or that, the sun would peak through just enough to catch on fire, and she would have to try and put it out with one hand and not moving the umbrella too much while she did it.

It all felt so impossible. But she looked at Daphne and explained it to her. As quickly as she could, with as much detail as she could muster. Even explaining the bit about her aunt visiting her, and everything she showed her.

Sure, it sounded crazy when she said it out loud. But then again, all of this sounded crazy when you looked at it for too long. The whole world had gone crazy. And she had to go crazy with it, in order to just survive.

41

THEY hid behind the slush mountains of half-melted snow. On either side of the front door to Something Old were vampire hunters, guarding the entrance like they were at Buckingham Palace. These ones were long and spindly, like four-legged spiders, roughly six and a half feet tall. They carried long bloodied hooks. Nix knew exactly what those hooks were used for, neither nor Daphne had to guess or even say it. They were used for deboning vampires. Much like the scythes were used earlier.

Nix shivered a little at the thought of it, her vampire flesh covered in tiny goosebumps. Something coiled and uncoiled in her stomach, making her feel nervous and nauseous all at the same time. Was it just nerves, or something else? Had the kid's blood been bad? Would it make her sick? How could that even happen, bad blood. And yet, she thought it and it added to her goosebumps, her whole mind reeling in fear. She looked over at Daphne and coughed, just a little.

"How are we going to get past them?"

Their entire bodies were covered in rough rags, almost like mummy bandages, torn and flittering around their bodies with every little movement. And between the edges of the bandages tiny, glowing red eyes looked out at them. Hundreds of them covering their bodies, searching out in the dark. Vampire sentinels, seeking out any of the bloodless, the death drinkers. To rip out their bones and leave them to die in the sun,

These ones did not look like they were made from wax, like the other vampire hunters they'd come across so far. These ones seemed to be made of discarded black rags, sewn together in the mockery of a human form, and probably filled with dead leaves and an armature of dead branches for bones. She could see these branch bones peaking out, the dead leaves rustling as they moved, sounding like a million locusts nesting in their bones. And when they moved, they jerked about, like a marionette being controlled by an unseen puppeteer. And these movements were even freakier, like they were being filmed in reverse and sped up somehow. Like strange claymation creations come to life.

"Why isn't anyone saying anything?" Daphne said, leaning over and whispering to Nix.

"Saying anything about what?"

"Look," and Daphne pointed at all the people along the street, cleaning the snow and trying to dig their cars out, now that the strange freak nightmare of a storm had finally ended. They either ignored the vampire hunters, or they waved hi to them or laughed and talked about them like they were no big deal at all. Like it was perfectly normal seeing them there, standing outside the bookstore.

For a moment Nix was taken aback too. Why wasn't anyone doing anything? Why weren't they freaked out or in awe? And then she remembered seeing Danny earlier, dressed like that demon from the Hellskin novel. Of course, they think the vampire hunters are just nerds in really elaborate costumes.

Probably characters from the Hellskin books that Danny was talking about so much. It seemed like the kind of thing supernerds would love. She told Daphne as much, and Daphne nodded and sighed elaborately and rolled her eyes. "Figures! Of course, of course, of course. It would be too easy for them to stand out and have the cops called on them, wouldn't it? No, our lives have to be difficult."

And Nix laughed. "Compared to our illnesses, though?"

And Daphne laughed as well and said, "Compared to our illnesses this still sucks and is still difficult as all hell. I was a dummy to ever think I could escape from Mister Brightbones and keep him away with those stupid scarecrows. I should've known he would've found a way, He always does. He always does."

Nix leaned back, making sure the umbrella still kept out the sun. She felt her legs burning a little, a little more, using up her blood faster than she would've liked. Damn. She did not want to feed again so soon, even though all of those warm bodies would make it so easy to do.

"Well, if this uses up as much of my blood as last time, you're going to have to just go in and stop Old Wick yourself."

"What are you talking about?"

Nix held up the palm of her hand, with her thumb ready to press against that keyshaped scar. "I've already lost too much blood just getting the chains off of me and burning myself up earlier. God, I'm so stupid. It's difficult Daphne because I'm making it difficult for us, because I'm so dumb."

"No, no you're not, Mom."

For once she actually liked the sound of that word in Daphne's mouth. It made her feel a little warm, even though it still carried some bad memories with it. She pushed past that feeling, shook her head no, and then said, "It doesn't matter. Look, I can take those vampire hunters out with a press of my thumb and that will be that. But the last time I did that I pretty much used up all of my juice. Understand?"

"Sort of. I still don't understand how it works, and why it does anything to them."

Shit, Nix felt something in the air, the temperature dropping. Her whole body covered in goosebumps now, her stomach like live worms squirming. Her mind had this panic sensation, all of her thoughts running around, trying to escape her skull and get out of here. It was the feeling of being prey, and she hated it. And it wasn't from old Wick, Mister Brightbones, or the vampire hunters. It was a wrongness in the core of reality itself, something pushing against the rotten skin of the world, trying to get into this one.

The Child of the Abyss. Shit.

"Look, promise me you will try everything you can to stop Old Wick, especially before he gets Mister Brightbones in the bone cage."

Daphne's face went white. "Oh shit, the bone cage you told me about? You think it's there? The one made from vampire bones?"

Nix shook her head back and forth, like trying to clear damp cobwebs from the center of her mind. "I don't know. I really don't know. All I know is that we can't let him put Mister Brightbones in the cage. We can't let him bait the Child of the Abyss into coming to this world, and doing the horrible things he wants to do to us. To everything. I promised my aunt, and now, Daphne . . ."

She looked at Nix with a mixture of fear and terror and regret and sadness and love. "Yes?"

Nix swallowed her words. Yes, she was manipulating Daphne now, but it was in the same way Daphne had manipulated her. "Be a good daughter and do this for mommy, okay? If I collapse leave me be. Even if it means the sun takes me away from the world, just do it. I need you to go in there, and destroy Old Wick. Can you do that for you mother? Can you do that for me?"

And Daphne nodded and said, "Yes, mommy, I can do anything for you, I love you."

And Nix closed her eyes and stopped every muscle in her body from moving. All those muscles you move without even thinking, without even needing to think about, she thought about them and stopped them. She paused that river of blood from flowing through her body, conserving all of her undead energy.

She didn't want to die. Not right here, not right now. Oh god, how she didn't want to die yet again. What would this be, the third time? The fourth time? How many more times? It would probably be the last time. The sun would probably take her if she fell over and the umbrella tumbled with her.

She only hoped Daphne listened to her and didn't save Nix first, and only charged in and put an end to all of this. She concentrated, connected in her mind to Old Wick and Mister Brightbones. She saw them in the bookstore, and felt the twisted psychic tentacles that lashed out, connecting Old Wick to all the vampire hunters. There were so many of them in the bookstore. So many! So many dead vampires now, too. The cage was completed, she saw it there in her mind's eye.

She had to do this now. If they were going to do this, she had to do this now. Take all the vampire hunters out in the store at once and wish the best for Daphne.

One, two, three.

She dug her thumb into her scar and poured all of her pain into that one thought. This had better work, my god. This had better work.

42

NIX pressed down hard, as hard as she had the last time she did this. She twisted her thumb, dug under the skin, felt that pain blossom. She wanted to rip the scar, become one with the pain, as she concentrated in the shadow of the umbrella, concentrated on Old Wick, on all of his vampire sentinels patrolling the place. She didn't think about the other dead vampires, she didn't think about the cage, oh god the cage. No, she just focused on him.

She brought his face into sharp focus, no longer a blur in her mind but instead a beacon. Long beard, wrinkled skin, that old wizard grungy Santa Claus look. His eyes were gold, somehow, yes, like two spinning coins in the dark. She reached out to him with her mind, with her memories, with the map of the store in her head, reached out with all of her pain, pointed right at him, like an arrow shot in the dark, guided by the connection between the two of them.

That's right, feel that pain, taste that sorrow on your tongue. It tastes like battery acid, doesn't it? The blood of that child burning through her body, feeding into the pain (but no, don't waver, don't think about the small husk of the corpse, think instead about Old Wick, yes, Old Wick. Focus on him. Do not waver!)

And oh shit, there he turned and looked at her. Across space, across time, across the arrows of thought. He stared directly at her through the scar, and there was an electrical feeling in her bones. Sprung now, alive, and she kept focusing on the arrow of pain sent his way, connected through the scar. Come on, come on, it worked before it had to work again, it just had to, come on, come on.

He smiled, all those strange sharp and crooked teeth. Tongue lashed out between the teeth and a laughter in his eyes, as they sparkled and then, yes, then in her mind's eyes she heard him. "Oh, you clever little vampire. I saw what you did last time, do you think I'm going to fall for that again? You took me by surprise, no more, no less. Last time I saw you, you were human. But I guess I lost you, too. Guess I'm going to have to use your bones as well. The cage is done, but I could always do with a few spare parts."

He laughed again and she focused that pain arrow, sharp, burning up as much blood as she could to ride that connection over and put a stop to him. Put a stop to him once and for all and get this done and over with.

He flinched, briefly, a second, a chink his armor. Yes, yes, she could do this, she could take him *down*. That will learn him to mess with her, to mess with this reality, to piss off her aunt. Yes, she whispered, her thoughts to his thoughts, this one is for my Aunt Doreen.

But all he did was flinch a little, like a tiny pinprick of pain, and nothing more than that. All it did was make him laugh some more, his eyes sparkling, wide now, focusing directly on her, reaching across the world and the scar and directly into her thoughts, glowing bright, as he laughed and said, "I told you, I'm not falling for that malarky anymore, little miss. Being a vampire now means you're just another parasite in this world. I might've saved you when the void came to devour everything, that delightful Child of the Abyss. But no, no you had to go and become one of them. One of his little grubby maggots, feasting on the corpse of this universe."

Face is bigger now, and she kept trying to send more pain his way, but it didn't do a thing, not a thing at all. And now Daphne was tugging on her shirt, and now she heard this sound, like rustling leaves and insects in flight, the wings a muttering voice of the dead, getting closer and closer. What was that sound? What did Daphne want?

But she couldn't break her concentration. Not now. She couldn't do it at all. She had to do this again, she had to shock him something fierce, get the vampire hunters to fall apart, and then cut off his head once and for all.

"Tsk, tsk, tsk. I can see your thoughts now, you know that? I can see you picture me headless, and that just won't do. What if I called the cops, or walked outside and alerted everyone to that little corpse you left behind? With a wight to clean it up you're royally screwed.

Murdering a poor innocent girl like that, with your fingerprints all over her."

No, no, she wasn't going to let him mess with her like that. She couldn't let him mess with her like that. She just had to concentrate, come on. Why wasn't this working? Why was he only flinching a little?

The sunlight. Like Daphne said, even in the shadow it burns more blood to do anything. Well, damn. She had to push harder, then, push more pain into it. Let's just hope that what she said before is true about children having longer deaths, deaths that burn slower since there is so much death left in their bodies.

And the sound of leaves rustling and insects got louder. And Daphne was saying something panicky, but she ignored her. She had to ignore her, she almost had it, she forced it in again, and watched him flinch, and the laughter was gone and there was anger now.

"You need to stop that, you're like an annoying gnat and nothing more than that. Stop that right now."

Yes! Yes! She was getting to him. Now to just turn up the juice, and if it makes her collapse and die in the sun, so be it. Daphne knew what to do, and she would be able to get it done now with the vampire hunters out of the way. Just fire off one big final missive, burn all her blood, use all of her pain, digging that thumb deep in now, deep inside, right into that key-shaped scar.

"You're forgetting one thing," Mister Brightbones voice was all hate and fire. "This connection goes both ways."

And a wall of pain hit her body all at once. Electrical shock in her bones and the connection was severed, and she fell to the ground, the umbrella thankfully tumbling over her as she collapsed and started twitching. Oh god oh no oh god, this hurt so much, every nerve felt like it was on fire. This was somehow worse than multiple sclerosis, it was like the time they did a nerve test and shocked her with electrical rings on her fingers. Her whole body shook and she wanted the pain to stop, she needed the pain to stop.

The connection was severed, and her body was burning more and more blood just to keep from passing out, just to keep from burning up, In the distance she heard Daphne screaming, but had no idea why, she was briefly blind from the pain and wishing for death (but there is no death for you anymore, you're undead now, it's all about the pain and nothing else, nothing but the pain. Not a cure, but a curse. And oh my god, what a horrible curse.)

And the sound of insects was so loud, directly above her, as someone ripped off the umbrella, the sun setting her skin on fire, as something picked her up like she was nothing more than a ragdoll. The rustling insect noise drowning out everything, even her screams.

43

NIX, screaming, on fire and up in the air, picked up by the spider tall vampire hunter. Hooks in the sun, hooks gleaming bright, and Nix was on fire and crawling, crawling and kicking and trying to get away as the hooks gleamed and came right toward her, eager to rip the skin and stick deep into the bone, and pull the bones from her body in one quick yank.

She pushed and screamed, the blaze of her face so bright it was hard to see anything at all. Just a blur of gold. And then she heard Daphne screaming, and felt the vampire hunter carrying her tumble down. Its rags caught fire, and it twitched and lashed out, with both hooks falling into the melting snow, and hissing from the heat of her fire.

That one twitched below her and she was in so much pain, oh god. Was this how Daphne felt when she caught fire the other day, running toward her? Was this how the others felt, their puddles of vampire skin lighting up nightmarish in the sun?

The smell of burning hair and flesh was everything now. Everything. She wanted to gag, and felt everything spin and it was hard to see beyond the gold of her burning body. She was feral now, near death and blood burning up, the child's death inside of her rushing out to heal what it could heal. But the sun was too strong, too bright, it was a losing battle. And she knew it, Nix knew it. This was it, she was going to fail her aunt, fail the universe, fail everything. And that made her crazed and feral and even more manic than before.

She wasn't going to survive this. She didn't want to survive this. It would be up to Daphne now, Daphne screaming, Daphne who came to her for protection. And all she did was make things worse and bring on the end of the world. But that didn't matter now.

The one vampire hunter burning on the ground wasn't going to get up. Those rags were lit up super quick, and pretty soon the tatters and dead leaves and broken branches were small infernos. It twitched a few times, and Nix hoped somehow Old Wick was connected to it, and he could *feel* it. Yes, yes, feel it you old bastard. Feel it, let it sink in and devour you.

But she didn't have time to think. Daphne holding her umbrella with one hand, knocking the second vampire hunter to the ground like a quarterback. Bits of her strayed beyond the umbrella shade and caught little bits of fire, them going out in the shadows almost immediately.

And Nix, on fire, wasn't going to waste this. She was going to be dead soon, she felt it. Felt her body scratching at that doorway of death. As a vampire would she become a ghost? Surrender to emptiness? Or was what she experienced earlier a glimpse of that kind of death? Her thoughts wandering around in an infinite emptiness, lonely and alone.

It didn't matter. What mattered was that she was on fire now, and that vampire hunter was pushing Daphne over, and down, and getting the hook under Daphne's skin, oh shit, pushing it in, hooking around bone, oh no oh god oh no.

Nix leapt and screamed, her body a brilliant ball of flame. She grabbed its head and pulled it back, the hook yanking Daphne, almost pulling her bones out. But Daphne cried out and rolled forward, rolling with the hook, so it wouldn't grab and pull back, pull out, yanking her bones out with it.

As the vampire hunter caught fire just as quick as the other one, their bodies like kindling wrapped up and brought to life. It screamed and the scream sounded like a trapped animal, cornered with a paw in a steel jaw. A horrible sound that gave Nix a queasy terrified feeling. Her body now one giant web of pain, every nerve on fire. It was worse than her worst relapse, And that was really saying something.

The vampire hunter twitched and became dying embers and then just a pile of ashes and soot and nothing more. They were both burned into the pavement, the snow melting into puddles around them. Their bodies left scorch makes on the sidewalk, like the shadows left after a nuclear blast.

Nix now crawled forward, pushing her burning body into the mountain of snow, and hearing it hiss all around her. Steam rising into the air, but at least for a cold brutal moment it kept her from the sun. It wouldn't last long, but she could stay in here for a second, and weep quietly as the pain made her numb to everything.

Now that she wasn't feral, now that she wasn't fighting for her life against those vampire hunters, all she felt was the pain. The pain along everything, her flesh crispy and aching as the child's blood rushed through her body, trying to heal her and grow skin back before the snow was all gone and she was just in the sun once again, burning up.

Her clothes were ragged and scorched and her skin was blistered charcoal. She heard footsteps, and daphne walking up to her, and draping her in something. A coat? A blanket? Something like that. It hurt her skin, but felt good getting it out of the sun.

And then in her hand, shoved the umbrella. It hurt to grasp it. She didn't want to grasp it. She wanted to scratch some more on death's door, like a stray cat begging to be let in. Please, please let her in. Let her go into that sweet nothingness beyond.

She was so weary and tired and done with this world, with this universe. What the hell was she trying to save anyway? A place that cursed her to chronic illness. One that each cure and remedy she tried came up snake eyes. Even the stuff that seemed to work for everyone, and even the dangerous, horrible last resort stuff. The stuff she risked death every time she took it. A risk worth taking if it actually worked, but no, more and more relapses.

Even this fucking cure here, this promise of being well and healed again. It barely lasted long at all. It seemed she was always feeding on death, feeding on murder. Could she live a whole life like this? A whole afterlife like this?

It wasn't fair. Why couldn't she just have a normal life, where she could dance and sing and run and jump? Why did she have all these things stolen from her? And why, why did everyone keep promising her a return to normal when no such thing was possible?

She let the umbrella fall, tumble down. Let the sun take her, let it.

But Daphne scoffed and said, "Fine, if you won't take it then I'll just expose myself to the sun and burn up as well. Mom, look at me, listen to me."

And Nix did, looking at her through the burned haze of her scorched eyelids, slowly regrowing themselves.

"Until I met you, I felt alone in this world. But I don't anymore, understand? I don't."

And she nodded, and understood, and grabbed the umbrella once more, adjusting the coat Daphne had draped over her head like a hoodie.

In the distance she heard grasps and murmurs, and remembered they'd had an audience the whole time. Oh shit. "Enjoy the early Halloween show," she said to them, "We're just cosplaying a scene from the Hellskin novels."

And everyone applauded, and then got right back to cleaning up the street.

44

THEY knew they couldn't just barge in the front door and put a stop to Old Wick, not like this, and especially not like how Nix was right now. She was about ready to fall apart, and she felt the edges of death, but knew she wasn't ready to go there just yet. The blood was still pumping fast and strong and moving out, healing the broken and burnt parts of her. She felt run down, and the pain was immense. She itched all over, every single part of her the sun touched and scorched away.

But she wasn't as bad as she was five minutes ago, when she wanted to just cross over already and get it over with. She was slowly, slowly healing. And the kid's blood was extra powerful, and long lasting, that she could tell. She wasn't getting that drained-up slurpy feeling she got before, when she was close to being drained of blood and ready for death.

But she knew this wouldn't last forever, and she was exhausted and bone tired and every part of her, just every part of her. And yet, her mind was wired and alive, and that manic feeling came back to her, that blood drunk feeling she thought had been fading.

She had to just get out of the sunlight, and here they were climbing the fire escape for Something Old, scaling it as best as they could. It wasn't easy climbing no, especially not like this, but at least this alley was ensconced in the shadow of the building next door. Nix even let her umbrella down, folded it up and slid it under one ragged arm. She'd taken Daphne's coat from her shoulders, so it no longer draped her like a hood and gave it back to her.

She only hoped the sun set a little early today, or maybe some winter clouds would roll over the sun? They didn't have to be the weird voodoo storm clouds of Mister Brightbones, just the natural normal ones would do. The ones they used to get a decade ago, before global warming changed the weather patterns and their autumn stretched out and smothered the winter.

They were climbing the fire escape because Nix knew of a way in through the second-floor window. It was easy to open from the outside, no storm windows and no screens. Danny did it that way on purpose, just in case he locked himself outside. He'd showed it to Nix awhile ago, back before her multiple sclerosis made stairs dangerous and impossible.

She thought about that as they climbed up and up. How good it felt to do this and not worry about *falling*. So many times she'd fallen down the stairs throughout her life. The worst time she cracked her spine, and it was another one of the long litany of pains that multiple sclerosis gave her.

But right here, right now? She was climbing. She was fucking climbing! It felt amazing. She hadn't done it in so long, and yes, even though her skin was still smoldering, and yes even though it hurt so much, every nerve still on fire, and yes even though it itched like hell, it was . . . well, it was wonderful.

Because it was an act of *healing*. It wasn't multiple sclerosis, it was it's opposite. And she felt grateful for that, grateful to feel somewhat normal, if only for a little bit. She chuckled to herself as they climbed, *somewhat normal*. As normal as a body full of someone else's blood could be. As normal as her skin growing back from being burned up by the heat of the sun.

Yes, there was nothing normal about it. And yet, in this moment, yes, she felt the most normal she'd felt in a really, really long time. It left a small ache in her heart, like a thorn had pierced her right there. A heart still racing and beating and sending that child's blood out to heal her.

Please, keep going, she thought. Please keep me going long enough to stop Old Wick. She trusted Daphne to be the one to do it, yes, but she wanted to be the one. She felt like she had to be the one to behead him. It was her right, after all, a promise she had made. And it would be so delicious to do it, so wonderfully delicious.

Huh. She never thought she would feel joy at the thought of beheading an old man before. But she never thought she would kill a child and drink her blood.

She was changing. Her soft edges were hardening, sharpening, becoming like knives. Her heart was spikey now, a vampire heart covered in thorns and spines. She was healed yes, but she was also *changing* in such a deepdown in the bone way. A way that, if she'd actually had time to set aside and think about it, might actually terrify her.

Had Daphne changed, too? Changed from the person she was when she was still alive and dying of cancer? Was that why she ran away from Mister Brightbones, to try and keep part of her living, breathing, human heart alive?

They were near the second-floor window now, on a little landing right outside of it. The fire escape jangled like windchimes made from bones as they moved, an ominous sound that she hoped they wouldn't hear inside. Did Old Wick know they were coming for him? Probably. He definitely felt them take out his sentinels, that was for sure.

But they hadn't left yet. Not by the front or the book door. They probably couldn't drive anywhere right now anyway, so they must be doing what he wants to do at the bookstore. though she didn't remember seeing them bring the bone cage here, and she didn't see it set up at the bookstore at all. Though it would've probably fit in with all the Halloween decorations, she swore she would've seen it.

What's his plan, then? In her visions from her aunt, it was always in that house, the Cannibal House on the hill. There was something there, she felt it. Like it was part of the plan, that even though Mister Brightbones was the bait, the house was . . .

Was what? A beacon? Telling the Child of the Abyss his brother is there, in the walls, waiting for him?

She didn't know. But she guessed they sure as shit were going to find out.

They stood now, on that landing right outside of the window. Daphne's hair was blowing, the shadow of the building stretched over them. Even though the sun wasn't setting them on fire, even in the shade here they were sluggish and slow. Especially with Nix being healed.

"Okay," Daphne said, "You said it was this window, right? So let's do it, Mom! Let's pry this sucker open and climb on in."

And Nix nodded and smiled. She hated to admit it, but yeah, she was seeing Daphne more and more like a daughter now. And it wasn't even that weird chemical thrall that she'd gotten when she was human.

Maybe she wasn't hardening quite as much as she'd thought. Maybe her humanity was still there, it was just changing. And maybe that was a good thing.

She nodded, said, "Here we go," and reached down and wiggled the window against the frame. It slowly popped up, and she shoved it the rest of the way, giving them enough room to crawl inside to the bookstore beyond.

45

THEY crept through the bookstore, and kicked off their shoes to keep extra quiet. The second floor was a mess of scattered books and splashes of ochre stains. Stains that looked like recently dried blood, some of it still glistening, still wet. Nix felt her mouth water, her blood sing to blood, that she wanted to lick it up. Not that it would do anything, she realized. The death was already used up, the blood empty of anything that could heal either of them. And yet, somehow she wanted it, somehow she needed it and desired it. So strong, her heart ached for it, and it took everything in her power to keep from leaning down and lapping it up, licking it and tasting it, just getting it on her tongue and lips. Even though it was drained of death and would do her no good, she felt it, aching, so strong, that ache.

Daphne next to her, silent in their movements, quick like shadows moving. The muffled sounds of voices drifted up to them from the first floor. Mister Brightbones whimpering and muttering, and Old Wick's crackling voice booming like lightning, like thunder.

Not enough to make it out. Not enough to even hear the basic gist of what they were saying. She guessed vampires didn't have super hearing after all. But that smell, oh that blood drunk smell. And a sound like a weak heart beating from one of the aisles, then another.

"Do you hear that?" she whispered to Daphne, hoping it was low enough that no one else could hear them.

"Yes. But ignore it now, we don't want to waste time gorging ourselves, we should be good for a little bit longer."

And she felt it, yes. There was still a panic in her heart that the blood might burn away and run out again, and leave her close to death once more, her multiple sclerosis coming back full on with a vengeance. It was hard to shake that panic, that it might drain away soon. Every second she felt like she was taking an internal pulse, to try and feel how much more of it was left.

And how much more of it she would go through before these burns would fully heal. She felt better the minute they got indoors and out of the sunlight. Even under the shade it was different than being indoors. And they avoided the windows on the walls, stayed in the center of the bookstore aisles, far away from the stray sunbeams stretching across the floors.

The light was diluted, filtered by overhead neon bulbs. That somehow scattered the sun with artificial light. It weakened it and weakened it some more. And she felt it the minute they climbed in, her skin cooling, like she dipped into refreshing, icy water. The itching soothed a little from the skin growing back, it was less fierce and terrible. She could finally relax a little. And the child's blood sparkled and sang as it moved through her body, electric. It felt thicker, stronger. The death so much greater inside of her, that promise of life powering her onward, healing her.

"You're right," she said, "We'll let them be."

Even though she could hear them mewling and crawling, sad noises of the slow dying and bleeding out. Were they traps for the vampires? Bodies used as bait?

And then she realized that no, she definitely did not want to go and see who was bleeding out in the dark corners of the bookstores, by the scattered and busted bookshelves. She didn't want to see if it was Danny, or any of the other people she'd known her whole life, in this rinky dink small town on the edge of nowhere. A little college town nestled in the center of middle America.

She remembered Anna. She remembered her wanting death, and the way she tasted. The emptiness they both saw, that great void waiting for them all. And then how good it had felt to drink her oldest and best friend to death.

How strong and wonderful it felt to kill her and be healed once again. The very memory gave her a shiver of horror. And they heard other noises as they crept through the second floor of the bookstore. Noises like bubbling water, gurgling sounds. Oh god. Boneless vampires, that's what that sound was, boneless vampires. She would always know that sound, it would haunt her nightmare all the rest of her life.

So these were traps then, yes. She wanted to tell Daphne, but they hadn't the time, nor could they speak too loudly. They didn't want to draw attention to them, they needed the element of surprise to be on their side. Especially since that little trick with her scars and the vampire hunters didn't work anymore. *Maybe it would work if it caught him by surprise? Maybe.*

As they crept forward, Daphne grabbed her hand, pulled her in, whispered to her. "If this is a vampire trap set by vampire hunters," she whispered, her voice low and hoarse, the sounds of vampire burbling and people moaning, begging for death suffocated the air with misery and death. "Where are they? The vampire hunters, I mean."

Goosebumps, raw terror. They could be anywhere, hiding, waiting. Or they could be hunting them now, following close behind, just out of sight, just in the shadows. All of Nix was on edge now, which made her heart beat faster and she gasped. Oh shit, oh no. Faster heartbeat meant that the blood would burn faster, that her new vampire heart would eat all that death and then she would be fucked.

At least there are bodies here to munch on, she thought. *So close to death. Even if they mostly bled out, it's the death that matters. If she could gobble it up in their blood, she could last a little longer, a little longer.*

No, no, wait. It's a trap. It's a trap. That's what they want her to do, to creep sneak creep over there and be ambushed. If she listened closely she could hear the sounds of the vampire hunters. So many different kinds. The slow bubble growl of the waxy vampire hunters. The low susurrus rustle of the ones made of rags and dead leaves. Those ones were like scarecrows, like the ones Daphne had set up on her property.

It all made some twisted sense that Daphne had made vampire hunters to protect her from Mister Brightbones. Ones obedient to her, ones that would not have killed her but instead kept him and the other vampires away. And yet, those ones weren't animated, were they? They were something else.

Focus, Nix, focus. That's not important now. Survival is. "I hear them," Nix said, "They're close by, but I don't think they're hunting us, not yet. I think they're waiting by the corpses for us to come to them."

Daphne scoffed. "Cowards." And then, there, they were near the stairs leading down, the voices louder. "Do you think you could do that trick again and knock them out? Or did Old Wick mess with you too much the last time?"

"Yeah, he definitely messed with me, but I'm also worried it would give us away. He would know where we are, and then we would be screwed blue and tattooed. Especially if my little trick backfired yet again."

"Good thinking."

And then they crept over to the top of the stairs, crept right over to the edge of the staircase, and looked down, hiding in shadows. Watching and waiting to see what was to come, and if there was any way to stop it and still make it out alive.

Alive, alive alive. That's not the case anymore. Nix thought. They need to make sure they make it out still undead and not all the way dead.

46

THEY leaned over the edge of the staircase together, looking down, glancing between the slats to the first floor beyond. This made Nix feel like a kid, that brief moment when she was little and sneaking up awake at the top of the stairs, to listen to the adult talking below. One time even her aunt and her mom talking about something in hushed tones and her mom getting mad and yelling at her, telling her aunt to get out. That ho daughter of hers would do any such thing as that.

She remembered it now, the moment bright and crystal in her mind. Her mom screaming that it was too much for a little girl to shoulder. That that kind of magic is too powerful for such a child. That it was obscene that she wanted to do that to her little girl.

And her aunt, words bitter on the tongue, acid in her memories. Was she remembering this right? She wasn't sure. She felt like she was, like she had to be remembering this right. And yet, memory was a strange thing, wasn't it? Constantly changing and morphing. Sometimes running away and hiding from you for decades, until that one moment when it came slinking back out and said hello. This was one of those memories, right here. A memory that had laid dormant, forgotten until now.

And her aunt holding up an egg. "We named her Phoenix for a reason, remember?"

And then she cracked that egg in her hand. Instead of goopy yoke sliding out between her fingers there was blood and bright red feathers, falling. "We didn't create the path she's on, we only saw it and are working toward making the best of it. You understand?"

Her mother's voice changed in that moment, was a guttural growl with a snarl on the edges. "Get out." She said. "Get out and pray that you are wrong."

And then she had to shake out of that memory, the strange sorrow in it still fresh and sharp in her mind. Did they see all of this? How much of this was planned? Daphne shook her and pointed, pointed down below. Pointed and hissed, "Look, come on, Mom, *look*."

Crawled over that edge to get a better view of things going on down below. corpses, surrounding a red candle. Humans and puddles of vampires all the same. And there, Mister Brightbones in chains. Iron chains, his mouth muzzled with an iron padlock. The same cold iron that bound Daphne and Nix earlier, and for a brief second she felt the sweet taste of justice dance on her lips. That would show him for binding them and leaving them for dead.

But that bitter justice was short lived. The horror of the moment, and the promise she made to her aunt shook it away like a soft fog drifting across her vision. Her aunt, her mom, what was going on. Was her aunt going to teach her magic? Was it somehow connected to all of this? How, and why, and she had no idea. And there was no time for sussing it out at all.

"There, that will keep you nice and wound tight until we get you back to the Lighthouse. You know the place I'm talking about, you do. It's where we fist met, isn't it? And it's not a lighthouse in the way these foolish mortals think of it, no, no."

And Old Wick bent over and put his foot against the crook of an arm of a corpse on the floor. "No, it's a beacon of a lighthouse, the kind that brings the darkness to it, like moths to a flame. Shadows flickering around its delicious light, wanting to eat it."

He pulled out a twig from his satchel, held it aloft. "I don't think this guy needs his arm anymore, do you?"

And for a brief horrifying moment Nix swore she saw that corpse breathe, and she thought it was Danny. Danny. It was hard to tell, he was face down and naked and scalped. She was rocked in shock, the moment freezing her mind in place, as her corpse heart picked up beat, pumping that child's blood faster and faster through her body, the fear of the moment uncontrollable, and somehow, yes, somehow? Making her hungry. So hungry.

"You know this one, old boy. I've seen you use this trick when you slum it with human magic. Dirty mortal magic you called it. Like attracts like."

And he tapped the corpses arm with the stick, still holding it there with his foot. The body seemed to squirm. Or was that a trick of the light? Was it dead? Was it alive? Nix didn't *hear* a heartbeat in the corpse, not like the rivers of blood still flowing in the traps beyond them on the second floor. So it must be dead, but then why was it breathing?

And Mister Brightbones struggled in his chains, and she knew they had to do something soon, but not yet. Vampire hunters were prowling down amongst the corpses, sniffing the air, looking for vampires. It would be only a matter of time before they saw them and came up and attacked. They had to sit here, quiet as mice, hoping their vampire scents didn't drift down too far. And that the vampire hunters upstairs by the traps hadn't noticed them either.

The ones down here were smaller, hopping monstrosities, with red glowing eyes and bodies made of clockwork and metal. Not wax nor cloth that could easily tear and burn. Like little steel creatures, full of haunted life and lust for vampire bones.

Old Wick snapped the twig in half and Danny's arm (yes, that was him, she saw his face now, saw the horror in his eyes at the moment of his death and it chilled her) yanked back with a wrenching violent sound. And it tore the elbow out of it's socket, thick corpse blood oozing out like gelatin from the now tattered wound where the forearm was once attached.

"There we go. Now, Mister Brightbones, I'm going to take the short way back to my little abode, the Cannibal House on the hill. Take you back to my beacon, my lighthouse, and put you in that cage that will bring your brother here, to me."

His eyes were manic, gleeful at the thought of it. Nix wanted to scream and run forward, to try and stop any of this, all of this. To lop off his head like she'd promised her aunt. But how? With what?

And the vampire hunters chittered in the dark, like clockwork insects waiting to feed. She wanted to cry, she felt so helpless and lost. Even here, now, healed and with vampire powers, she felt so useless in the face of terror.

She couldn't even push against her scar. To try it would be to drain herself dry, she knew it, and then if it failed? She failed.

Old Wick walked over the eastern wall, the one that was bare and without any bookcases lining it. He took the corpse's hand and pushed down the knuckles in a way that made it point. Then he dipped that pointer finger in the coagulated blood, lifted it up, and drew a ragged door on the wall. The outline of the door was messy, smeared, with thick chunky blood. It dripped slowly, oozing down into gloopy puddles on the ground.

"And when that Child of the Abyss gets here and demands I let you go free? You know what I'm going to ask for? Do you know?"

And Mister Brightbones said nothing, only stared.

"I will give him what he wants. I want him to devour this world, destroy it completely, and let me rebuild it. It is a sour, rotten world. A world that has a worm in its core, slowly eating its way into every heart and soul. I will make a beautiful world, a perfect world, and it will be mine. Only mine."

Daphne sobbed next to her and said, "I get it now, I get why you had to stop him."

Oh no, oh no. She was too loud, wasn't she? Daphne was too loud, why did she have to talk at all?

Mister Brightbones turned and looked at them in wide-eyed horror, blaming them for all of this. And Nix knew, she knew, in some way he was right. Yes, yes, he was right. But that didn't mean she couldn't stop it.

Even without that dark magic her aunt wanted to each her. And Old Wick turned and raged, his face bright red with anger. His veins sticking out on his forehead, his eyes bugging out, his lip quivering and coated in the spittle of the enraged. "You!" He howled, "You! I should've taken care of you when you came to my house last time. Oh, I will not make the same mistake twice., Get them, debone them, and leave them in deathpuddles for the sun."

And then he pointed the corpse finger at Mister Brightbones, saying "Don't forget to bring him with us."

And then he walked up to his bloody door and knocked.

47

THUNDERCRACK, knuckles knock and a brief flutter of lightning across the edges of the wall. A deep distant bellowing sound rang out from the walls, like the heartbeat of a giant. The walls themselves undulating, then the sound of ripping flesh. Blood, skin, meat and tearing sounds. the bloody door ripped a hole in the wall, like meat tearing muscle. Strings of blood and sinew tore away from the wallpaper, ragged strips like tattered flesh dangling down. Was it wall, or was it meat and muscle? And beyond that, glittering, shimmering, was a place Nix recognized and it stopped her heart. All those years of dreaming of it, of being there with the horrible yellow wallpaper getting in her head, of visiting there with her aunt when she was on the threshold of death. The Cannibal House. There, it was the living room she remembered so well. There, it was the bone cage, standing upright and vibrating with an unseen, mystical power.

Nix trembled, her mind racing. Fear at seeing that wallpaper again, remembering how she felt the last time she saw it. Her palms began to sweat blood, and she gasped. No, no, don't let the fear burn through that blood. Children may have a long death to power her vampire heart, but eventually she'll hit the end of it, and then she'll be running on empty, and her multiple sclerosis will be back on and brutal again. Her heart raced at the thought of that, the terror of being sick and relapsing making her burn through the blood even faster and faster. It was like a spiraling out, the panic creating more panic creating more panic.

She wished she could stop herself, wished she could shut up her brain weasels once and for all. But that wallpaper in the distance started moving, the women crawling across it, and she felt the urge to join them, to creep into the dark beyond the walls. No, no, no.

She was so lost in terror she didn't even notice Old Wick and several vampire hunters carting Mister Brightbones through that door, and towards the bone cage beyond. She was so lost in her own spinning mind that she didn't notice the other vampire hunters moving towards her, nor did she hear the click click clicking of their metal carapaces as they sulked toward her, their mechanical limbs moving in herky-jerky unnatural motions. Breathless, hypnotized by the terror of the wallpaper, of her own burning blood and rapid heartbeat, of the failure of her body.

Completely frozen and paralyzed in fright. Even with the whispering sound of the rag and bone vampire hunters moving away from the dying human traps behind them. The blood sticky and strong in the air, but she didn't notice it at all, didn't even feel the urge to run into the traps.

She only felt that bright echo of terror in her own internal feedback loop. Brought on by that yellow wallpaper, and the crawling women in chains, the ones who wanted her to follow them. Follow them, follow them into the deeper heart of the house. The thought of that cannibal house heart made her sweat and cry out, still unable to move. Heart beating so fast, blood burning out of her, oh god. Any minute now, any minute now and she'll be empty again.

She can't go back to that. No way she could ever go back to that again. She couldn't. She didn't want to drink to kill or murder. She didn't want to be sick or ill or broken anymore, either. She wanted to be healed completely and without the need to feed. She wanted to be alive, really truly alive, not undead. She wanted to be everything she never was, a normal person with a normal life and without any struggles at all. The promise of the vampire had been that, and it had been a lie.

So let the vampire hunters come, the women in the wallpaper told her, their voices like the wings of insects in her ears. *Let them come and take you away from this cruel world. Let them bring your bones here, into the house. Let us nurture you in death, your spirit joining us beyond the wallpaper. That is where love lives, true healing lives. Beyond the rusted shores of death. Beyond the haunting gates of infinity.*

Beyond, beyond, beyond.

And then, *ow*. And then, *shit*. She felt a pinch on her arm and the sharp pain brought her back to the world. *Ow, ow, ow.* She turned her head, rubbing her arm, and saw Daphne there, pinching her, pulling on her skin, knocking her out of this trance. It was like the pain of the scar, it had the ability to bring her back down, into this place once again. Lodged in the real, and no longer spinning out of orbit into her own fear and anxiety.

"Sorry, so sorry mom! So so sorry, but I had to do it, I had to try and knock you out of it. We need to go! We need to get away from these vampire hunters!"

Almost there, almost completely surrounded them, like a ring closing in, closer and closer. Nix trembled, sighed, and whispered, still in a sick dizzy daze from the wallpaper beyond. "You should have just gone, escaped and gotten away and left me here."

She knew it wouldn't matter, but Nix felt like she had to say it anyway. If they didn't stop Old Wick, didn't chop off that head and leave him for dead? Well, then the whole world would be right and well fucked. So it didn't matter of Daphne stayed or left, not in the larger picture. She knew that, she did, but in some other way Nix still wanted to save and protect Daphne, even if all was lost and hopeless.

"Not a chance, Mom. No way I'm leaving you for those monsters."

Nix nodded. She would do the same for her. Even after all they'd gone through, yes. She would do the same for her, so she understood it.

But what were they going to do? Time was running out, they were caged in on all sides. Nix decided to give the scar one last chance. She would try and burn all of her blood and all of her pain all at once, to reach out and take down all the vampire hunters at the same time.

Closer and closer. The clicking and clanking was so loud in her ears. And she heard a voice crying out, someone in a trap for vampires and felt horrible, it was all her fault. Danny and Anna, and then that little girl, and so many vampires dead now, and so many of the people she'd grown up with and spent her life with in this small town, all dying here, right here, in this bookstore. Some where bleeding out in vampire traps, and others were just cruelly cut down and left on the floor like discarded toys.

And it was all her fault. She leaned into that emotional pain, tears of blood streaming down her cheeks. The blood was hot, burning up, an inferno on her face. Emotional pain, physical pain. Hand on that scar, digging in fingers now. She needed to go further, farther, more pain. Sun still out and setting now, bright amber sun beams streaming in through the windows along the walls. She ran over, holding her breath. Closer and closer.

Emotional pain. And now, yes. The hand in sunlight and damn, it caught on fire and she felt it once again. All that burning pain. She had been healing it, been fighting it back, but here it was once again, on fire yet again.

Would she ever be able to heal herself completely?

The pain of the flames. The emotional pain. The fear of her heart beating, the blood burning up inside of her. No, don't try and heal that arm. Instead, yes, indeed flow to the scar. Flow toward the magic I need you to work. Flow like fire and ice. Find that bastard Old Wick. Find him, find him find him.

Connected, like a silver thread, hooked under her skin and his, pulling them together. Closer, together. Closer. And also all tied in and knotted to her was Mister Brightbones as well, the scar connected to him, she felt him. That presence hooked into her mind, her heart. Scar and vampire bones all mixed up now. Brightbones, Wick, and her. And then blammo, she let it all out. Every last bit of pain and suffering and energy. Her world dimmed like a supernova eclipse, a detonation in her heart, all that blood burning up at once so fast. It felt like her heart was exploding, was bursting out, the veins under her skin a riot with fire and pain, as she collapsed to the ground, completely blind and convulsing.

She heard the sound of bodies collapsing. The vampire hunters, yes. Hopefully Old Wick, too. She wasn't sure, she couldn't be sure. Not until she could see again.

48

BLINDNESS came and went quickly, a rotoscope twist of darkness and light, blindness spinning through her eyes and then back into sight again, like her vision effects from multiple sclerosis were put into hyper drive. What she could see felt like a dream, one tugging at the corners of her mind, as her body twitched, broken, her blood on empty again, her vampire heart sluggish and wheezing. Even though those kids had a long death inside of them, she used it all, right now, just to knock out those vampire hunters.

And it worked, sort of. Not as well as she would have liked, but it was something, something. Her legs were immobile now. The cramps in both of them making it impossible to move even a little bit. Rigid, flat behind her, like mermaid legs. Unable to ease up those muscles, unable to relax even a little bit.

Damn, damn, damn. When she was a living, breathing, human being, her multiple sclerosis had the courtesy to only attack the left side of her body. But here, now that she was undead? It attacked every last bit of her. How rude, how very rude indeed.

She felt that heart sluggish and meandering. The blood pretty much gone, the heart wheezed, and then coughed, and then rattled like bones in the wind. All gone now, not even a slurp slurp to push her through. This was it for her, yeah. This was the end of it all.

She knew it. She felt it in her bones. She better make it count, then. Yes, yes indeed, she better make it count, then. The half-healed burns all over her body itched now, charred and crispy with her weak movements. Her left hand, the one with the scar? That one was the worst.

All the skin was crispy, crunchy. And it fluttered away from her when she moved, like burned paper. Tattered, ashen, fluttering away. Her bones bare beneath her baked flesh, shining white.

She tried to move forward, closer to the edge of the stairs. Everything hurt as she pulled herself closer, closer. She had killed almost all of the vampire hunters, almost.

God, what a scene she saw before her, her watery vision still strobing between blindness and sight. Everything a zoetrope around her, as one of the last vampire hunters dragged Daphne down the stairs, screaming. His hook in her back, using it to move her, to force her to go where he wanted her to go, towards the sunlight? No, no. Toward the the door, that open pulsing meaty door. The door that squished and gurgled as it moved, undulating in the shadows.

Breath caught, she reached out, tried to stop Daphne, to grab her leg, to grab the vampire hunter, anything.

How did that one survive? look at all the others, all dead. Just that one survived, just that one.

Down there she saw Old Wick, pulling something toward the bloodied door. Hard to make him out in the blindness strobe, but there he was, Old Wick. His face was half burned, and he looked even older than he had before. Like twenty years older.

The burns looked fresh, like he survived a bomb going off, and his one eye dangled out of its socket, ruptured from the explosion. His hair gone, his beard still burning a little, with tiny smoldering flames. And Nix smiled, oh yes, Nix smiled. She'd done that. Yes, she'd done that. She hadn't enough death in her to take him out altogether, but *she did that*. And right now? Right now that was almost enough. Almost.

Because he was still strong enough to pull that body of a little blind boy across the hardwood floor. Mister Brightbones. He was on fire, yes, he was burning up. Or rather, that little boy's body was on fire? Even though the fire didn't seem to be burning him. Just his clothes, but not his skin.

Mister Brightbone's face twisted up in the horror of everything going on around him, his mouth screaming, senseless. "No, no, no, I will not do this, I will not do this! I will not be your bait, you idiot! Don't you know what will happen when my brother gets here? Don't you understand?"

Nix pulled herself down another step, painful, still unable to move her back legs. The spasms were so tight, so harsh. The pain absolutely brutal. But she couldn't let it get her now, she couldn't succumb to that pain. She had to keep going, crawl down those stairs, one step at a time.

And what would she do when she got down there? How would she stop them like this?

She had no clue. But somehow, someway, yes, she had to. She had to.

But, alas, Old Wick was faster than her, faster and faster, ungodly fast, moving like a video sped up ten times fast.

"Don't you understand," Mister Brightbones hissed again, his body making a horrific sliding sound as he tried to crawl away. "Don't you understand at all what will happen when he comes here, to this world?"

"I do," Old Wick said, quick and sharp. "But I can control him."

Mister Brightbones laughed. "No, no you won't. Not even with me, he's not coming here to save me. He's coming here to stop me, and to stop this world. We're siblings, don't you know, and our rivalry runs deep. We hate each other," those words spit out, poison on the tongue. "Deep in the bone and the marrow. We despise each other."

And then, before he could say anything else, Old Wick picked him up like he was nothing and tossed him through the undulating bloodied door. Over he flew, and for a brief moment Nix thought he would miss, that this would all end so quickly because he would miss and that would be that. The bone cage would be knocked over, collapsed, scattered into a million pieces like a Jenga explosion.

But that didn't happen. That didn't happen at all. His body slid right into the open door of the cage, and he tumbled inside, banging up against the bonewalls. But they held tight, they didn't budge, they didn't slip. And he seemed weaker somehow inside of there, like he aged a billion years in one second, all of the energy draining out of that little boy's body completely.

And Mister Brightbones was stuck there, in that body, in that cage, as Old Wick slammed the door shut. The vampire hunter was right behind, pulling Daphne across the floor by the hook in her spine, and Daphne screaming in pain, reaching around, trying to pull it out, kicking and screaming to no avail.

As Nix crawled down the stairs, everything hurting so much. Her muscles from multiple sclerosis, her skin from being burned in the sun. Her eyes were starting to sharpen a little, no longer fluttering through darkness and light. It was just light now, thankfully. She was just glad it didn't turn into vertigo again. Not now, not today. She would be so lost if that happened.

And Old Wick turned away from the bone cage, and sauntered up to that door, the throbbing meaty door, the bloody edges of it oozing and dripping. He grabbed onto the flesh of the wall and said right to her, his eyes like laser beams in her vampire heart, "It seems like you lived long enough to die again, I warned you didn't I? I warned you about that little mouse in your house, but you didn't listen. And now she'll pay."

And then he snapped his fingers and grinned, his eye bouncing against his cheek. As the vampire hunter picked up Daphne, hook in hand, digging in deep into her spine. She wiggled and cried out, and Nix felt this slow-moving terror crawl up her spine. She felt sick and broken, and unable to do anything more than crawl, meekly across the floor, and hope against hope that her eyesight wouldn't give out yet again.

The vampire hunter was going to yank, and Daphne would be nothing more than a puddle of boneless vampire flesh, writhing on the ground like all the others. Hear them now? Moaning and crying out in pain. The ones still alive, after the fight with Old Wick. The one she had missed.

A chorus of the dying and the damned. She heard the dying humans as well, in their vampire traps, bleeding out and begging for help. The world oozed in pain, and everything slowed down to a crawl. Time, stopping.

The vampire hunter was going to do it, he was going to . . .

The sound of a gong, somewhere in the distance. Or was that a bell? Nix wasn't sure, she couldn't tell what that noise was, all she knew was that it made her vampire heart try to beat a little faster. It struggled, looking for any blood still in her body to slurp up. But it wheezed and sputtered and came up empty.

Fear, fear in the air. An air that felt stale and somehow empty. As if the empty spaces were draining of all essence, the void in the room and the shadows shrinking and swirling, giving life to something, something horrible.

A child crying, sharp and brutal, it echoed through the two buildings, connected by an open wound.

As the darkness and the emptiness spun itself into a form, right there, right in front of the cage where Mister Brightbones weakly pushed against the bones. Not inside the cage, mind you, just right to the left of it, not far from Old Wick. Old Wick, who was grinning manically, his face twisted into a grimace of joy. "Yes, yes! He is coming! He is here! The Child of the Abyss! Help us build a new world!"

She'd failed. Nix had failed. The Vampire hunter fell to the ground the minute the Child of the Abyss coalesced in front of him, a pile of rags and sticks and nothing more. Daphne on the ground next to him, in pain, pushing back, crawling back.

If only Nix had someone to drink up. She didn't have the energy or the strength to stop this. She could only watch it mutely as it happened. As the shadows turned into something horrible.

A giant, screaming fetus. It was the size of an elephant. The head was large, and you could see all the veins pulsating beneath its paper-thin skin, the body still bloodied with the viscera of the unborn. It crawled towards the cage, howling muttering, screaming its long brutal baby scream. A scream that cuts through the guts of any living human, no matter how much they despised children.

It crawled past Old Wick, toward his bait, toward Mister Brightones.

"Yes, yes! I'll give him to you, just like this, all neat and nice and wrapped up in a bow. All you have to do is help me remake the world, do you understand? And I can tell: you want to do it. You do! I can feel the hunger inside of you, and the hatred of all things living and breathing. You want only emptiness and nothing more, I can see it in you."

If only her aunt had a chance to teach her that dark magic her mom refused to let her learn. If only she could find some way to stop this. She was dying now, yes. No longer undead, her own mortality caught up to her.

Well, no not dying exactly. After all, she was already dead. This was just her death catching up to her. This was it, it was all over.

And then Daphne grabbed the hook, the one that was in her back, and rose up, hate and fury in her eyes. She watched as Daphne sunk the blade directly into Old Wick's back, and with one smooth motion, hooked onto his bones, and then yank. Yank. Yank.

Just like they'd seen his vampire hunters do a thousand times. He fell to the ground, spineless, boneless puddle, shaking, screaming, dying, then dead. Humans, even a long-lived magus like that old bastard, still couldn't last as long as a vampire after their bones were removed. It was so fast, so brutal, Nix didn't even have time to register what had happened. A gasp. How fast, how simple it was to kill Old Wick. Even after all those long-lived years, just a corpse, right there.

And the giant fetus crawled up, and began to feed on the corpse with nasty, slurping sounds that gave Nix shivers of fright. Her skin felt colder than cold, the blood gone now, her body a yellowing decay. She had to feed. She had to. She was starting to rot while she was still alive.

Nix crawled forward some more. No human bodies down here, all the vampire traps were upstairs. She wasn't going to last much longer, no not at all. She felt it wheeze, wheeze, wheeze, and every part of her trembled to feed, trembled at the horror as the Child of the Abyss fed on Old Wick's body. This was how the world ends, this is how the world ends. Not with a bang, but a shiver.

And Daphne opened up the cage. And she stepped inside, and walked up to Mister Brightbones.

"Your cure was a lie," she said, and then chopped his head clean off with the hook. So quick, so clean, a flash of light as the afterimage sunspot of Mister Brightbones faded. Everything shook for a moment and Nix wondered how any of this could be so easy. So simple. The violence like a cough in the dark, nothing more than a split second of brutality and then nothing. She was losing control of her arms now, too. Unable to even pull herself forward. Her heart couldn't beat anymore, not enough blood to do it. Her burns no longer healing, but instead spreading and fluttering away from her corpselike body.

Nix knew that wouldn't be the end of him, not exactly. Just the end of him in this body. And yet, it felt good to see her do this. It felt good to see Daphne put an end to all of this. He'd lied to them. This cure was no better than any of the cures for her chronic illness. It was only a temporary reprieve between feedings.

She heard the Child of the Abyss crying starved, infantile howls. She saw that Old Wick was gone completely, all that was left of him was a greasy smear in the shape of his body. So long, Oliver Haddo. May the afterlife be an endless void of suffering for you. And for a moment she thought, this was it. It was over. The Child of the Abyss would devour the world and there would be nothing left but emptiness. But it seemed like it was hungry for something else, something that was taken away from it. The way it looked at Mister Brightbones's headless corpse, now decaying in high speed as it rotted and the cancer crawled over every part of its severed head. It was looking for the after-image spirit of Mister Brightbones, that skeletal glow, now gone from this world after being pushed out of its body.

And as it howled it struggled to keep itself together. It was the void, after all, it did not want to be physical. It wanted to be emptiness. It sloughed off skin and sucked in on itself and oh no, oh no. Was it turning into a black hole? Would it suck us all into its empty void?

She wished she'd been as strong as her aunt thought she'd been. She wished she could've stopped this sooner. The world rattled, as the giant fetus collapsed in on itself, turning into a flash of darkness, the shadows all around them longer, and then, and then?

And then, it was gone.

Just like that. Gone. Where had it gone? Back to where it came from? Was it Brightbones's death that had done it? Now that he wasn't physical anymore, was the Child of the Abyss hunting his brother in the shadows between worlds? The place where the dying go to wander?

The whole room felt quieter, emptier. The ghostly echo of a baby crying hung around in the air for moment or two more, and then was gone. Like a whisper of an explosion, and nothing more.

And then Nix passed out from hunger and lack of blood, the emptiness a dark comfort behind her eyes.

49

THE blood still worked. Thank god, thank god, the blood still worked. They were at a motel now, off of some random interstate in some random midwest small town. The kind of place where the sea seemed so far away and the ground stretched out in long plains around them. They'd been on the run for awhile now, yes. Nix hated it. She hated not having any money, she hated the way they had to burn through some of the blood just to make sure no one asked too many questions. Just to make sure they would take their cash without asking for a credit card, without asking for their IDs.

There were some small places scattered across the world that still worked in that way. They were seedy and run down but you knew you had your privacy, and Daphne kept saying how they needed their privacy.

"We don't have the time to build a scarecrow," she'd said, "no way to keep something from spying on us."

And Nix would remind her that Mister Brightbones was dead. But Daphne just shook her head, a haunted look in her eyes and say, "I still dream about him, though."

And Nix would nod and agree. She'd dreamt about him too, and wanted to believe that didn't mean anything. That didn't mean Mister Brightbones was still around, hunting them with a new body, a new group of vampires out to tear them down and get revenge. But she knew better. She knew that he always came to them in dreams before. And here he was, coming to them in dreams now.

Though this time he wore the skin of an old man covered in scars and carrying an IV drip in one hand. How long would this body last? They had no idea. They just knew he was out there, somehow, still hunting them. Wanting to get revenge for their betrayals.

And so that meant they could never rest. It meant they could never stay still, and they had to always keep moving. At night, at day, always moving. Always keeping their trail hidden as best as they could.

But, but, but. She felt a connection to him in that burnt-up hand, a lingering shadow of that old scar that he'd given her in a dream a long time ago. And no matter how much death she drank up, that hand never seemed to heal. The rest of her did, sure. But that burnt-up charred hand will always be there, reminding her of what she'd been through, and what she'd done.

Oh god, and they'd done so much. Murder was nothing to her these days, and she even started to enjoy it, in a tiny cruel way. That rush of the dying, of feeling it come and wipe away all of her sickness and all that other bullshit thrilled her each and every time. It left her tingling and raw, and after awhile, yes, it felt so sexual. Like a million orgasms all at once ripping through her body. A holy communion of death that healed her right up.

Daphne didn't seem to share her new love of murder, though. She kept to the rabbits and foxes when she could, and went after the old and dying when she needed death with a little more juice to it than they could provide.

And she knew Daphne looked at her with horror each time she did it. Shame shivered in her bones from that look, but Nix didn't care. That orgasmic mania that followed death took over every inch of her. Blood singing, laughing with a face covered in gore.

Two kids were asleep and waiting for them in the motel room right now. Drugged and passed out and Daphne was going to do it this time, Daphne would join in with her. Nix would make sure of that. After all, mother knows best. A grin in the dark as they walked across the parking lot, toward their motel room, key cards in hand.

"I got you a present," Nix said, "Found them while you were off trying to get us a ride out of this shit town. I think you'll like it."

And when they opened the door the two kids squirmed in the shadows. Daphne gasped. Her eyes were wide and her lip trembled, and a lone quiet tear slipped across her cheek and down her chin. Drip, drip, drip.

"No, no, no. Mom, what did you do?"

And Nix smiled, all teeth in the shadows of their room. The only light the dim harvest moon shining ochre through the windows, coating the two boys in a bloodied light.

"They were lost, wandering around in the back behind the motel, looking for their parents. I tried to help them out, help them find their parents and everything. But they weren't here anymore, and they said the car was gone. I guess they were abandoned here, left to the elements. I figure we could use their blood right now really badly. Can't you feel it? They have such a long death inside of them, it could sustain us for a year, maybe more. Can't you feel that?"

And the two kids squirmed and cried out in their sleep. And Daphne sobbed and said, "No, Mom. No. Not after all of this, after all we've been through, I can't let you do this."

And then Nix turned to her, her eyes reflecting that bloody light of the harvest moon. "You don't get to say that to me. Not after what you did, you understand? You gave me a taste for the long death."

And Daphne sobbed, softly, a sound almost like laughter in the moonlight. "All right, Mom," she said. "All right."

And then they both crawled across the bed and fed. And in the morning Nix woke up all alone with the two corpses, the sun streaming in an open window and burning the edges of her bare legs. She yelped, moved them aside and put out the fires. She called out for Daphne, once, twice, but no answer followed. Just a whisper of gravel as new cars pulled into the motel parking lot. She could barely see out the window, the sun too bright for her vampire eyes, but she knew, oh yes, she knew. A sharp pain in that scar on her hand, like she was being stabbed repeatedly. Hurt so badly she winced and swore under her breath.

Mister Brightbones. She'd dreamt of him again last night, and she had a feeling now that he'd finally followed her here, through that connection of scar and dream. Followed her here to pay her back.

ACKNOWLEDGEMENTS

I would like to give thanks to Natania Barron, Michelle Muenzler, and Jonathan Wood for reading it over as I wrote it and giving me killer notes. Also like to thank my editor, Darin Bradley, for helping me edit the hell out of this and bring it back from the dead. This book would be half the book it was if it wasn't for you guidance and suggestions as an editor. It was a lot of work, but in the end this book is a million times better thanks to you. Thanks to Mark Teppo and Underland for giving this book a home and tossing it out into the unsuspecting world. Little do they know what terrors awaits for them! And thanks to my kids Ashlyn and Liam Jessup, for putting up with my odd hours of writing weird horror novels, and then listening to the plots in my own rambling ways. Also thanks to Victoria Dovensky for being awesome and supporting me in tons of different ways. Thanks also to Werner Books, for always supporting local authors (including yours truly) and being the best bookstore in Erie, PA.